Love You Still

A Second Chance Small Town Romance

AJ Alexander

LOVE YOU STILL by AJ Alexander
www.authorajalexander.com
aj@authorajalexander.com

Copyright © March 2024 by AJ Alexander
First Print Publication: March 2024
Photo provided by: Cadwallader Photography, LLC
Cover Designer: Wildheart Graphics
Developmental Editing: Made Me Blush Books
Line Editor: The Ryter's Proof Editing Services
Proofreader: Crystal Clear Author Services

dedication

To those that believe everyone deserves a second, third, and sometimes even a fourth chance.

content warning

These content notes are made available here so readers can inform themselves if they want to. Some readers might consider these as 'spoilers', particularly for the detailed trigger warnings.

In this case, most of the triggers listed below happen prior to the events in the book, but are discussed in length by the characters throughout the story.

Complications/Death During Childbirth
Childbirth
Death of a Parent(s)
Death of a Loved One
Grief
Pregnancy

one
selina

"Are you sure you want to do this?" my mom asks for what feels like the millionth time in the last week.

"We've been over this, Mom. I don't have a choice." I sigh as I stuff my favorite sweatshirt into my backpack.

"There's always a choice." My mom rolls her eyes, pulling my sweatshirt out and folding it nicely before placing it on top of my bag.

My mom and I have been having this same conversation for weeks, ever since I was awarded a scholarship to the Juilliard Summer Dance Intensive. I've been trying to land a spot in this program since I was a freshman in high school, and I'd almost given up hope when the letter finally arrived.

All I've ever wanted to do was dance, ever since my mom signed me up for dance classes to help me get ready to go to school and make some friends. What she didn't know was that those classes would ignite a fire in my heart for dance that still burns to this day. Everyone assumed I'd grow out of it, my focus shifting from dancing to boys, but for me, that never happened. Sure, there have been boys, well one boy in particular, but he has always come second to my dancing. All my hopes and dreams are finally coming true, but it feels as if I'm being ripped into a million tiny pieces.

"You're already starting classes at Juilliard in the fall. Can't you just wait a few more months? I don't want you to regret the time you missed with your friends."

"My friends will be here when I get back." I flop onto the bed beside her, turning my attention out the window.

"Maybe. But you need to at least tell Vance you're leaving, hun." My mom wraps her arm around my shoulder, pulling me to her side. "He's your biggest cheerleader after your dad and me. He'll understand."

My heart aches at the mention of Vance's name. He's been the only boy in my life since, well, forever. Vance and I have been connected ever since our first day in kindergarten. He walked right up to me with a bright smile on his face and pulled me in for a tight hug before announcing to the entire class that I was the girl he was going to marry. I obviously had no idea what any of that meant, but he slowly wormed his way into my heart. First as one of my best friends, then becoming something else entirely.

"I remember the day he came over and declared to your father he was going to marry you."

I giggle softly. "We were, what? Eleven or twelve years old?" My mom nods as I lay my head on her shoulder, unshed tears collecting in my eyes. "He tried to kiss me under the old black willow tree in front of the church. I told him the only boy I planned on kissing was the one I'm going to marry."

"He marched right up the front steps, knocked on the door, and asked to speak with your father." My mom shakes her head slightly, planting a kiss on the top of my head. "Your father had no idea what to say, but he took his tiny hand in his and shook it. He told him that if he was man enough to speak to your father about his feelings for you, then he was all right in our book."

"And I've been stuck with him ever since. Too bad things aren't really that simple." A lone tear streams down my cheek as I reach up and angrily swipe at it. "Will he still want to marry me when I live over thirteen hours away?"

This is the million-dollar question. Vance and I have lived in the same town, only a few miles away from each other, our entire lives. Now I'm moving almost a thousand miles away. How can we expect our relationship to last? I've tried to talk to Vance about my concerns numerous times, but he always smiles brightly and promises it will all work out. He's the hopeless romantic in our relationship, believing that since we were meant to be together, everything will work itself out. Love conquers all, and all that other nonsense. But unlike him, my feet are planted firmly on the ground.

Attending Juilliard is going to be harder than anything I've ever done. I can put in the work; I know I can, but it won't leave much time for anything else, let alone traveling back and forth between New York and Tyson's Creek. How can two people have a relationship like that? A clean break is what's best for both of us—at least, that's what I keep telling myself.

"By plane, it's only two hours and some change,"

"Be serious for a second, Ma." I sigh, pushing off the bed and strolling toward the window. "We barely spend any time together now. There's no way we can make it work with me being so far away."

"I am, sweetheart." I don't even bother to turn around and look at my mom as I shake my head, which causes her to sigh loudly. "Look, I know having a long-distance relationship isn't ideal, but if you love him as much as I believe you do, then it's worth it.

"Then at least break up with him. Vance will never let you go unless you make him."

"I can't do that either." I wrap my arms around my waist, holding myself together. "This isn't something I can do over the phone, but if I see him..."

"Can't or won't?"

"Do you think any of this is easy for me?" I screech, tears flowing freely down my cheeks. "This is all I've wanted ever since I took my first dance class. I want my chance to be a prima ballerina. To dance *Swan Lake* in front of millions of people. But my heart feels like it's being ripped out of my chest at the thought of leaving him. Why can't you understand that I have to do this and just be happy for me?"

There's no way I can make anyone understand the indescribable pain running through my body as the time gets closer to leaving Tyson's Creek and Vance behind. It's selfish and childish to want to have it all while giving up nothing, but there's a part of me that's afraid of losing everything if I choose between the two things I love the most in this world.

"It's not that we aren't happy for you, Seli." My other best friend, Lydia, sighs as she comes strolling through the door and plops down on my bed beside my mom. Her dark hair hangs loosely around her shoulders as she narrows her eyes in my direction. "We are sad for us."

Lydia and I met around the same time Vance and I did. Her mom had the same bright idea as my mom to put her in dance class to help her make friends before school started. She spent most of the time in the corner, her eyes cast down on the floor, as if the studio was the last place she wanted to be, but something about her called to me. During the first break in class, I went over and sat beside her. I didn't say a word, just sat there, letting her know that someone saw her and was there when she was ready.

I repeated the same steps for the first three classes until she finally told me her name. She was so shy, preferring to blend into the background instead of being front and center on the stage during dance class, but somehow, I managed to convince her to at least give dancing a try. She didn't stay in classes for long, but we were inseparable. We played at the park and went to the library together and told each other our secrets.

When we started school, we added Connor and Vance to the group, and we all became fast friends. As we grew older, she naturally gravitated to Connor, the same way I did with Vance, but the four of us remained the best of friends, not letting relationship drama get between the four of us, or at least, that's how it used to be. With me leaving tonight for New York without saying anything to Connor and Vance, I may end up tearing our group apart at the seams.

"I just want to make a clean break. It's better that way," I mumble, swiping my cheeks and turning back toward the window.

"Better or easier?"

"Not you, too." I try not to lash out at Lydia, but I don't know how much more of this I can handle.

I stare at Lydia, willing her to understand the emotions raging inside of me. I don't know how to put into words the desire to keep everything exactly how it is right now, but also the fear of losing a part of myself if I stay here in Tyson's Creek. I want to have it all, but how is that fair? I may be able to get everything I've ever wanted, but someone is going to miss out. Someone is going to have to change their plans and dreams to fit mine, and then what happens? Will they all hate me for choosing myself over them? Or if I want to keep things as they are now, will I regret choosing to follow my dreams and resent them? There is no clear winner in this situation, no matter how much I want there to be. Right now, I just want to cause the least amount of damage to all our hearts as possible.

"Speaking of Vance, he's expecting to see you at Connor's party in a few hours."

"I can't, Lyds. You know I can't," I whisper before looking down to check my watch again. "We still have a few hours. Do you want to come with us to the airport?"

"As if I would say no. Although I don't agree with what you're doing, I'm going to miss you." Lydia wraps her arms tightly around my waist, laying her cheek against my back.

Leaving home for the first time is always difficult, but this has to be a new level. I've spent my entire life in Tyson's Creek. Everyone person I know lives here, but if I want to be a prima ballerina, I need to go to New York. This is the chance of a lifetime. I know deep in my heart that I need to take advantage of this opportunity, but there's another part of me that wonders if I'm making a mistake.

My phone vibrates in my pocket, and my entire body tenses. I already know who's calling without even looking at the caller ID. The familiar chorus from "I Got You, Babe" fills the room. "Speak of the devil," I choke out as Lydia gives my shoulder a squeeze. "I gotta take this."

"We'll give you some privacy. Meet you downstairs in a few minutes."

I take a deep breath, attempting to rein in my emotions before accepting the call. "You just saw me a few hours ago. What could possibly be so important that it couldn't wait until Connor's party in a few hours?"

His deep chuckle comes from the other end of the line. "Is it weird that I just wanted to hear your voice?"

"I sound the same as I did when we talked after graduation." I shake my head back and forth as another sob bubbles up from my throat. Each breath feels like pure agony as shivers rack my entire body. "There's nothing special about my voice."

"Everything about you is special, Seli," he whispers, his feeling for me clear in his voice.

My mind is screaming at me to run to him. To cancel my trip to New York and give up my scholarship to Juilliard in the fall. To stay here in Tyson's Creek for the rest of my life with Vance. But I can't do it. My heart continues to scream in agony as I grip the phone tightly in my hand. Tears stream down my cheeks as I plaster a smile onto my face.

"You're too good for me, Vance Kirkland."

"No. I'm a better person *because* of you, Selina Grymes. I love you."

"I love you, too," I mutter into the phone before hanging up and crumpling to the ground. "I deserve this. I do. I do."

My heart feels as if it's crumbling inside of chest as I think about what I'm about to do. I thought I could handle talking to him one more time, but clearly, I was wrong. I can feel my entire soul yearning for one more hug, one more kiss, anything that I can get to remember Vance by. After tonight, he'll hate me and never want to have anything to do with me again, as he should. But there's still a part of me that hopes he'll understand why I'm doing this to him. To us. He's the other half of my soul and always will be, but I need to follow my dreams. Unfortunately, those dreams are leading me away from him.

A set of arms wrap tightly around me, pulling me into someone's lap. "Breathe with me, Seli."

I turn and bury my nose in my father's chest, inhaling his scent. It takes a few moments, but I follow his instructions and try to draw breaths into my tight lungs. Slowly, it becomes easier to breathe. The tightness in my chest dissipates, but my heart still cries out in agony at what is going to happen next. Vance has no idea. He believes that I'm going to remain here for the summer before heading off to New York to start at Juilliard. He has said numerous times how proud of me he is, but he has a life here. His family is here, and there is no reason for him to move to New York, other than me.

I've thought about asking him to come with me a million times, but I couldn't. I can't ask him to come with me for the same reason he hasn't asked me to stay. I don't want to resent him, turning our love for each other into something twisted and full of resentment and pain.

"Daddy, why does it hurt so much?"

"I want to tell you that this will pass." He lays his cheek on the top of my head, tightening his hold on me. "That the pain you feel will heal after some time, but I don't want to lie to you."

"Can't you try? Just this once."

"Sorry, Princess." He chuckles humorously. "You two are like magnets, orbiting each other, lost in your own little universe. You two are meant to be, no matter how much I hate to admit it."

"Do you think he'll ever forgive me?"

"Yes," he answers without hesitating. "That boy will love you until the end of time."

"That's what I'm afraid of."

My emotions keep fluctuating between soul-crushing sobs and numbness. I keep waiting for the pain to subside, calming to a bearable ache deep inside my soul, but it doesn't. What started out as an amazing morning with the promise of a happy ending has come crashing to the ground.

"Selina..." I can hear my mom choking back emotions as I turn my focus toward the door. She and Lydia have their arms wrapped tightly around each other, tears streaming down their faces. "It's time to go."

I nod, unwrapping myself from around my father and pushing to my feet. My eyes remain focused on my feet as I grab my backpack off the bed and shuffle to my bedroom door. I want them to lie to me. To tell me everything is going to be okay and that the pain will disappear with time.

"Seli." Lydia reaches her hand toward me, but I shake my head, knowing that if she touches me, I'll break.

I can barely breathe.

The walls are closing in around me.

But I continue to put one foot in front of the other, carefully making my way down the stairs and out the front door. I can hear my parents whispering behind me as I open the car door and slide into the back seat. Pain beyond anything I could imagine rips through my body with each movement. And I pray things will get easier with time.

"Are you sure you don't want to at least stop by and

see him before leaving?" Lydia asks as she climbs into the back seat beside me and grips my forearm tightly, tethering me to the seat.

"I can't, Lyds. If I do—" My voice breaks off, and searing pain flows through my entire body as waves of agony pull me under. Tears pour down my face as my parents climb into the front seat and start the car. "I just want the pain to stop." I bury my face in my hands and cry, trying to make sense of what has now become my life.

"Okay," she whispers, threading her fingers through mine and giving my hand a squeeze.

I turn my head, staring out the window. I find comfort in the familiar scenery as it goes by. I send up a silent prayer, yearning for numbness to cut me off from all these feelings that I'm so desperate to forget.

two

Vance

"**Y**ou're so whipped." Connor chuckles as I tuck my cell phone into the back pocket of my jeans.

"Maybe." I shrug before running my hand through my hair. "But she's leaving in a few months for New York. I need to get as much of her as I can."

My heart constricts in my chest at the mention of my and Selina's pending separation. When she told me she got into Juilliard, I was ecstatic for her. Dancing has been her passion for most of our lives, and she deserves this chance, but there's a small part of me that wishes things were different.

"You two are meant to be together, just like Lyds and me." Connor slaps me on the back before flopping onto his bed. "Everything will work out."

Connor and I have been best friends since birth— well, not really, but he's the brother I always wanted. We both grew up here in Tyson's Creek, living only a few blocks away from each other. He's also the only person who understands my feelings for Selina because he feels the same way about Lydia.

I knew the moment I laid eyes on her that we were going to get married. It was a crisp fall day, the sun filtering through the tree in front of the local elementary school. Connor and I were roughhousing, as boys do, shoving each other back and forth as we made our way into the building, but the moment I saw her, everything else ceased to exist. Her chocolate-brown hair was pulled into two pigtails nestled on either side of her head. Each had a red bow tied around the top with long spiral curls brushing her shoulders. Seli was talking to someone—I have no idea who—but then she smiled. Her entire face lit up with joy before she giggled softly at whatever they were saying, and then our eyes locked with each other. In that moment, it felt like I'd been struck by lightning. Every muscle in my body froze in place, and my eyes widened in surprise. It was at that moment I knew I had found the missing piece of my soul.

Most five-year-old children would've ignored whatever happened between us, but not me. I strolled right up to her, introduced myself, and promised her we were going to get married someday. We've been inseparable ever since. Our parents and friends swore things would cool off as we got older. That I was just sweet on the first pretty girl I saw, but I knew in my heart that she was the only girl I'd ever love. It wasn't until

Connor and Lydia fell in love that I had someone else who understood how I was feeling. I love Selina Grymes beyond all reason, and I wouldn't have it any other way.

I flop down onto the bed beside him. "I know, but I just wish I was going with her."

And that is my only problem. Juilliard is one of the most prestigious fine arts colleges in the country, but it's also in New York City, 935.5 miles away from my house. Yes, that is exactly how far away we'll be from each other for the next four years. I googled it. Seli and I are soul mates. There's no denying that to anyone, but how can two people function being that far away from their other half? I hate leaving her at her front door to walk the few blocks home after our dates. I'll completely lose my mind if I have to go months without seeing her. So, the day she told me she was going to Juilliard, I applied to every college in New York City. My grades are good, so it wasn't too hard for me to snag a spot in next year's incoming freshman class. All I was waiting for was for her to ask me to go with her.

"There's nothing keeping you here, Vance. You got into NYU and snagged an amazing scholarship. You're the one who chose to stay here in Tyson's Creek."

"She didn't ask me to go with her," I grumble, rubbing the spot over my heart on my chest.

A part of me wanted to tell her I would go with her, but a much bigger part of me wanted it to be her decision. We've been together for most of our lives in some manner. First as friends, then as boyfriend and girl-friend. Maybe she is hoping for some time away from me to spread her wings and fly. I know Selina loves me with all her heart. Not only has she told me a million times, but she also shows me every day with her actions.

"Did you ever think she was waiting for you to offer?"

"The thought crossed my mind, but Seli would've said something if she wanted me to come," I reply with conviction.

Selina is a straightforward and to-the-point type of person. If she wants something, she tells me, even if it's supposed to be a gift. So why wouldn't she ask me to come with her if that's what she really wanted? But that doesn't stop the nagging voice in the back of my mind from wondering why she never asked me to go with her.

"Do you think she's going to break up with you?"

"No," I sigh, trying to make sense of all the swirling emotions running through my mind.

I don't, for one minute, doubt that Selina and I are meant to be together. She is going to be my wife, the mother of my children, but is there a chance she's having second thoughts? Is she still as much in love with me as she was a few years, months, or even weeks ago?

I shake the negative thoughts from my head. "Selina loves me. End of story. New York isn't that far away; we'll figure it out. We only have a few more months to spend together, and I plan to make the most of them."

"Sounds like a plan to me." Connor smiles, grabbing an Xbox controller off his bedside table and tossing it to me. "Now, enough with the heavy. Let's blow some shit up."

"I thought you'd never ask." I smile before focusing on the television and waiting for the game to boot up. "Are you planning on giving that ring to Lyds tonight?"

"How did you..." Connor spins toward me, his hand immediately going to the bulge I noticed in his pocket since graduation this morning.

"I'm your best friend, man. Do you honestly think you could do anything without me knowing?" I wink in his direction before throwing my arm over his shoulder and pulling him to my side. "But you also haven't stopped touching the square-shaped bulge in your pocket since this morning. If you don't want to give it away the minute Lyds walks through the door, you need to stop."

Connor sighs, reaching into his pocket and pulling out a small black box. "You don't think this is stupid?"

"Seriously? I'd ask Selina to marry me right now, but she has things she wants to do before we get married and start a family."

"What if Lyds..." His voice trails off as I shove him hard in the side, sending him tumbling off the edge of the bed. "What the hell was that for?"

"I was hoping you'd hit your head and come back to your senses." I push to my feet, reaching my hand toward him. "Do you love her?"

"Yes."

"Then that's all that matters." Connor eyes the black box skeptically before gripping it tightly in his hands. "Ask her."

Connor nods before dropping onto the bed beside me, focusing back on the television, effectively ending our conversation.

We play *Call of Duty* for what feels like hours as we wait for the girls to arrive. I can't stop myself from checking my watch and phone, hoping for any sign that they are on their way, but come up empty. Finally, Connor snatches my phone away and shoves it into his pocket, claiming that they will get here when they get here. Usually, zoning out and playing video games helps the time go by faster, but I can't shake this nagging feeling in the back of my mind that something is terribly wrong.

As we are finishing another round of matchmaking in *Call of Duty*, Connor's phone dings loudly, signaling an incoming text. "Is that Lyds? Are her and Seli on the way?" I ask, throwing the controller on the bed beside me.

"She'll be here in a few minutes."

"She? What about Selina?" I question around the lump forming in my throat.

"She's gone." He places a hand on my shoulder, giving it a small squeeze. "Lydia and Selina's parents just got back from dropping Selina at the airport. She's on her way to New York."

I shake my head, unable to form the words. My heart feels like it's been ripped out of my chest, indescribable pain radiating through my body. My mind goes back over our last conversation, searching for any clue that something was wrong, but I come up with nothing. No hint that she was going to leave without even saying goodbye.

"She left," I mutter to myself as my entire world comes to a screeching halt.

I should've known when she never asked me to go with her that this was coming, but I thought our love for each other was enough. That because we are soul mates, we could survive the distance and time away from each other, but it seems she may have had other plans.

"I'm such a fucking idiot!" I scream, throwing the Xbox controller against a nearby wall. "All this time I was talking about our future together, and she was just searching for a way to let me down easily."

"That's not true!" Lydia shouts as she comes running into Connor's bedroom, tears streaming down her cheeks. "She was afraid that you'd ask her to stay."

"But I've never once asked her to give up her dreams for me. I know the only thing she has ever wanted was to be a ballerina. To dance across the stage as a prima ballerina. Why would I ask her to give all of that up for me?"

"Did you tell her that?" Connor questions, wrapping his arms around Lydia and pulling her to his side.

I slam my fist into the wall, chunks of drywall crumpling to the floor around my hand as I pull back and slam my fist into the wall a second time. I unleash all my fury and anger on the wall, wanting to rage against the world for what is happening.

"You know you're going to have to pay for that, right?"

"I know, and fix it, too," I reply through clenched teeth as I pull in a deep breath. "I would have done anything for her. She knows that. I told her a million times, showed her every day we spent together. I have been planning to spend the rest of my life with her since we were five years old. What else did she want from me?"

"But all your plans were here, in Tyson's Creek. From wanting to fix up the old farmhouse near the edge of town to our plans of starting a construction business together." Connor pushes Lydia behind him, and I lean forward, barely missing his chin with my fist.

"You need to stop and think, Vance. Have you ever thought about these things happening anywhere but here?"

"She would have stayed if you asked her to. That's why she left without telling you. If you'd asked her to stay, she would have, but then what? She would have spent the rest of her life wondering what could have been. Resenting you for holding her back from her dreams," Lydia says, stepping around Connor and wrapping her arms tightly around my waist. "So instead of growing to hate you, she put you first, breaking her own heart in the process."

Tears spring to my eyes as I wrap my arms around Lydia, clinging to her body like an anchor holding me together.

"She asked me to tell you she loves you, always," she croaks as I tighten my hold around her.

Bitterness courses through my veins that fate could be so cruel. That it'd allow this angel to light up my entire world before ripping her away from me and plunging me back into darkness.

I should've pushed her harder about what she was thinking, about going with her to New York, anything I could to make her understand *she* was my dream. That being with her was the only thing that mattered to me. Everything else was just background noise. Ensuring that she knew with every fiber of her being that she was it for me, that the way I love her is all-consuming and bigger than anything else in the world. But I failed, and now she's gone.

I wasn't kidding when I said I was happy for her that her dreams were coming true. The only thing I ever wanted in life was for her to be happy. I wanted her to live out her dreams. The only thing I wanted was to be by her side as she did so. I know in my soul that Selina and I are meant to be together. That this separation is only temporary, no matter how much it's tearing me apart inside. I need to be patient and believe that someday we'll find our way back to each other.

"Can I have my phone?"

"She's on the plane, Vance. She won't be able to answer," Lydia says as she pulls away from me, stepping directly into Connor's open arms.

"I know."

My eyes lock with Connor's, and we stare at each other for a few moments before he places my phone in my palm. I take a deep breath, pulling up Selina's number, wanting one final connection to her before I let her go. Opening a text message, I leave her one parting message.

I love you to the moon and back, Seli. Always and forever.

I don't wait for a response. My eyes burn with unshed tears as I shove my phone into my pocket and stride out his bedroom door.

three

Vance

two years later

"This better be good to be calling me at two a.m. We have to be at the job site in a few hours," I grumble, sitting up in my bed.

I look around my small bedroom. It's not much, but it's all mine. This isn't where I planned on being at this point in my life, but it's a roof over my head, so I can't complain.

True to our plan, Connor and I have been working on getting a construction company started here in Tyson's Creek. Right now, it's only the two of us and a few other guys, but we always have steady work coming in. We are one of the few companies in the area. Choosing to keep our prices affordable and working on word-of-mouth referrals is working in our favor, but we want to take our small business to the next level. That's why Connor and I started taking business classes at the local community college. It's been hard trying to juggle a new business and classes, but I doubt it's any easier for Connor with a baby on the way.

"Did you pocket-dial me again?" I chuckle, flopping back on the bed. My eyes droop slightly, but I fight the urge to go back to sleep. When he doesn't answer me for a second time, I know something is wrong.

"Connor? Are you still there?"

"She's gone, Vance. She's gone." Connor's voice breaks as he sobs into the phone.

My body moves on autopilot. I slide my bare feet into my boots that are lying on the floor near the end of my bed before making my way into the living room. "What do you mean? What happened?"

Connor still says nothing. I can't hear any other sounds in the background that would let me know where he might be. *She* could be anyone. *Gone* could mean anything. Bile rises in my stomach at the idea of something happening to his mother or Lydia.

Those two women have been my rock since my mother passed. I always said she was going to work herself to death, and I was right. She had a massive heart attack during her shift at the grocery store. The doctor I spoke to told me it was quick, and she felt no pain, which to me, was a blessing. But most twenty-year-olds don't have to worry about burying their parents. I had bills to take care of and a funeral to plan, all while going to community college and starting a business. Mrs. Bennett helped me with all the legal stuff, helping me get everything situated with my mom's insurance, and since our house was mortgaged, the bank took care of all the paperwork for me, as well. Lydia helped me find my apartment, saying she wanted to keep me close so they could keep an eye on me, but I knew it was for my benefit.

I've been a mess ever since Selina left for Juilliard. I miss her. My soul yearns to be near her, but it's too late now. I should've told her before she left that I'd follow her anywhere, that I got into NYU and wanted to come with her. But I was naïve. I believed that our love would stand the test of time and that the distance between us meant nothing. At first, it didn't, but then her phone calls became sporadic, trickling down to nonexistent.

She always calls on my birthday, our anniversary, and on major holidays, but our conversations are always stilted and filled with a lot of uncomfortable silence until she makes an excuse to get off the phone. When she called after my mom passed, she listened to me sob into the phone about how much I missed my mom and blabber on and on about how much I missed her, too. She was ready to rush home, but I told her she needed to stay in New York, that hearing her voice was enough for me. What a crock of absolute shit. I wanted to beg her to come home immediately, but it felt wrong.

After that, Selina was always practicing or off somewhere with her new friends. I keep hoping that once Connor and Lydia have the baby, she'll come home. We can talk more, and everything will be fine, but who knows? Selina is living her dream, a dream much bigger than a small town near the Tennessee-Alabama border. I don't know how I ever thought she'd be happy staying here with me. At first, I hated her for leaving the way she did, but I know I'd have asked her to stay, but I will always wonder if she'd have said yes.

"Connor. Connor. Are you still there?" I plead as I search my small coffee table set in front of a faded leather couch for my keys, wallet, and shirt. Thankfully, I fell asleep in my jeans after a long day of work at the construction company. I find one of my shirts draped across the back of the couch before shoving my keys and wallet into my pocket.

"Just tell me where you are. I'll be in the truck in a few moments." I make my way down the stairs and quickly unlock my truck, waiting for Connor's response. My mind is racing with all the things that could've gone wrong. Connor doesn't answer, just keeps repeating the same phrase as he sobs loudly into the phone.

"Is it Lydia? The baby?" I choke out, my hand tightening on the steering wheel. I suck in a shaky breath and hold it, bracing for him to answer me when I hear someone else on the other end of the line.

"Hello? Vance, are you still there?" The soothing sound of Mrs. Bennett's voice sets my mind at ease. Relief courses through me, knowing that, whatever happened, Connor isn't alone.

"Yes, I'm here, Mrs. B. What happened?"

"There were complications during childbirth. Lydia..." Her voice trails off, but I already know what she is going to say.

"Lydia is gone."

"Yes."

"How's Connor?" I ask, already knowing the answer. He's devastated.

"As well as can be expected. Little Jade is doing fine, but she has to stay here at the hospital for a few days for observation."

"What can I do?"

Emotions clog my throat as I drop my head onto my steering wheel and clench my eyes shut tightly. I need to keep it together and make it through this phone call with Mrs. B. I need to be there for my best friend and both their families. I will not break. I will stay strong for them, and when I know things are okay, then I'll deal with my own emotions.

"We're bringing Connor to our house. Can you call everyone and let them know what happened?"

"Do her parents..." The tears I was trying to hold back stream down my cheeks as my heart cracks in two. Today was supposed to be the happiest day of all three families' lives instead of one of the worst.

"Yes. They were here at the hospital."

"Okay. I'll take care of everything. Once I finish

making phone calls, I'll come to the house. I'm bringing breakfast."

"You don't need to—" she begins, but I cut her off immediately.

"But I want to," I reply, and Mrs. Bennett sighs loudly into the phone.

"Okay. I'll see you at the house soon. If anyone wants to come over, let them know any time after lunch would be best. I want to see if I can get Connor to eat something."

"You got it, Mrs. B." I quickly hang up the phone, dropping it onto the seat beside me.

My hands clench tightly around the steering wheel as indescribable rage fills my veins. I want to scream into the universe. Curse the powers that be for taking such a beautiful soul before she had a chance to live her life. Lydia was going to be a mother, grow old with Connor, and continue to make the world a better place for everyone around her. But that's no longer possible.

"Fuck!" I shout, my voice echoing around the tiny cab of my truck as I tug at the steering wheel repeatedly.

I want to rip it out and destroy everything in my wake as I try to imagine a world without Lydia in it. Blood-curdling screams rip out of my throat as I release my pent-up emotions. I scream for the loss of my friend, for the baby girl who will never know her mother, and for Connor, who lost everything in a single moment.

Jade. That was what Mrs. B said her name was while we were on the phone. Connor and Lydia were determined to keep the sex of the baby a surprise, but Connor secretly wanted a baby girl who looked just like her mother. I wonder if he still feels the same. Little Jade is a blessing. A little life that was born of this tragedy and the last piece of Lydia all of us have. But how are any of us going to be able to look at her, knowing what happened? How can Connor love the tiny human that took the love of his life? All these questions swirl through my head as my arms drop to my side. My muscles burn and ache as I reach for my phone on the seat. I take a deep breath as I try to get control of my emotions before I find the number I'm looking for and hit send.

It took me a few hours to call all our friends and let them know what happened. Somehow, I kept my emotions in check, only allowing a few tears to escape as I delivered the news. I listened to everyone as they tried to process what happened before making promises to come visit the family as soon as possible, but I've yet to call Selina or her parents. I don't know what to say to either of them, knowing that the minute I open my mouth, the torrent of emotions I've been keeping at bay will come rushing to the surface like a tidal wave. So, I put it off for a little longer.

As the sun peeks over the horizon, I move on autopilot and climb out of my truck and head back inside to shower. My mind is completely blank as I strip naked and step in. I don't know if the water is cold or warm. My entire body is numb from all emotions as I lather my body with soap. I take the time to wash my hair thoroughly before climbing out and wrapping a towel around my waist. Once in my room, I go into my closet and grab the first pair of pants and shirt I find.

I should pay closer attention to what I'm putting on, but right now, I can't bring myself to care. I have clothes on, and they're clean. Besides, I doubt anyone is going to notice what I'm wearing. My entire body feels heavy, making it almost impossible to move as I struggle to get dressed. The pain becoming almost unbearable, I slide down to the floor. Dropping my head to my knees, I breathe in deeply. My fists clench tightly on my knees as anger and sadness continue to fight for control. I've never been a religious person, but right now, I have questions for the higher power in the universe.

"Why?" I croak, my eyes once again filling with tears. "Why her?" I'm met with silence, not that I was expecting an answer. I don't know what I was expecting, but I continue speaking, letting all my questions drift into the universe. "You could've taken anyone else, but why her? Why now?"

A sense of peace settles over me, as if someone is wrapping their arms around me. Comforting me. The smell of Lydia's favorite perfume fills my nostrils, and I sob loudly, my heart cracking open, and every emotion

I've been trying desperately to keep control of comes pouring out of me. Soul-deep pain overtakes me as I give in to these emotions.

My hands clench tightly around my shoulders as I try to keep hold of these feelings, to hold my friend right here with me. "Please don't go. Please, just..." My voice trails off, searching for the right words.

Is this really Lydia? Did she come to me, knowing that I'd need comfort? I don't know, but right now, it doesn't matter. Right now, I want to tell her how much she has meant to me.

"I'm shit with talking about my emotions, but I know you knew how much I loved you. You're one of my best friends and the glue that kept me from completely falling apart over the last year. I promise to take care of them. To let Jade know all about you."

A sense of comfort settles over my soul, soothing the jagged edges of my pain as the presence disappears. Loud hiccups wrack my body as I let go of one of my best friends. I meant every word I said. I will make sure that Connor is okay, that he finds a way to move forward without her beside him and that Jade will know about her mother. We'll tell her stories about how her mother brought joy to everyone she met and made them better people for having met her.

My entire body shakes as I whisper into the void, "Goodbye, Lydia."

I don't know how long I sit on my bedroom floor,

but slowly, my tears subside, and I push to my feet. The pain feels a little less than before as I finish getting dressed and head back to my truck. As I climb in, I call in and order breakfast from Just the Drip, informing them I'd be there in a few minutes before pulling out of the driveway and heading toward the center of town. I drive in silence. No music, just the sound of the birds greeting a new day and a gentle breeze coming through my half-open window. The sky turns a beautiful shade of pinkish blue as the sun rises higher into the sky. Main Street is still quiet—most of the shops not even opening for hours still—and everything goes on as if nothing has happened. As if our lives haven't been completely turned upside down.

I pull into a parking spot in front of Just the Drip and take a deep breath before picking up the phone and dialing a familiar number.

"Vance? Is everything okay?" Mrs. Grymes's voice brings another wave of tears to my eyes.

"No, Mrs. G."

"What happened, sweetheart?" Her voice softens, wrapping around me like a warm blanket. She has always had this effect on me. Just the sound of her voice calms the restlessness in my soul, just like her daughter's.

A sharp pain shoots through my chest, thinking about Selina. I know I should've called her instead of her parents. She was Lydia's best friend—those two were more like sisters—but I couldn't bring myself to do it. I wouldn't be able to listen to her sob into the phone, wondering if she was going to make the trip home to be with all of us. Her friends. Her family. The people that care about her the most. Would she jump on a plane to comfort Lydia's parents, to meet her best friend's daughter, to comfort all of us? I'm not sure if she would or wouldn't, so I didn't call.

"There were complications during childbirth, and Lydia passed away this morning. The Bennetts are all at their house and ask that people refrain from coming by until after lunchtime." I repeat the same message I gave everyone else, with no emotion, trying desperately not to say anything else.

"Oh, no," she gasps, and I hear the phone clatter to the floor. A guttural scream filters through the phone, followed by a set of pounding footsteps.

"Hello. Who's this?" Mr. Grymes shouts into the phone, the panic clear in his voice.

"It's Vance. I was just calling to let you both know that Lydia passed away this morning," I choke out, my knuckles turning white as my grip tightens around the steering wheel. The thin walls keeping my emotions at bay threaten to fall.

There's silence on the other end of the line. Neither of them speaks for a few minutes as they process what I've told them. "Did you call Selina?"

"No. I couldn't. I didn't know how..." My voice

cracks slightly as I clench my eyes shut tightly. "How to tell her."

"Okay, son. We will take care of letting her know."

"Do you think she'll come home?" I give voice to the question lingering in my mind since I picked up the phone.

"I don't know, but we will make sure there's a ticket waiting for her."

"Thank you."

"Anytime, Vance. We'll see you later," Mr. Grymes replies before ending the call.

A fresh wave of emotions fill me as I climb out of my truck and make my way into Just the Drip. Selina may come home. I may have a chance to talk to her face-to-face for the first time in two years. I wonder if she looks the same. If I'll still get butterflies in my stomach at the sight of her. Are things going to go right back to how they used to be now that there isn't such an immense distance between the two of us, or will they still be awkward, forcing me to accept that things between us are over?

"Good morning," someone says as I enter the café, bringing me back to the present.

"Morning. Order for Vance Kirkland," I respond, still lost in thought.

I know I shouldn't be excited about the possibility of seeing Selina, especially under these circumstances, but I am. I need her. She's the only other person in this world besides Connor who understands what I'm feeling over the loss of Lydia. Maybe even more, since they were like sisters.

Although Selina stopped contacting me frequently, she and Lydia still talked regularly. Lydia would tell me about all the things Selina was doing in the city, keeping me up to date on everything she was doing. I never asked questions, not wanting to know if she had found someone else or if she was homesick because I knew both reasons would send me running right to New York.

"Here you go, sir." The clerk hands me a stack of boxes before stepping around the counter, carrying two large boxes full of coffee, and striding toward the door.

"I haven't paid yet."

"It's on the house." They flash me a smile before pushing the door open and holding it, waiting for me to follow through.

"Thank you," I whisper as I pass them, thankful for the people in the sleepy town. "We all appreciate it."

Usually, I would make a snarky comment about being in everyone's business, but this isn't the time. I used to hate how my mom would know I got in trouble at school before I even got off the bus, or that without saying a word to anyone, they knew Selina had left for New York. Living in a small town makes it almost impossible to keep secrets; everyone knows everyone.

But it's times like these that the true meaning of small-town living comes to the surface.

I'm sure word has spread across town about Lydia's death. Although she may not have known them personally, or ever interacted with them before, everyone in our town is mourning her loss. That's what it means to be a community. We come together in times of need to support each other in any way we can.

I place the boxes on the hood of my truck before going to the other side and pulling the passenger side open. "If you could place that in the footwell, I'd appreciate it."

They bend down and slide the boxes of coffee into the car before grabbing the other boxes off the hood of the car and placing them on the car's seat. "Please let the Bennetts know that if they need anything, to let us know. You, too." They reach over and give my shoulder a squeeze before stepping back and closing the door.

"I will. And thank you again," I pull them in for a tight hug, their arms wrapping around me.

We stand there in complete silence, just holding on to each other. Silently telling each other that things will be okay. That the pain is deep now, but we will get through this.

"You're welcome," they say before taking a step back and returning to the small café. I make my way to the driver's side of the car, climb in, and head to Connor's parents' house.

I'm not in the car for long before I arrive. Mr. and Mrs. Bennett's house is a few blocks from Connor and Lydia's. Lydia's parents live a few blocks in the opposite direction, putting their house directly in the center of the two. I asked Connor why he wanted to live so close to his parents, and he said he wanted their child to be able to walk to their grandparents' house, just like he did before his grandparents passed away.

I pull into the driveway and shut off the car, wanting a few more minutes to collect my thoughts and get a hold of my emotions. After a few deep, cleansing breaths, I climb out of the car, making my way over to the passenger side to grab breakfast. After a few failed attempts, I manage to carry everything to the front door and use my elbow to ring the doorbell.

Mrs. B opens the door. Her salt-and-pepper hair hangs loosely around her shoulders. Instead of her usual attire, she's wearing a pair of dark-colored jeans and one of our high school football sweatshirts. Her face is completely devoid of makeup, which is also unusual for her, but understandable, given the circumstances. Her eyes are bloodshot from crying, and dark circles appear under her green eyes. She barely manages a smile as she reaches for the boxes in my hands. "Hey, honey."

"Hey yourself," I reply, stepping around her and striding directly to the kitchen.

"Did you plan on feeding an army?" Mr. Bennett chimes in from his place at the table.

His wire-rimmed glasses are perched on the end of his nose as he takes a sip from his mug. Mr. Bennett and Connor look almost exactly alike. Connor is a few inches taller than his dad, but they have the same green eyes, strong jaw, and messy dirty-blonde hair. His normally clean-shaven face is covered in stubble, new growth since he shaved sometime yesterday morning.

"Nope. The ladies at Just the Drip hooked us up," I answer, placing all my goodies on the island in the center of the kitchen. "They also said if we need more food to let them know." Okay, that isn't exactly what they said, but I'm sure they'd be happy to oblige.

Once I have everything open and grab plates for the three of us, I take a seat at the island. "Is Connor sleeping?" I ask, my eyes scanning both of them, searching for any hint of them lying to me.

Mrs. B takes a sip of coffee and hums softly. "Yes, finally. He just sat on the couch for a few hours, staring out the window before we convinced him to get some rest." Her voice catches slightly as tears stream down her cheeks. "He's so lost, Vance. I don't know how to help him through this."

"You're doing exactly what you can, Mrs. B. Being there for him. It's going to be hard on all of us, him most of all, but we will all get through this." I push to my feet and wrap my arms around her shoulders from behind. I rest my chin on the top of her head, just like I've always done since I discovered I was taller than her in the sixth grade, hoping that a simple act could give her some comfort.

"When did you get here?" Connor's gruff voice echoes through the silent room.

"Just a few minutes ago. I brought breakfast," I say, a fake smile on my face as I take in my best friend's appearance.

His hair looks like a rat's nest is sitting on the top of his head from sleep, dark circles under his lifeless eyes. Connor looks like a zombie, someone going through the motions for the sake of others, but he's dead inside.

"Oh. Thanks for coming," he mutters as he shuffles toward the table and plops down in the empty seat beside his father.

"I wouldn't be anywhere else but here," I reply, grabbing a plate off the counter and piling it high with food.

It is at this moment I realize that nothing else matters besides my best friend. I will help him through this. I'll remind him he has a tiny piece of his soul mate with him. That their daughter will be the most loved and spoiled little girl on the planet, if I have anything to do with it. And that I'll be here for both of them, no matter what. This will probably be the second hardest thing I've ever done, but I have no other choice. Connor and Lydia got me through the worst days of my life. It's time for me to return the favor.

four

Vance

"I'll take these into the kitchen," I say, for what feels like the millionth time today. "I don't want to speak for Mr. and Mrs. B, but I'm sure they appreciate your kindness." I force a smile before placing the container of food on the table and returning to my seat beside Connor.

I haven't left this spot for more than a few moments since people began arriving around lunchtime. Everyone wants to pay their respects and let Connor know they are here if he needs anything. I'm sure deep down he appreciates it, not that he has said as much, but he can't bring himself to do anything besides stare out the window. His eyes remain focused on the large tree in the backyard. The tire swing his dad hung for us when we were kids blows gently in the wind as the sun sets.

"This was Lydia's favorite time of day," Connor says, only loud enough for me and his parents to hear him.

Mrs. B cries loudly, burying her face in her hands as Mr. B wraps his arms around her shoulder. "It sure was. She said that sunset was the time to let all your worries and concerns from the day free and embrace the chance to start over again tomorrow."

"Too bad it doesn't allow you to go back in time," Connor croaks, tears silently streaming down his cheeks.

My eyes fill with tears at the mention of her name, my chest tightening with emotions I refuse to let break free. My mind races to find the perfect thing to say. That one phrase that could ease all his pain, but there's only one thing that comes to mind. "I'm sorry. So sorry, Connor."

"Why are you sorry?" he questions, his fist clenching tightly on his knees. "Did you kill my wife?"

He pushes to his feet, his entire body pulled taut as his pent-up emotions come exploding from inside him all at once.

"No, you didn't. It was some fluke allergy that only one in a million people have that did it. How fucking lucky for us. Maybe I should go buy a lottery ticket. I'll win the jackpot with this kind of luck."

All eyes in the room lock on him, watching him crumble under the weight of his loss. No one says a word, their eyes filled with unshed tears as they watch him slowly self-destruct. I knew this moment was coming, the moment Connor was going to lose all control of his emotions, but I assumed it would have been when we were alone, away from the prying eyes of all our neighbors and friends.

"Maybe we should get some fresh air. You've been cooped up in this house for hours." I reach for his arm, attempting to lead him from the prying eyes. "If anyone understands..." I begin, but Connor's eyes widen in horror as he snatches his arm away from me.

"Understand? You think you could possibly understand what I'm going through right now? I lost the love of my life on what should have been the second happiest day of my life. How can you possibly understand how I'm feeling? Please, enlighten me."

"I didn't mean it like that."

Tears stream down Connor's cheeks, his eyes light with pure fury as he steps toward me. "Then how did you mean it, Vance? Are you trying to compare Lydia dying to Selina leaving? Lydia is gone. She's dead and is never coming back. You can go to Selina whenever you want. Hell, you could have been with her right now if you didn't let your fear of being rejected get in the way. All you needed to do was tell her you would follow her wherever she wanted to go."

I know he's in pain and that he doesn't mean to lash out at me, but his words still hit the mark. I could have saved myself a load of heartache if I had just told Selina I wanted to go with her, but I was a coward. More worried about what it would feel like if she told me she didn't want me there with her than about keeping the two of us together.

Connor grips the neck of my shirt tightly in his hand, pulling me towards him. His entire body shakes with anger as our eyes lock with each other. "Do you really know how that feels, Vance? Do you? Do you have any idea how it feels to have live wires running through your entire body? That the act of breathing feels as if it's going to kill you and force you to keep living all at the same time?"

"No, I don't," I croak, my eyes remaining locked on his face. "I wish there was something I could do to ease all your pain, Connor. I really do. I know there's nothing I could say to make you believe things will get easier, but they will. You have your little girl, a piece of Lydia, for the rest of your life."

"I'd rather have my wife." Connor sobs as he releases his hold on my shirt. I take a step forward, wanting to wrap my arms around him, but he places a hand on my chest.

"Did you know they asked me to hold her? Something about skin-to-skin bonding or some bullshit, and I wanted to vomit. The thought of touching the thing that took my wife away from me made me sick to my stomach."

"You don't mean that, Connor. I know right now it seems like it, but you love Jade. You love her because she is a part of Lydia you can carry with you for the rest of your life."

"Right now, I don't know anything." Connor flops back down onto the couch and is immediately enveloped in his parents' arms.

I stand by and watch my best friend cry, letting go of all the pain of losing the love of his life and the idea of having to go on without her. Bitterness courses through my veins that fate could be so cruel.

"We're all here for you, Connor. Whatever you need, all you have to do is ask." I sob before I spin on my heels and head to the back door.

My vision blurs as I grab the handle and fling the door open, gasping for air as my chest tightens. I don't know where I can go to escape the pain that radiates through my body, but just being in that room, surrounded by everyone's grief, is suffocating me. I know I should've stayed by Connor's side and helped him work through everything, but right now, I can't get his words out of my head.

He's right. I can't possibly understand what it would be like for Selina to no longer be here. Sure, she's miles away in New York, probably having the time of her life, but she's still there. There's still a chance that I'll be able to see her again. To know what it feels like to have her wrapped in my arms, to beg her to forgive me for deserting her. For making her feel as if she had to choose between me and her love for dancing. All I have to do is pick up the phone.

"You seem like you have a lot on your mind," a voice sounds from beside me.

"Yeah," I mutter as I notice a tiny slip of a girl standing beside me. She has shoulder-length brown hair, her green eyes smiling softly up at me before she shifts her attention toward the setting sun. I take a few moments to try to figure out where I know this girl from. She looks to be around my age, so we probably went to high school together. She's almost a full head shorter than me and is wearing a pair of tight-fighting jeans and a plain black top—nothing out of the ordinary when coming to visit a friend.

After staring for a few moments, unable to place where I know her from, I open my mouth and ask, "Do I know you?"

"No. Not really," she answers, not giving me any further information. "We went to high school together, but we weren't really friends."

I narrow my eyes at the girl, trying to put her face with a name but come up empty. "Sorry," I grumble, not sure if that was the response she was looking for.

"No need to apologize. We live in a small town, sure, but you can't be expected to remember every person you've ever met, especially when you only had eyes for one girl." She giggles softly, her hand stretching toward me. "Emily."

"Vance, but I have a feeling you already knew that."

"Yeah, I did," she responds as she turns her attention forward.

We stand there, both of us lost in thought, before I break the silence. "What do you mean that I only had eyes for one girl?"

"Selina Grymes was your world. Just like Lydia was Connor's. You two circled those girls as if they were your sun."

"She is—I mean was. Honestly, I don't know what we are anymore." I chuckle humorously. "Either way, she moved off to New York to attend Juilliard right after graduation. It feels as if she's forgotten all about me and everyone here in Tyson's Creek."

"I doubt that very much." She turns to me, her arms crossed over her chest. "Did you ever stop to think that she's been hurting just as much as you are?"

"How the hell am I supposed to know what she's thinking when she doesn't talk to me?" I huff, confused about why I'm even having this conversation with a stranger. "I'm not a mind reader, you know."

"No, you aren't, but neither is she, Vance Kirkland. If what Connor said was true, you have been keeping some things from Selina. Things that would have made it so much easier for you to be together."

I open my mouth to respond but quickly shut my mouth and think about what Emily just said. Would things have worked out differently if I had just told Selina about my scholarship to NYU? Would we be living happily in New York together, or would we have met the same fate? There is no telling how things would've turned out, I know that, but if there was even a slight chance that things could have worked out, I may have done things differently. In the end, it all boils down to me being afraid to take the chance of putting myself out there for Selina. If there was a way to guarantee the outcome would have been different, I know in my heart I'd have done it in a heartbeat. But without that guarantee, here we are.

Selina and I had been so worried about stopping each other from making our dreams come true that we never took the time to include each other in those plans. Selina always planned on going to New York on her own, just as I always planned on what our lives would be like here in Tyson's Creek. Not once did either of us make room for the other. No wonder she didn't bother to ask me to go with her. She never knew I'd be willing to do so.

"It sounds like you're speaking from experience," I retort as I run my hands through my hair.

"Maybe the exact opposite." She scoffs, pulling her hair up into a messy bun on the top of her head. "Instead of telling me he wanted to spread his wings while at college, he cheated on me. I found out last weekend when I went to surprise him."

"Ouch." I grimace, trying to imagine who would do something like that to someone they claimed to care about.

"Yeah. Wasn't fun, let me tell you, but deep down, I knew there was something wrong." She shakes her head before shifting toward me. "The moral of the story is, don't be afraid to tell someone you love how you feel. That way you don't spend the rest of your life wondering what if."

She raises on her tiptoes, planting a soft kiss on my cheek before pulling me in for a hug.

I stand there stiffly, my entire body rigid before I relax. I wrap my arms around her waist and hug her back, letting everything else melt away but the feel of her arms wrapped around me. After everything that has happened over the last twenty-four hours, I don't want to live with any more regrets. It's time that I tell Selina Grymes the truth. That the only thing in life I need is her.

five
selina

She's gone. Never coming back. One of the few people in this world that knows all my secrets. I just talked to Lydia on the phone a few days ago. She was bursting with excitement about her and Connor's little one on the way. I had begged her for the millionth time to find out the sex of their baby, but she refused. She claimed it was one of the very few surprises we were given during our lives, and she was determined to keep this one.

When my mom called to tell me the news, I was running late to class. I tried to rush her off the phone, claiming to be too busy to stop and talk to her, but there was something in her tone of voice that made me pause and listen to what she was saying. My world came to a screeching halt. My best friend, partner in crime, and hetero life mate, Lydia, had died giving birth to a beautiful little girl.

In that moment, I wanted to rage against the world and demand to know what went wrong and who was to blame for this tragedy, but the only thing I could do was stand there, frozen in place, as a few people stared at me, wondering what had happened. Everything else around me faded into the background. The voices of the people around me asking me if I was okay became nothing but background noise as my mom told me she'd purchased me a plane ticket to leave in the next few hours.

I didn't stop to tell my teacher that I had an emergency and had to go home. I didn't think about what disappearing in the middle of the semester was going to do to my scholarship. The only thing that mattered to me was getting home and being there for Connor and Lydia's family and holding the only piece of Lydia I had left.

Everything after that conversation with my mom was a blur. I went back to my small dorm room I shared with a girl I barely knew and shoved some things into a bag before rushing off to the airport. Now, here I am, sitting in the back of my parents' car, wanting the only person I know who can take the pain away.

"Where is Vance?" I question, wrapping my arms tightly around my middle, trying to hold myself together. "Didn't he want to come with you to pick me up?"

I know I sound selfish right now, asking for him to be here. We've barely talked since the night of our graduation, but that's my fault. It took a few months, but I came to regret leaving Tyson's Creek early. I put on a brave face for my friends and my parents, telling them how amazing things were in New York, but I felt utterly alone. I had a few acquaintances, girls I took classes with over the summer, and my roommate, but we really had nothing in common besides dancing. We took classes, ate together sometimes, went to sleep, and then started the process over again. I missed having lazy days where I could read a book or go to the movies with my friends. Dance was beginning to feel like a job instead of something I enjoyed doing.

Every time I got a call from home, my heart yearned to be home with them, going to bonfires and just being with them like it had always been. Every time I tried to tell any of them how I was feeling, I clammed up. Mixed into their stories about what was happening in town, they were also telling me how proud they were of what I had accomplished and how they couldn't wait to see me dance across the big stage like I'd always dreamed of.

Speaking to any of them became almost painful. Our almost daily phone calls turned to weekly, then monthly, and then quickly trickled down to a random text asking how each other was doing or sending a funny meme. But Vance never stopped reaching out to me. He'd call and leave me encouraging messages or just tell me how much he loved me. At first, I'd listen to each message, letting his words wrap around me like armor before starting another day, but soon, even that became too much. Every time I heard his voice, I wanted to come home. I wanted to feel his arms wrapped tightly around me, telling me that everything was going to be okay. I wanted to be there with him and all our friends, but at the same time, I didn't want to disappoint them either.

"He's staying with Connor," my mom whispers, reaching her hand between the seats and gripping mine.

"Makes sense." I squeeze her hand back, forcing myself to smile slightly. "Connor needs him right now."

"You should call him and let him know you came home."

"Yeah," I mutter, reaching into my back pocket and pulling out my cell phone. My finger swipes across the screen, bringing it to life, but there isn't one missed notification, text message, or call. Not that I'm surprised. There are only a few people that even have my phone number, not that any of them use it. The only people who call me are a little preoccupied right now. "I'll just see him when we get there."

Just as I'm shoving it back into my pocket, we pull up in front of Connor's parents' house. Tears immediately pool in my eyes as I look at the familiar sight, remembering all the time the four of us spent here, making plans for the future. A future that won't be coming for one of us.

"You don't have to do this right now, baby." My dad's deep baritone echoes around the interior of the car. "You just got home. No one will fault you for wanting to get some rest and process what happened. We can come back in the morning."

"No." My voice cracks slightly, but I continue. "I need to do this."

Neither of my parents say a word as I open the door and climb out, going right to the front door. I don't even knock before the door swings open, and a familiar body comes crashing into mine.

"I'm so—" Leia whimpers, but I cut her off.

"I know," I croak, wrapping my arms tightly around her tiny waist and laying my cheek on the top of her head. Leia isn't short. I'm just taller than most people my age. The end of her long blonde hair tickles my forearms as I tighten my arms around her waist, letting the pain and sadness over the loss of my best friend overtake me for the first time since I heard the news.

"I didn't think you'd get here so quickly," she states as she pulls away from me, her wire glasses foggy from our tears.

Lydia was my person, but Leia Armstrong was always a good friend to both of us. We never intentionally left her out of things or tried to make her feel unwelcome, but I'm sure she felt that way at some point since we met during our freshman year of high school. Leia's parents own the small farm and inn in the hills surrounding town. I can remember all the nights we spent there, looking at the stars and wishing to grow up as quickly as possible. If I could go back in time, I'd tell my younger self to cherish those moments, because they'd be gone before you know it.

"My mom arranged everything before she called." I sniffle, swiping at the tears on my cheek. "How is everyone?"

"As well as can be expected. Connor hasn't said much since his parents brought him back to the house. Their little girl needs to stay in the hospital under observation for a few days, but she's going to be okay."

"A little girl," I whisper, a fresh round of tears collecting in my eyes. "Lydia would have loved to have a little girl."

"Yeah." Leia wraps her arms around my shoulders and pulls me into the house.

We move into the house in silence. The air is thick with sadness and something else I can't place. Everything looks exactly as it did when we were in high school. Family pictures are hanging on every available wall; the large oversized sectional couch is sitting in the center of the room. Everyone is huddled around Connor; his mom has her arms wrapped around him as she cries silently.

"Hey, Connor. Guess who's here," Leia whispers, laying her hand on his shoulder and squeezing it. "Selina is home."

Every nerve ending in my body is on high alert. My breathing is shallow and short as my body inches closer to him. The room becomes eerily quiet as we all brace for Connor's reaction to me being here. Lydia was my best friend, the sister I never had. Connor doesn't need to be reminded of what he lost right now.

"I'm sorry," I say as I struggle to suck in a breath.

My chest tightens as if all the air is being sucked out of the room and someone has wrapped their fingers around my neck. I struggle to take a breath as panic bubbles up from my stomach and settles in my chest. Beads of sweat dot my forehead as my eyes snap shut, my lips moving slightly as I try to find something else to say to my best friend's love, but I can't think of a single thing. There are no words that can help soothe the pain of what he's feeling, what we're all feeling, at the loss of Lydia in our lives. I clench my eyes closed tightly as I try to pull in a breath, willing my body to calm down as I wait for Connor to say something, anything. To even acknowledge my presence, but he doesn't move a muscle. He continues staring off into space as if none of us are in the room.

I need to find Vance. He's always been the one to keep me grounded, to stop the walls from closing in around me when I start to panic. My eyes snap open and search the room for him, but he's nowhere to be found.

"Vance went outside to get some fresh air after him

and Connor got into it," Leia whispers, answering my unanswered question before giving my hand a small squeeze and releasing it.

I nod as I turn on my heels and move to the back door, needing to get to him as quickly as possible. I can barely focus on anything but the pain radiating through my chest as I try to focus on the last time Vance and I saw each other. That was one of the happiest and saddest days of my life. I knew I was leaving for New York, but I couldn't bring myself to tell him. To let him know I was choosing my dreams over spending the rest of my life stuck in Tyson's Creek. That I was choosing to remember the good times we had together instead of growing to resent him for not being able to fulfill my dreams.

Now is my chance for a do-over. I can tell him all my regrets from that night. That even though I pushed him away, being here with him is what I really wanted. I can dance anywhere, but I'm only whole when he is standing there beside me.

In and out. In and out.

I gasp for breath, my cheeks and chest feeling like they're on fire as I allow the air to slowly fill my lungs, easing my panic. I reach for the door handle, ready to pull it open as the tightness in my chest subsides, allowing me to breathe easier. With my heart rate slowing, I pull the door open as I catch sight of Vance standing near the deck railing. The warm glow of the patio light illuminates his silhouette standing a few feet away from me.

Just as I'm about to open my mouth and call his name, I freeze. My eyes widen in horror as I see a pair of slender arms slide around his neck before planting a small kiss on his cheek and pulling him toward them. Vance goes willingly, his entire body sagging into this person's embrace. My heart recoils at the idea that Vance is wrapped in the arms of someone else, seeking the comfort that only I used to give him, screaming that there must be an explanation for what I'm seeing right now. But my mind knows what happened. He got tired of waiting for me to come to my senses, to realize that the only thing I've ever wanted was to be with him.

Gasping in shock, I stumble backward and pull the door tightly shut behind me. My entire body shakes with sadness as I step back inside, wishing for the ground to open and swallow me whole.

"That was quick," Leia jokes. "I expected you two to be out there for hours."

My entire body recoils at her statement, but I stand my ground, not wanting to bring any attention to what I just saw. Out of all the things that I thought could have happened with me coming back to town, this wasn't one of them. Vance promised to always love me, to be there for me in every way possible, but I guess that was all a lie. I never gave him any inkling that I was having second thoughts about leaving or told him I wanted to come back home and be with him. Instead, I kept all those feelings locked inside, and now it's too late. He's moved on like I always hoped he would, but it still hurts.

"Did you know?" I manage to spit out between clenched teeth as I try to get a hold of all the emotions running through my body.

"Know what?"

"Leia, stop playing games. Did you know he was seeing someone?"

"Seeing someone?" Leia's blue eyes lock with mine, her eyebrows pulling down in confusion, as if she has no idea what I'm talking about. "Selina, I don't understand what you are talking about."

"Vance was outside, getting very cozy with a girl I've never seen before."

"Selina, you..." Leia begins, her hands reaching toward me, but I take a step back. Knowing that if she pulls me in for a hug, I'll break.

"You know what? Don't tell me. I don't want to know what he's been doing and with whom. It's my fault for leaving without a word. I should've broken up with him properly instead of hoping that he'd be waiting for me like he always promised."

"Selina. I don't think you understand."

"I saw them, Leia. It's over."

"Seli, it's not what you think. Just go talk to him."

"I can't." Leia takes a step in my direction, but I raise my hand. "Please, can you just take me home?"

I love him, but I hate him. It's a tricky situation that even I can't explain to anyone, especially not now. I want to get out of here, to deal with the loss of my best friend and my greatest love in the safety of my old bedroom, away from prying eyes. I can attend Lydia's funeral, pay my respects to my friend's memory, and go back to New York, forgetting about what I had hoped my future would be with Vance and instead, create a new one.

"Please," I beg her, tears streaming down my cheeks as I stare into her eyes. Emotions flash across her face as if they were on a movie reel before she sighs loudly.

"Okay. But promise me you'll talk to him. Give him a chance to explain what you saw." She gives me a sympathetic smile before grabbing my hand and pulling me out the front door.

"Just get me the fuck out of here as fast as possible," I mutter as I climb into her car and pull the door shut tightly behind me.

Leia starts the car, pointing it toward my house a few blocks away, but never once repeats her question. I don't want to lie to her because I don't plan on ever speaking to Vance Kirkland again.

six

fourteen years later

"I never thought I would find myself here, of all places," I mumble as I look around my old dance studio.

"Things don't always work out how we plan," Ms. Cassandra replies as she leads me from room to room. "I haven't been able to keep up with things for the last couple of months, but with a little sprucing up, I think it will be good as new."

I scan the room, searching for the place I used to call my own. The once-vibrant blue walls are now dingy, with paint peeling in different places. The shiny wood floors are now covered in gouges and scuff marks, no doubt from the hours of dancing that have taken place on them. The room, once filled with mini ballerinas ready to dance across the stage, is now nothing but a dreary reminder of dreams lost.

"When your mother told me you were back in town, I knew what I wanted to do with the space..." She pauses. "I'm not getting any younger, you know. And with my son..." Her voice trails off, and my heart breaks for her.

Ms. Cassandra has been the only dance teacher in Tyson's Creek since the studio opened when I was five years old. She's the reason they accepted me into Juilliard. This place was my home away from home, and Ms. Cassandra has always been more than just my dance teacher—she's family.

Although I've been shit at keeping in contact with people here in Tyson's Creek, besides my parents and a few friends, I never once imagined I'd come back and Ms. Cassandra would not be here, teaching classes to the future dancers of the world. This dance studio gave a lot of us a place to belong, a place to call our own. My heart broke for her when my mom told me her son died in a car accident a few months ago, leaving his wife and young daughter alone. I never thought I would see the day that Barre Studio would close its doors, but her family needs her.

"I need the space to train," I answer, still unsure of what my future as a ballerina will be.

I had spent years training and finally landed the position of my dreams with the New York City Ballet. I'd danced with some of the best dancers in the world before finally being cast in the lead role of Princess Odette in *Swan Lake*. It was two weeks until opening night, and we had a rehearsal. Everything was going great until I made the last leap, coming down wrong and snapping my Achilles tendon.

That one mistake ended everything in the blink of an eye.

I had surgery, and now it's time to start the long rehab process. The doctors expect it to take about six months to a year for me to heal but give no guarantees that I could ever dance professionally again. I've known dancers who had lesser injuries, and they never completely recovered. Their turns weren't as tight, and their leaps weren't as carefree as before. The fear of another injury always lingered in the back of their mind. People would talk about how they lost their edge, and everyone knew what that meant: the beginning of the end.

The company gave me a leave of absence for a year to get back into shape, and at that point, we would test whether I could come back. Since I was in my mid-thirties, my career was close to ending anyway, but that was my chance to be center stage for the first time. Chances like that don't come along often, and I wanted to have one more shot at making my dreams come true.

But there's a part of me that's thankful for my injury. It's given me a chance to slow down and think about what my life has become and how it isn't anything like I had hoped it would be. Don't get me wrong, I love dancing in front of hundreds of people, living out my dream of being a ballerina. There is a certain thrill about being on the stage that I've never been able to find in any other place, but I don't have anything else but dancing.

I've been lost ever since I got on that plane after graduation, leaving a piece of myself here in Tyson's Creek. I threw myself into my training and schoolwork, hoping to dull the ache deep inside my soul, but the pain never lessened. I believed if I trained harder and became the best ballerina I could, I wouldn't regret my decision to leave. And for a while, it worked, but I didn't find the same joy in dancing. Instead of it setting my soul on fire each time I stepped on stage, it felt like a chore. A job. Something I had to continue doing to survive. If I'm being honest with myself, a part of me was happy when I got injured. I was given a second chance to find my passion again, to take the time and fall in love with dancing again. Time to work on getting rid of these feelings of incompleteness that have been bubbling beneath the surface for a while now.

I didn't hesitate to plan to come home after my injury, knowing that I'd need the support of my parents and friends to get through this, but there was also another reason I came home. To find myself. To find that piece of my soul that shattered into a million pieces the last time I stepped foot into this town after my best friend died. The last time I saw him and found out that everything I believed was true was nothing but complete and utter bullshit.

"It would mean the world to me if you'd take over the studio." Ms. Cassandra grips my hand, giving it a small squeeze, bringing my mind back to the present. "This isn't what either of us wanted in life, but it's the hand we've been dealt."

I pull my hand from her grasp, heading toward the wooden barre attached to the wall. As I run my fingers across the rough wood, memories of the many hours of rehearsals for different programs run through my mind. This old dance studio was my home away from home, my escape from the dull existence that Tyson's Creek had in store for me if I'd stayed.

I can see it all playing out in front of me. All the younger dancers I can foster and grow into the next generation of prima ballerinas. I can give them a place to call home, like I had. I can teach them how dancing is more than moving your body. It's a passion that can let you soar if you only let it. I can rehab my injury and repair my heart at the same time, putting the pieces back together and finding a way to move forward. A way to create a life that doesn't revolve around what part I get in the next production, but rather about what brings my heart joy.

"I'll take it," I say.

She wraps me in her arms, giving me a tight squeeze. "I knew you wouldn't be able to let this place go." She pulls back from our embrace with a smile.

"Connor Bennett is on his way here to give you an estimate on the few repairs that are needed."

I open my mouth to protest, but she cuts me off.

"Don't you worry. I'll deduct the cost of the repairs from the sale price of the studio."

I give her a tight smile, trying to process her last few sentences. I just bought a dance studio in my hometown, which should be causing me to panic. But instead, I feel a sense of peace for the first time in years. However, right now, my biggest cause for concern isn't the studio. It's Connor Bennett.

Well, not him specifically. I haven't seen or spoken to him since Lydia's funeral, wanting to close off any chance of hearing anything about what was going on with a certain someone. I didn't want to hear how good he was doing, how he had forgotten all about me and the promise he made to love me forever. Vance Kirkland is the one person I have no desire to see now that I'm back in town.

My heart still aches when I think about him. His smile. The way it felt to have his muscular arms wrapped around me. His wavy dark brown hair and soulful brown eyes that pierced my soul whenever he looked at me. He said that my happiness meant more to him than his own life, but that was all a lie. How quickly he forgot all his claims about us being soul mates. I've spent years wondering how different things would be if I had stayed. If I had gone to Connor's graduation party and said yes when he asked me to stay. I wouldn't have been able to tell him no. All he had to do was flash me a smile, and all my resolve would dissolve.

If I had stayed here, we would have had the life that everyone wanted: a big family, a white picket fence, the whole nine yards. But would that have changed anything? Sure, we'd be together, but I don't know for sure that I would've been happy. I always believed I was destined for something greater than this small town on the Tennessee-Alabama border, and when I was accepted into Juilliard, I knew I had to leave, or I would suffocate.

The one thing I regret about all of this is that I never explained to him what I was feeling. I don't know if I could have put it into words for anyone, including Vance. Even if I did, would he have understood? He was so focused on making plans for our future here in Tyson's Creek that I'm not sure he would've listened to my concerns.

He's always been the hopeless romantic type, refusing to believe that there was any other outcome for our relationship but marriage. So, to him, my leaving to go to New York was only a small roadblock on our path to happiness. At the time, I believed that, too, but instead of waiting for me like he promised, he shattered my heart into a million pieces.

Just as I'm about to open my mouth and make an

excuse to hightail it out of there, the bell over the door chimes.

"Well, as I live and breathe. If it isn't Selina Grymes." Connor's voice echoes through the studio.

"Shit," I mutter before spinning around and plastering on a fake smile. "It's so good to see you, Connor."

Connor looks exactly like he did when we graduated from high school, just with a little gray sprinkled throughout his hair. He still has that chiseled jaw and arms the size of my head, more than likely from throwing lumber around all day. Being part owner of the local construction company, Connor has his fair share of business.

"We both know you don't mean that, Seli." He wraps his arm around my shoulder, pulling me in for a one-armed hug.

I cringe slightly at my old nickname. Ever since I was little, everyone in town has called me Seli. But I'm not that girl anymore.

"No one has called me that in years," I grumble, stepping out of his embrace.

We stand there awkwardly, sizing each other up. My eyes flick across the room, looking anywhere but at Connor. I'm sure he wants to ask a million questions about where I've been or why he hasn't seen me in fourteen years. My parents and Leia are the only people who know that I saw Vance with someone else that night, and I swore them to secrecy. When I got on the plane that night, I was determined to forget about everyone who lived in Tyson's Creek besides my parents, but Leia wasn't having it. After she saw me here, she made a point of calling and texting me more, even wrapping me into her weekly calls with her room-mate and one of her friends. I grumbled about it every time she called, but secretly, I yearned for those phone calls. For a small connection to the last time I felt alive, even though it would have been easier to forget. But here I am, standing in one of my favorite places in town, after buying it from my second mother. Of course, he has questions, but I have no intention of answering any of them.

"Connor already has a list of the repairs I figured you would want to be done before the sale goes through, but if there is anything else you want, just let him know," Ms. Cassandra chimes in, breaking the silence as she strolls toward the desk and grabs a set of keys. "Here are the keys. Come and go as you please. This place is yours now."

"But we haven't finished any of the paperwork yet..." My voice trails off as she scurries out the door.

"Don't worry about it. We all know you're good for it. Besides, it's time for her to pick up her granddaugh-ter, Piper, from preschool," Connor reassures me as he pulls a piece of paper out of the folder he's holding. "This is the list of repairs Ms. Cassandra gave me, but if there is anything else you want, let me know."

He waits patiently while I look over the list.

"Can we refinish the floors? They're a little worse for the wear," I ask as I hand the list back to him.

He squats down and runs his hand across the floors before standing to his full height. "I don't see that being a problem, but you will have to close the studio for a weekend to get them refinished. Everything else on the list, we can get knocked out at the same time."

We take a few minutes to walk around the studio, and Connor explains to me how they plan to renovate it. The list isn't long, but it is going to be a lot of work, although I know Connor will get it all done.

"How's the little one doing? Jade is her name, right?" I question as we make it back to the front.

"Yeah. Jade is fourteen now. She's been a student here for the past few years."

"Connor..." Emotions clog my throat as I think about the day I heard I'd lost my best friend. Although I made a point not to come back to Tyson's Creek often during my first year in New York, Lydia and I kept in touch. She kept me up to date on everything that was going on in town, including how Vance was doing. When I heard she was pregnant, I was ecstatic for my best friend, promising to be the best aunt ever. Too bad I let my broken heart get in the way of that promise.

"I know. I know." He gives me a soft smile as he rests his hand on my shoulder. "She'd be so excited to have you home. Jade can't wait to meet her famous aunt from New York."

"Aunt?" My voice trails off as the emotions I've been struggling to keep in check overtake me. Tears stream down my face as painful sobs wrack my body. Connor doesn't hesitate to wrap his arms around me, pulling me tightly into his chest.

"You've always been a part of our family, Seli. Even with all the miles between us and the years without phone calls and texts, we've all been here, cheering for you and waiting for you to find your way home."

Connor plants a kiss on the top of my head as I continue to release all my pent-up emotions—sadness, regret, and guilt. I've kept all these emotions trapped inside me for years. I continue to cry, tightening my hold around Connor as I try to find the words to tell him how much his comment meant to me.

"Thank you," I croak out as my tears turn into sniffs, and I step out of his arms. "I really needed to hear that."

Connor smiles at me, his eyes shining with unshed tears. I don't know what I expected when I saw him for the first time, but this wasn't it.

"I can't wait to meet my niece, either." I sniffle, swiping at the remaining tears on my cheeks and stepping out of his embrace.

"Like I said, the feeling is mutual," Connor replies as he opens the front door.

"Does he know I'm here?"

"Not yet, but you know how news travels." Connor runs his hand down his face before stuffing it into his pocket and pinning me in place with his stare. "He never really got over you, Seli."

"I'm sure he's been fine without me. Plenty of fish in the sea. Isn't that how the saying goes?" I swallow around the lump in my throat.

Searing pain shoots through my body as I remember what I saw that night on the back porch of Connor's parents' house. A girl I'd never seen before with her arms wrapped tightly around him, her lips pressed gently against his cheek. To most people, it would have seemed innocent, but I saw his face. The look of pure bliss as he melted into her arms. He never used to look at anyone like that but me. And I thought he never would, until that night.

"Maybe for you..." Connor's voice trails off, then he sighs. "It was nice seeing you, Selina. Someone will be here on Monday to get started on the work."

"Someone? I thought you would do the work."

"We have a dependable crew of guys that can get the job done. Either Vance or I will probably stop in during the day to make sure everything is going okay." He reaches into his back pocket and pulls out his wallet. "Here's our card. Just call the office or my cell if you have questions."

I take the card from his outstretched hand with a smile. "It was good to see you, Connor. I really mean that."

"It was good to see you, too, Seli." He smiles before pulling the door open and stepping through it.

As the door closes softly behind him, I flop down into one of the chairs and try to imagine what it will be like to see Vance again for the first time since I left. My heart broke the night I left Tyson's Creek without saying goodbye, and it broke a second time on the night I caught him with someone else. However things played out for the two of us, I can't help but believe it was easier this way.

The time apart allowed us to grow up and see the world clearly. No one meets their soul mate when they're five years old. Seeing him in the arms of another woman on one of the worst days of my life was a wake-up call, reminding me I made the right decision to go to New York. To choose my career over what we had because I would've died if I had to stay here and watch it fade into nothing more than a dream. If I could turn back the clock, I know I would have given anything to be the woman he wanted, the woman that was meant for the future he had painted for us, but sometimes things don't work out the way we want them to.

Sometimes the past is best left in the past. I came home to get back into shape and rekindle my love of dancing before going back to New York. I left Tyson's Creek with a dream, and I won't let Vance Kirkland or anyone else stand in my way of achieving it.

seven

Vance

I've spent most of my day working on paperwork, trying to finish our quarterly taxes before the deadline next month. I lean back in my chair, glancing out the window at the guys as they leave for the day. I always wanted to be the owner of my own construction company, because working with my hands has always been something I've been good at.

"Hey, man," I say to my best friend as he walks into the office. "How was your afternoon with Ms. Cassandra? Did she find a buyer for the studio?"

Silence fills the room as I look up from the paperwork on my desk and notice the serious look on his face. Immediately pushing my chair back from the desk, I stand and make my way toward Connor.

"Is Jade all right? Your parents?" I ask, placing both my hands on his shoulders to get his attention. "Whatever it is, man, you'll get through it. *We'll* get through it. Together, like always."

Every muscle in my body tightens as I brace myself

for whatever he has to say. Connor was there for me when my entire world came tumbling down around me, even when he should have been focusing on himself. I was a complete mess when Selina left without a word. At first, I hoped that she'd come to her senses and come back to me, finally understanding that the distance between us was nothing and that if we loved each other, we could make it through everything. But when she didn't even look in my direction at Lydia's funeral, I knew I needed to try to move on, putting that part of my life behind me, but that was easier said than done.

Connor was there for me, helping me pick up the pieces of my broken heart while also learning how to take care of his daughter without the love of his life beside him. Jade and his parents are the only things he has left in this world. If something happened to them, I don't want to imagine what that would do to him.

"My family's fine. It's you I'm worried about right now." He steps to the side, heading for his desk.

My shoulders sag in relief as I wait patiently for Connor to collect his thoughts. He takes off his jacket and sets his tool belt and keys on the desk. If it was anyone else, I'd be peppering them with questions. Connor and I have been friends our entire lives, and I know he won't tell me anything until he gets his thoughts in order. No amount of pestering from me is going to make him process whatever he's about to tell me any faster, no matter how much I'd like it to.

"Why are you worried about me?" I question nervously, reaching up and gripping the back of my neck. "The most stressful thing I've done all day is work on our quarterly taxes."

"Why don't you have a seat?" His gruff voice is laced with sympathy as he pulls out the chair in front of his desk for me to sit.

The hairs on the back of my neck stand up straight as a sense of impending doom overcomes me. I don't know what has Connor so riled up, but whatever it is, it's obviously serious.

"You're freaking me out, man." I chuckle as I sit in the chair in front of his desk. "Rip it off like a Band-Aid and just tell me."

I try to make a joke out of this situation, but in reality, I'm sweating figurative bullets. Since Connor says there's nothing wrong with Jade or his parents, that only leaves one other reason for him to be this concerned about my well-being. Selina Grymes. I grip the arm of the chair so tight that my knuckles turn white from the pressure.

"Selina's back."

That small phrase feels like a punch in the gut as I buckle over and rest my arms on my knees.

"Fuck!" I shout, dropping my head into my hands.

Of all the things I thought Connor was going to tell me, that wasn't one of them. I haven't seen or heard from Selina since Lydia's funeral. She didn't say a word to me, just sat in the back of the church, her head cast down with tears streaming down her cheeks as she mourned the loss of her best friend. I had tried desperately to keep the connection between us alive after that, but she shut me out, leaving me with another scar on my already damaged heart.

Our sporadic phone calls and text messages turned into nothing. Finally, about a year after Lydia's death, I gave up and wrote her a letter to say goodbye. It tore my heart to shreds, admitting that our love wasn't strong enough to survive the distance, but I needed her to know that I'd always love her, even if it was from a distance.

I've spent most of our time apart wondering what went wrong, imagining how things would have gone differently if I'd had a chance to talk to her face-to-face when she'd come back to town. I should've tried harder to get her to come back, but when she didn't even bother to speak to me at our friend's funeral, I knew it was time to let her go.

We spent so many nights rocking on the old porch swing at her parents' house, making plans for our future together. Sure, we were young, but I knew the moment I laid eyes on her that we were meant to be together. Hell, I still do. Although my mind decided it was time for me to move on from Selina, my heart never got the memo. Just the mention of her name brings back all those feelings I've shoved deep into my soul, trying to forget how things could have been if I had only manned up and asked to go with her. To be a part of this new life she was creating for herself outside of Tyson's Creek and away from me.

"Does she look happy?" I question, wanting to know everything about her life since she left town all those years ago.

"She looks good, but the light she once had in her eyes has dimmed." Connor leans against his desk. "She plans to take over the dance studio from Ms. Cassandra. I was giving her an estimate on some repairs she wants to make before she starts teaching classes again."

"How long is she in town?" I murmur as I lift my head and stare at my friend.

My heart pounds loudly in my chest as I try to focus on what is going on around me, but my mind is only on one thing. Get to Selina before it's too late. Before she leaves again without a word.

He pulls out his own chair and pauses, probably attempting to gauge my reaction to the news. "I don't know."

A sense of longing fills me as I stand quickly, knocking the chair to the ground. Turning quickly to my desk, I grab my keys and rush to the door.

"I have to go," I say over my shoulder as the door slams behind me.

A few of the guys try to get my attention, but I'm focused on one thing: seeing Selina. I've imagined for years what I'd say to her when she finally came back to town, but right now, I can't think of a single thing. Instead, my mind is swirling with a million questions. I want to know everything that has happened during every moment of her life since she left me broken-hearted without a word.

I should be angry, ready to demand answers for her behavior, but right now, the only thing I feel is longing. My soul is crying out in pure joy that she has come back to me. I tried to forget Selina, to forget what we shared, but it was no use. We belong together, and now I finally have my chance to prove it to her.

With my mind made up, I climb into my truck and speed over to the dance studio, pulling quickly into a parking spot. I freeze as I glimpse her locking up the studio. My chest aches with a longing I haven't felt in years. Gone is the tall, skinny girl I once knew, replaced by a stunning woman. She's wearing a fitted red top with her long dark hair pulled back in a tight ponytail. The perfectly round globes of her ass are covered in tight-fitting jeans, just begging for me to smack them. Images of my handprint on her bronze skin filter through my mind, sending a surge of pleasure directly to my cock.

"Down, boy," I mutter to myself as my eyes travel down her body.

Unable to stay away any longer, I climb out of the truck and step around to the front.

"Hi," I say, loud enough for her to hear.

The last thing I want to do is scare her. She just got back to town. I don't want to send her running for the hills again. She spins around, and her eyes widen in surprise when she sees me.

"Hi." Her breathy voice caresses my skin, pulling me closer to her.

I take a step forward, but she holds up her hand, halting my movements. Her eyes clench shut tightly as if she's trying to brace herself for my anger, for me to unload years of pain and questions at her feet, but that's the furthest thing from my mind.

When she doesn't look up at me, I take a step closer, causing her eyes to snap to mine. My chest tightens at all the emotions swirling in her eyes—pain, regret, sadness, and most importantly, love. Selina still loves me—I can see it in her eyes—but there's something holding her back, stopping her from making both of our dreams come true.

"Your parents told me you were coming back to town to recuperate from your injury." I motion toward the small building behind her. "But Connor told me you were here because you bought this place."

Her eyes widen in surprise at my admission, causing my cheeks to heat in embarrassment. When we were younger, I was always invited to Selina's house for family dinner. We discussed everything under the sun; no topic was off-limits. Those dinners gave me the family environment I always wanted. My dad took off before I could walk, and my mom worked two jobs to keep a roof over our heads and food on the table. I spent more time at Connor's and Selina's than I did at my house.

When Connor and Lydia got engaged, I didn't want to be a third wheel. I didn't want to watch the two of them be happy together when the only person I wanted was miles away, so I gave them some space, making up excuses for the reason we couldn't hang out the same way we did before Selina left.

I assumed I could do the same with Selina's parents, but her mom wasn't having it. She demanded that I continue spending every Sunday evening with them. It was weird at first, but the longer Selina was gone, the more I wanted to cling to that part of her. I never asked too many questions, but her mom told me anything she thought was appropriate.

"You still talk to my parents?" she questions, her head cocking slightly to the side as if she's trying to solve a puzzle.

"Yup. I still have dinner with them every Sunday. Old habits die hard." I chuckle humorlessly.

"I needed a place to practice," she replies as she twirls her keys around her finger, a telltale sign of her nerves. "I couldn't let them close this place."

"Makes sense." I pause, awkwardly searching for something else to say. "How have you been?"

Her eyes flick back and forth, looking anywhere but directly at me before she answers, "Fine."

"Are you going to keep the classes going?" I blurt out, wanting to keep her talking and prolong our time together.

"Yes."

I reach up and rub the back of my neck. "Can I at least get *something* more than one-word answers from you?"

"Yes," she replies, and her cheeks pink in embarrassment. "I'm sorry. This is a lot harder than I imagined it would be."

I smirk and take a step toward her as she backs away and bumps into the locked door. Tears collect in her eyes, but she quickly bats them away.

"Do you want to get some coffee and catch up?" I question, not bothering to hide the longing in my voice.

"I don't think that's such a good idea," she whispers as she walks past me.

Our shoulders brush slightly, and an electric current runs up my arm and directly to my heart, igniting the love I once had for her all over again. It's been years since we've seen each other, but in some way, it feels like she never left.

"It was nice seeing you," she calls over her shoulder before hitting the unlock button on her key fob and climbing into her car.

I stand as still as a statue as she pulls out of the

parking lot and drives off toward her parents' house without a second glance.

I tried to move on, to be with someone else, *anyone* else, but I finally admitted it to myself: There is no one else on the planet that I'll ever love more than Selina Grymes. And based on her reaction to me a few moments ago, I'd wager she still feels something for me, as well.

"You got away from me once, Seli. I'm not about to let it happen again," I whisper into the wind as I stride to my truck.

eight
selina

"That did not just fucking happen," I mumble to myself as I aimlessly drive toward my parents' house.

I knew deep down the moment Connor walked into my dance studio that Vance would end up there eventually, but I didn't think for a minute it would be so soon. I haven't seen him since my parents dropped me off at Connor's after Lydia passed away, the night that changed the trajectory of my life forever. Okay, maybe I'm being a tad dramatic, but the moment I saw Vance with his arms wrapped around some random girl, it felt like the world was ending.

"Why are you sitting in the car, staring off into space?" Leia says through my open window, causing me to jump slightly.

"Holy shit, Leia! Are you trying to make me have a heart attack?" I grumble, shutting off the car and pulling the keys from the ignition.

"That's not something to joke about." Leia's voice

softens as tears pool in her eyes, and she steps away from the car.

"I'm sorry, hun. I didn't think before speaking, as usual." I immediately climb out of the car and wrap my arms around her.

Not only does Leia have to deal with all my emotional baggage about being back in town and seeing Vance again, but she also has her own family drama. Her dad has had a handful of health scares over the last few years, and now it seems he also has kidney failure. He's never taken the best care of himself, claiming that he's been on this earth long enough that when it's his time to go, he'll be ready, but he hasn't once thought about what it might do to his children. After her mother passed away a few years ago, it's like he has given up. It's as if he's only biding his time until he can see her again.

"Sorry. I'm not usually this weepy," she huffs out before stepping out of my embrace. "But enough about me. How did it go with seeing the love of your life for the first time again?"

"He isn't the love of my life," I grumble, brushing past her as I walk to the front door.

"Yeah, keep lying to yourself. That's why you haven't done anything but dance since the day of Lydia's funeral."

I wince slightly before turning the handle and walking inside. "Can we not talk about this right now?"

"Talk about what? The fact you saw Vance this morning at the dance studio?" my mom chimes in as she comes around the corner, her silver hair piled high on the top of her head, a sly smile on her face. "Does he look as good as you imagined?"

He looks better than I imagined, but there's no way I'm going to tell my mother that. He's no longer the same baby-faced teenager he was when I left Tyson's Creek. A chiseled jawline with a perfectly groomed beard covers his face. Although he works in construction, he isn't as muscular as I had imagined. His arms are really the only difference I noticed. His dark brown hair is a lot longer than I remember, making it almost impossible for me not to run my fingers through it. His chocolate-brown eyes still seem to be able to stare into my soul, exposing all my secrets and making me wish I had more time to prepare before seeing him for the first time after all these years.

"I haven't been imagining Vance in any way. But how do you know that we saw each other already?" I question, dropping my bag and key onto the small entryway table near the door before striding into the living room. "I only saw him maybe ten minutes ago."

They both scurry after me, neither wanting to let me out of their sight for fear that I won't tell them about my conversation with Vance. My mom grips my arm, pulling me toward the couch and forcing me to take a seat.

"Well, Mrs. Jenkins saw the two of you when she was coming out of Just the Drip and texted Connor's mom, who called me."

"And how did you find out?" I shift my attention to Leia, already knowing the answer to my question.

"Your mom called. She assumed you might not tell her, so my job was to get you talking." Leia flashes me a smile before plopping into the chair across from us and putting her feet on the coffee table.

"Feet belong on the floor," my mom snaps, causing Leia to grumble as she lowers her feet to the floor.

"You two are ridiculous." I laugh softly while shaking my head. "There's nothing to tell. He came to say hello and get our awkward first meeting out of the way."

"That was almost a believable lie, Selina. Now, tell us the truth," Leia retorts, pinning me in place with her stare.

"That man has not stopped asking about you every chance he got since you left town. There is no way he only stopped by to say hello," my mom chimes in, reaching for my hand. "I know that things didn't end the best between you two, but I know you know he still cares for you."

"I don't know anything, Mom," I whisper, pulling my hand from her grasp and balling it into a fist on my thigh. "He's moved on. I knew it was going to happen—hell, I wished for it at one point. Now we just need to figure out how to be in the same place together."

"Vance Kirkland move on?" Leia scoffs, pushing to her feet and coming around the coffee table. She kneels in front of me, grabbing both of my hands in hers. "Vance has not moved on, Selina. Just like he never cheated on you. He's always been here, waiting for you to come home."

"It's been sixteen years since I left town. There's no way he has been waiting for me all this time."

I want to believe every word that she's saying with all my heart, but my mind knows better. Vance and I were only kids when we made all those promises to each other. Sure, he spent every day telling me how we were meant to be together and that nothing could keep us apart, but the moment I stopped answering his few phone calls, he went running into the arms of someone else. Okay, that isn't entirely true either, but I'm sure he's found someone else since then. Gone on dates and tried to forget all about the love we shared.

Lord knows I did, but nothing worked. My stomach turned every time I agreed to go on a date with someone, because no one could live up to Vance. He was my first everything, and after a few years, I realized he was going to be my only. I hoped that he felt the same way, but after seeing him with that girl, I knew he had had enough. He was ready to move on and repair the damage I had done to his heart. Unfortunately, it wasn't that easy for me. I'll love Vance Kirkland until the day I die.

"She isn't lying to you, sweetheart. He's never once wavered in his feelings about you. You are the girl he's going to marry and spend the rest of his life with."

"I know you two are trying to help me, but there's no way Vance is still in love with me. Too much time has passed. There's no way to repair the damage that was done. We are just another sob story. We grew apart, went our separate ways."

"You're full of shit, Selina Melissa Grymes, and you know it."

Sometimes I forget how perceptive my mom is to my feelings. Sure, she's my mother, but she's also one of my closest friends. We had our problems as I found my way toward adulthood, but there was never anything we couldn't talk about. Even when she didn't agree with my choices, she was always there for me, supporting me even when she knew I was 100 percent wrong in my choices, and she was also there when I figured out I had fucked up, helping me work through my issues to find a solution I could live with.

"Damn, she said your whole name. She means business," Leia jokes before giving my hand a squeeze.

"There is more to your love story than just growing apart, Selina. When you're ready to face the fact that fate has given you a chance at love again, you know where to find me. We are all here to help you two find your way back to each other."

We sit there in silence for a few minutes, both of them giving me time to process what they have said. Is it really that easy? We can just start over? Get to know each other as we are now and hope that the memory of what we once were is enough to bring us back together? No, it can't be.

"I'll think about it," I whisper, not wanting to give them an answer either way. They've given me a lot to think about, but nothing has to be decided today.

"That's all that we can ask." My mom smiles at me before pushing to her feet and walking toward the kitchen. "Are you staying for dinner, Leia?"

"Depends. What are you making?"

"I haven't decided yet. That depends on if you are staying or not."

"No can do, Momma Grymes. Selina and I need to get moving or we'll be late," Leia jokes as she checks her watch.

"Late for what?" I question as she pulls me to my feet and drags me toward the front door. "Where are we going?"

"Umm, today is Friday. We need to get to Bristol's for our weekly call with Audrey."

Audrey and Bristol are the newest editions to our friend group since I left for New York. Leia ended up going away to college and met Bristol during her junior year. Leia and I had been chatting more regularly by then, and I immediately fell in love with Bristol. It seems she felt that same way about me, declaring I was her new sister. She introduced the two of us to her best friend, Audrey, shortly after that, and we have been chatting once or twice a week ever since.

When they graduated, Bristol followed Leia home to Tyson's Creek and opened a yoga studio instead of chasing her parents around until her dad retired from the military. Business has been good for her, mostly because everyone immediately fell in love with her bubbly personality. Ever since Bristol told us she was pregnant; it's been her life's mission to get all her sister in one place to help her raise her child once they're born. Now that I'm back in town for the foreseeable future, Bristol is working overtime trying to convince Audrey to move here with her daughter, Love.

"Ugh, do we have to?" I whine as she grabs my bag from the end table and shoves it into my chest. "I would much rather go upstairs, put on some pj's, and sleep until Monday."

"Are you that excited to see Vance again?" Leia jokes, shoving me out the door and pulling it shut behind her.

"No. Connor said he was sending a team over to work on the floors. I want to make sure I'm well rested and have a plan written out of everything that I want done so they can get finished quickly." I throw my bag over my shoulder and follow her to her car.

"Control freak."

"I'd like to think of it as being prepared. I don't want to waste their time. I'm sure Vance and Connor don't have time to waste between projects," I say, knowing that it's a complete lie.

I'd rather anyone but Connor and Vance's company be doing the work for the studio. The desire to avoid Vance and all the feelings that seeing him have stirred up after all these years is strong. I need to focus on getting better and reminding myself why I started dancing in the first place. The last thing I want or need is to be dealing with the emotional baggage that comes with being around Vance Kirkland. I know I can't avoid him forever, but I'm damn sure going to try. At least for the time being, that is.

"You really think Vance won't be the one to do whatever you need done at the studio?" She eyes me skeptically over the roof of her car before opening the door and climbing inside.

"Yes. No. Maybe." I sigh as I pull the door shut behind me and buckle my seat belt. "I'd prefer him to send someone else. I don't know if I'm ready to be in that close of proximity to him right now."

"Because you're still madly in love with him and would rather stay here in Tyson's Creek with him instead of going back to New York and making all your ballerina dreams come true."

"I wouldn't go that far," I grumble, shifting my attention out the window.

As I watch the familiar scenery go by, I think about how easy it would be to start my life over here in Tyson's Creek. I'm on a leave of absence from the ballet, whether or not my injury heals. It would be all too easy to get out of my obligations. I have a business here; my family and friends are here. My parents always told me I could dance anywhere. I didn't believe them when I was younger. My need to be in the spotlight was the only thing I could focus on. Now that I'm older, I understand that dancing is something you do because it's a need deep inside your soul, not because of fame and fortune. If I'm no longer a part of the ballet, is there really a reason for me to go back to New York?

"I would, but I won't. Right now, we need to brainstorm some very good reasons why Audrey needs to dump that douche canoe, Ian, and move to Tyson's Creek."

"That won't be hard. We're here," I answer quickly. "Besides, there was something off with her the last time we chatted."

"Maybe her cards told her she needed to run in the opposite direction, and fast."

"Maybe. All I know is if that asshole did something to them..."

"We'll be on the next plane to Texas to kick his ass." Leia finishes my statement as we make our way across town to Bristol's place.

We drive in silence, neither one of us finding the need to fill the space with noise. But when we come to a stop in front of Bristol's house, Leia turns to me. Her mouth opens and closes a few times before I laugh loudly.

"Just spit it out already."

"Can I just say one more thing about whatever this is between you and Vance?" I nod, waiting for her to continue. "I know that a lot of time has passed since you and Vance were together, but I know he still loves you. He never stopped, and by the look on your face right now, I can tell you still feel something for him, too."

I open my mouth to rebut her observations, but she holds up a hand. "It's none of my business, but if you wait too long to show him you still feel the same, you might lose this second chance. I doubt fate is going to give you another one. Just think about it, okay?"

"Okay," I retort as she flashes me a bright smile.

"Now, let our girls' night begin!" She fist pumps the air before climbing out and striding toward Bristol's front door.

Now that I'm back in town, it's inevitable that Vance and I will be pushed together at some point. I never got over Vance. Not that I wanted to. Leia and my mom are right: Most people don't get a second chance at love, especially with the love of their life. I tried to say goodbye to him once, but fates have crossed our paths again. I owe him an apology, among other things, but is it fair of me to ask him for a second chance? Is it as easy as showing him how much he still means to me, and then everything will be okay?

I'm not delusional enough to believe everything will go back to the way it was, all roses and sunshine. We are both older and are different people. We need to take our time and get reacquainted with each other again.

But so much time has passed. I'm not the girl I once was. Fuck, I don't even know who I am anymore. How can I be someone's everything when I don't even know who I am? The girl Vance fell in love with is still inside me somewhere. I know she is. I just need to take the time to find her. To find out who I am as a person, and then once I know, I can go to Vance and beg his forgiveness for being a silly girl afraid of being hurt and ask for another chance. If what Leia says is correct, Vance will flash me one of his patented smiles, wrap me in his arms, and tell me how much he missed me.

nine

Vance

"Are you sure this is a good idea?" Connor asks me for what seems like the millionth time over the last few days.

"No, but am I going to do it, anyway? Yes." I don't bother to look up from my desk as I search for the plans we sketched out for renovations to the dance studio.

I spent most of the weekend weighing the pros and cons of seeing Selina so soon after our run-in at the dance studio. I hadn't seen her since Lydia's funeral, but the connection between the two of us was still there, as strong as ever. The moment I laid eyes on her, it felt like everything was right with the world, soothing the deep ache inside me for the first time in years.

"Usually, I'm all for telling you to just rip off the Band-Aid and get it over with, but this time is different," Connor replies as he takes a seat on the edge of my desk, the plans I've been searching for in his hand. "She hasn't picked up a phone, sent a text, or even a smoke signal to you in years. To me, that makes it glaringly obvious she probably wants nothing to do with you."

"Would you be saying the same thing if this was Lydia we were talking about?" I growl, snatching the plans from him and stuffing them into my bag.

I know he means well, but if the roles were reversed, I know he wouldn't listen to anything anyone had to say. Lydia and Connor were, *are,* soul mates, just like Selina and me. It doesn't matter that we haven't seen or spoken to each other in years or that she just disappeared from my life without a backward glance. None of that changes the fact that she's a part of me, the other half of my soul. A love like that doesn't always come around for someone. Now, fate has given us a second chance. A chance to start over and learn from our mistakes. I'd be a fool to let this go. No matter what her reasons were for cutting off all contact with me all those years ago, we can figure things out.

"I know you..." My voice trails off as I notice the pained look on Connor's face. His shoulders roll forward as if he's trying to protect himself from my words. *Fuck.* "Sorry, man. That was a low blow."

"It's all right." He gives his head a shake before he forces a smile. "And if I'm being honest, no, I wouldn't. If it was Lydia, I'd tell you to mind your business."

I open my mouth to respond, but he grips my shoulder, giving it a squeeze to get my attention, and I snap my mouth shut.

"But this isn't about Lydia and me. This is about you and Selina. The situations aren't even remotely the same."

"True, but..." I sigh, trying to put into words exactly what I'm feeling. "There's something still there, Connor. I can feel it. After seeing her again for the first time a few days ago, I finally feel whole for the first time since she left."

"But are you sure she still feels the same way?"

"I don't know. But I need to find out. If I don't try, I'll regret it for the rest of my life."

"If she asked, would you leave?"

"What do you mean?" I eye him skeptically, waiting for him to explain himself.

"Selina told me she was going back to New York once her injury healed. If she asked you to go back with her, would you leave?"

"Yes."

"You'd leave the only life you've ever known. The business. Me and Jade. You'd leave us for a chance to be with Selina again." He repeats himself, wanting to ensure I understand what exactly he is asking me.

I promised Connor when Jade was born that I'd always be there for him when he needed anything, no questions asked. He doesn't ask a lot, but when he does, I drop whatever it is I'm doing to help him. Whether it be grabbing something from the store he forgot, picking up or dropping off Jade at her dance classes, or working every weekend so he can spend time with Jade instead of being stuck here in the office. If I leave, I won't be able to be there for him like I have in the past. Could I do that to him? He wouldn't be alone, but can I really break my word?

"I know it sounds selfish, but yes." I sigh. "I've regretted not going with her since the day Lydia told me she wasn't coming to your graduation party. I've spent years asking myself what if. What if I had gone to New York with her? What if she had stayed home for the summer instead of leaving right after graduation? What if she had come home for good after Lydia had passed away? I don't want to keep wondering. I want to know I did everything I could to convince her she should choose me this time. I wouldn't make her give up her dreams or force her to stay here in Tyson's Creek. All I want is for her to let me love her."

Connor and I stare at each other for a few moments before he sighs loudly and shakes his head. "Okay."

"That's it?" I question, wondering what brought about the sudden change of heart.

Connor has been trying to talk me out of supervising the work on Selina's studio ever since I brought it up over the weekend, but now, he's suddenly changed his mind. He can be just as, if not more, stubborn than me when he digs his heels in about something.

"Yup. That's it. I know you, man. Once you've made up your mind about something, there's no changing it." Connor pushes off my desk and heads toward his own before taking a seat behind it. "And I agree with you. There is something there between you two. It was clear as day when she asked me how you were."

"She asked about me?" I question, feeling like a teenage boy wanting to know what the girl he likes had to say about him in the lunch line.

"Yes, she did." He chuckles as he types something on the keyboard. "Now get out of here before you're late. I'll send a few guys over to help you get the floors sanded and prepped for refinishing in about an hour. That should give you enough time to talk to her and let her know where you stand."

I throw my bag over my shoulder and grab my tool belt off the hook on the wall beside my desk. "Thanks, man. I appreciate it."

"Don't mention it. But can you do me a favor?"

"Sure."

"If this doesn't work out, let her go this time. I get you want answers, but once you get them, it's time to let go."

I open my mouth but quickly snap it shut, taking a moment to really think about what he said. It took me a while to accept the fact that Selina wasn't coming back to Tyson's Creek. Every time her parents told me she wasn't coming home for a visit or took classes over the summer to get ahead, my heart broke a little more until finally, I'd had enough. Connor and I got completely wasted, and I wrote her a letter, saying goodbye. I meant every word I wrote, and still do, but maybe it is time to think about truly letting her go.

"I'll try."

"That's all I can ask. Now scram; some of us have work to do."

I give Connor a mock salute before turning toward the door. I'm about halfway there when I pause. "It will happen for you at some point, too."

"What?"

"You'll find love again, Connor. And if there's anyone in this world that deserves love, it's you and Jade," I say over my shoulder, silently asking the universe to send someone for my friend.

Connor and Lydia planned to grow old together, but because of some unexplained medical anomaly, she was taken from us. He's dedicated his life to raising their daughter, Jade, and this business. But he needs someone in his corner. Sure, he has me, his parents, and all our friends, but he needs someone for himself. A woman who will love him and his daughter unconditionally, the same way Lydia would have.

"We'll see," he answers as I turn and walk out the door.

As I climb into my truck and point it toward downtown, I try to imagine how this meeting with Selina will go. For years, I hoped Selina would come home, and things could go back to how they were before she left, but as the years passed, I knew it wasn't possible. I'm not the same almost eighteen-year-old boy I was when she left, and I'm sure she isn't the same either, but that doesn't mean our love is going to rekindle on its own.

Now I'm faced with the scenario I waited all these years to happen, and I have no clue what to do next. I spent a year imagining how our first meeting again was going to go and what I wanted to say to her. I rehearsed it, ready to demand to know why our love wasn't enough and why she left without a word. However, when the time came, I had nothing to say. All the words I rehearsed disappeared, and the brokenhearted boy came back to the surface, reminding me I was just as much at fault for what happened to us as Selina was.

I always knew it wasn't completely her fault, but for a while, I still wanted to blame her. I want to be angry that she chose to put us through the pain of separation. But as I got older, I realized I could've just as easily told her I was moving to New York with her instead of waiting for her to ask. I could have chased after her when she slipped out of Lydia's funeral without saying a word to anyone. There are so many things that I could have done and didn't. But now, fate has given me another chance, and I won't waste it.

My grip tightens on the steering wheel as I get closer to the dance studio, hanging on to the small hope that Selina truly still loves me. I haven't been with anyone since Selina left. I've dated, but it was mostly to help Connor. I refused to let him close his heart off to the chance of finding love again. I wanted someone to love me the same way I loved Selina, but I knew that I'd never be able to give my heart to them. Even after all these years, my feelings for her are still as strong as they have always been. I'd do anything, give up anything, to be with Selina, but I can't help but wonder if she ever felt the same way about me.

"Now is my chance to find out," I mutter to myself as I pull into a parking spot in front of the dance studio and take a deep breath, centering myself.

My heart beats loudly in my chest as I climb out of the car and walks to the door. I can't help but feel as if this moment will change everything. It will either set the course for the long-awaited reunion with Selina or shatter all my chances of getting her back. I don't know how things are going to play out once I open the door, but I need to try. For both our sakes.

As I pull open the door, a familiar melody filters through. "Some things never change." I chuckle, noticing the soft piano sounds of "Sweet Child of Mine" filling the room. As I come around the corner, I glimpse Selina's reflection in the mirror. Her eyes are closed, a soft smile spreading across her face as she moves to the music. Her arms move gracefully through the air as she raises onto her toes, her feet dancing across the floor as she spins.

I freeze in place, mesmerized, as I watch her move across the room. I've always enjoyed watching her dance. The way all the tension in her body disappears as she moves to the music, as if she doesn't have a care in the world, feeling this music as if it was a part of her soul. I continue to watch in silence as she glides across the floor before she leaps into the air. Her legs are outstretched in an almost straight line parallel to the floor, making her look more like a graceful bird than a human being, but the moment her foot hits the floor, everything changes. A grimace of pain crosses her face as she stumbles forward, her ankle immediately buckling under the weight. I rush forward, dropping everything in my hands, my arms outstretched as I grip her arm in my hand and pull her toward me, stopping her body from collapsing onto the floor.

"Are you all right?"

"Fine," she retorts quickly, her eyes wide with surprise. "What are you doing here?"

"We're supposed to start work on refinishing the floors this morning." I chuckle, my hand sliding down her arm and resting on her small waist. "I'm sorry I didn't say anything when I came in, but I didn't want to disturb you."

"Oh." Her tongue peeks out as she licks her bottom lip.

"I've always loved watching you dance," I whisper

into her ear, inhaling her floral scent as she steps out of my embrace.

"I thought Connor was sending some guys to do the job," she whispers, spinning on her heels and striding to the front of the studio.

"He is. I'm just here to make sure everything goes smoothly." I follow behind her, my eyes tracking her movements as she stops behind the receptionist-type desk in the front.

"You didn't need to come all the way down here for that." Her eyes remain downcast, focused on the few papers she continues to shuffle around to make herself appear busy.

I step behind the desk and place my hand on top of hers, halting her movements. "I know, but I wanted to see you, Seli."

"Don't call me that." Her voice cracks as I grip her chin, forcing her to look at me.

Her eyes are full of so many different emotions that I can't make sense of what's happening. She looks anywhere but at me.

"Look at me, Selina," I command, her eyes snapping to mine. Maybe she isn't the same person who left me all those years ago, but that doesn't make me love her any less.

There are two things I know at this very moment. First, any chance of me ever getting over Selina Grymes and moving on with my life is out the window. She is and always will be the woman who holds the key to my heart. Second, there is no chance in hell that Selina doesn't still love me. I feel in my heart that they're true. The other half of my soul has finally returned, reuniting with its other half.

I scan her face, trying to commit every detail to memory: the color of her eyes, the way a few strands of her hair fall into her face. But neither of us makes a move. It's as if we're in our own world and nothing else exists but the two of us.

"Welcome home," I grunt, brushing my thumb across her bottom lip as I lean forward, my eyes focused on hers. The need to claim her lips is almost over-whelming as I lean forward, brushing my lips softly against hers.

"Vance," she mumbles against my mouth before nibbling on my bottom lip and running her tongue along it, begging for entrance. "Please."

"Hey, boss." The sound of Easton's booming voice breaks the spell between us as Selina places both her hands on my chest and shoves me away from her. I stumble slightly, catching myself on the end of the desk before scowling at the two men coming into the tiny waiting area.

"Connor told us we could wait an hour, but I know how much you hate wasting time." He smiles at me before his eyebrows pull down in confusion. His eyes flick between Selina and me before he shifts his attention toward me. "Are we interrupting something?"

"Yes."

"No."

We respond at the same time, my eyes snapping to hers as Selina slides past me, her head cast down to the floor. "I'll be in the back if you need anything."

I watch as she scurries to the back of the studio before disappearing out of sight.

"Damn it," I curse softly under my breath before turning toward Easton and Jasper. "You can get started with sanding the floors in the back."

"You got it, boss." He gives me a mock salute before striding back out the door to get the equipment they need to get started.

Just as I'm about to follow them out the door to clear my head, a feminine "FUCK!" filters through the walls of the shop. A smile comes across my face. I've planted the seed; now it's time to wait for it to grow.

ten
selina

"**Y**ou are one of my best friends, Leia. It's your duty to come!" I whine into the phone as I hold another shirt in front of me and examine my reflection. My lips turn up in disgust as I throw it on the massive pile of clothes on my bed and go back into my closet.

"When did getting dressed become so difficult?" I grumble as I look through the remaining clothes in my closet and find nothing suitable to wear.

I just want the perfect outfit that says *I wish we hadn't been interrupted when you kissed me in the dance studio earlier this week, but I'm glad we were because my heart couldn't take it*. Although I'm not really interested in being in a relationship. Is that too much to ask?

It's been almost a week since our kiss, and I can't stop thinking about it, which has been very inconvenient. Not only that, but I've also been avoiding him like the plague. I should've been at the studio, overseeing the renovations, but when Vance showed up again on Tuesday morning, I hightailed it out of there, asking him to text me if they had any problems. There have been no issues, but that hasn't stopped him from sending me cute little texts throughout the day, and it's driving me insane.

"It became difficult the minute your mom announced your ex was coming to dinner tonight," Leia scoffs, reminding me yet again of the problem at hand.

When my mom announced Vance would be coming over for family dinner, I protested, but she wasn't hearing any of my excuses. When I threatened to take my dinner upstairs and hide in my room while he was here, my mom put her foot down and said in no uncertain terms that I will have my ass at the table at 6:00, end of story. I immediately ran upstairs and called Leia, wanting to have someone else there as a buffer between the two of us. The only problem is I haven't asked her yet. I have no doubt she knows why I called her in the first place, but in true Leia fashion, she's going to make me ask her before putting me out of my misery.

"No one asked you." I grab a wrap dress my mom got me last year for Christmas from off the bar in my closet before turning to the mirror.

"That was the exact definition of a question, Selina." Leia snickers into the phone as I hold the dress in front of me, turning left to right. "Now, are you going to tell me why having Vance come over for family dinner has you in such a tizzy?"

I toss the dress on top of the pile and take a seat on the end of my bed. "I just don't want to be with him alone, with both of my parents. My mom has been dropping hints she would be more than happy for the two of us to pick up where things left off."

"She isn't the only one."

"Whose side are you on anyway?"

"Yours. And that's why I refuse to come to dinner unless you can give me a very good reason why you need someone to run interference between you and Vance." Leia pauses, and I hear a rustling noise and the sound of a door opening and closing.

"What are you doing?"

Leia completely ignores my question as she continues. "You still love him, Selina. We all know it. Is it really that bad for you to spend some time getting to know each other again?"

"Yes, because I'm leaving. He has a life here. He can't just pick up and leave Tyson's Creek just because we get back together, and it's naïve of me to think he'd do it."

"You don't have to leave, Selina." Leia sighs as I hear a door slam shut in the background. "No one knows what the future holds. Instead of worrying about things that might happen, worry about the here and now."

"You're starting to sound like Audrey," I grumble, flopping back on the bed.

Audrey Wilde is Bristol's longtime best friend and the resident free spirit in the group. She reads tarot cards to help "guide" her to make the best decisions for her and her daughter, Love. I don't pretend to understand how a deck of cards can guide your decisions, but Audrey finds comfort in the cards, so who am I to say whether they help or not? The more time we all spend chatting about the universe and how everything is connected has gotten me thinking about fate, wondering if there really is a driving force that leads us down the path that we are meant for. Was it my misstep or was it the universe intervening and leading me down a different path than the one I had chosen for myself? I'm not saying it's not possible, but if I admitted that, then maybe giving Vance another chance is what is meant for me.

"Although I don't believe in reading tarot cards and the universe giving us signs like her, there's nothing wrong with living in the moment." The sound of Leia's voice brings me back to the present. "So again, I ask, why are you so afraid to see Vance?"

"Why isn't *I don't want to* a good enough reason?"

"For someone who doesn't know you're still madly in love with him, sure. But for me? Not a chance."

"We kissed when he came to the dance studio on Monday."

"You what?" Leia screeches as I hear someone storming up the stairs. My bedroom door flings open, slamming loudly against the wall.

I bolt up from the bed, all my attention focused on my door, ready to scream bloody murder at the intrusion, but I immediately cackle loudly at the look of pure shock on Leia's face. Her cell phone is pressed tightly to her ear, her mouth opening and closing like a fish as she scans my face.

"Why the hell am I just hearing about this now? You're supposed to lead with that type of information." Leia marches into my room, dropping a small duffle bag onto my bed, along with her purse and cell phone.

"What are you even doing here?" I question, quickly ending our phone call and shifting my attention toward her.

"Vance is coming over for dinner at your parents' house. Do you honestly believe I'd leave you here on your own?" Leia rolls her eyes at me before flopping down on the bed beside me and throwing her arm over my shoulder. "Besides, how else am I going to give Bristol a play-by-play of what happened if I'm not here to witness it firsthand?"

"How nice of you."

"I aim to please. Now, please explain to me, in detail, what happened when he came to the studio."

"We were talking about the renovations I wanted, and the next thing I knew, we were kissing. If it wasn't for the guy from his crew coming in and interrupting us, something more may very well have happened." My cheeks pink from embarrassment, a sense of longing settling over my soul.

My fingers brush against my bottom lip as I remember what it felt like to have his lips pressed against mine. It was like I was eighteen again. The same butterflies in my stomach reappeared, making it impossible for me to think of anything but the way his body felt pressed against mine, the woodsy scent of his skin filling my nose.

"It seems as if someone is more upset about being interrupted than the fact he kissed you at all."

"I don't know what you're talking about," I respond as I roll my eyes, wishing I could rebut her comment, but I can't. There's no telling what Vance wants from me, but I need to decide if that's what I want and, more importantly, if I want to try being with Vance again.

When I was younger, I felt I had to choose between being with Vance and following my dreams to be a prima ballerina, but is it possible for me to have both? Can I find joy in staying here and fostering a young girl's desire to dance the same way Ms. Cassandra did for me? Will that be enough for me? If someone had asked me that a few months ago, before my injury, I would have said no in a heartbeat. However, now that I've had time to think about how I feel about dancing and the lack of joy I find as I glide across the stage, I don't know my answer.

"Okay, enough with the heavy." Leia grabs my hands and pulls me to my feet before shoving me toward my bathroom door. "Go take a shower and wash your hair. By the time you get out, I'll have picked out the perfect outfit for you."

"Everything in my closet is right there, and none of it will work." I motion to the huge pile of clothes lying in the center of my bed.

"That's why I came with reinforcements." She winks, holding up the small duffle bag she brought in with her. "Now go."

I shake my head as I turn around and walk into the bathroom, pulling the door shut tightly behind me. I don't waste any time starting the shower and getting to work, keeping my mind focused on washing my hair and not seeing Vance in about an hour.

Things with Vance were so much easier when we were younger. Being with him was like breathing— effortless and something I needed to survive. But now, everything feels so complicated. I feel like I'm walking on a tightrope, trying desperately to keep from leaning one way or the other. If I say or do the wrong thing, it can tip me one way or the other. The problem is I don't know which way I want to fall. Do I want to see where things could go between Vance and me, or do I want to stick my head in the sand and continue denying my feelings for him?

"Are you almost finished in there?" Leia shouts through the door. "Bristol sent a 9-1-1 text to both of us."

"Did you go through my phone?" I mumble as I climb out, dry off quickly, and wrap a towel around my body before opening the door.

Leia's eyes focus on her phone as her fingers fly across the screen. "No. I saw the notification pop up. You should praise me for the herculean effort it took to not check for text messages from Vance."

"Good job." I giggle nervously as I grab a pair of underwear from my dresser and slide them on under my towel before turning my back and putting a bra on. "Are you going to tell me what the 9-1-1 message was about?"

"Audrey called her, crying hysterically about Ian."

"Holy shit!" My eyes widen in surprise as I rush to the bed and grab my phone.

My finger swipes across the screen, unlocking my phone, and I read all my missed messages from Bristol.

I always had a bad feeling about Ian, but I never thought something like this would happen. It seems Ian has a wife and kids somewhere on the East Coast. Now all his impromptu business trips make sense. He had a whole different life that he was hiding away from Audrey, and none of us had any idea.

"His wife called her?" I screech, burning rage filling my veins as I continue reading.

"Yup."

"We need—"

"Oh, no, you don't! We aren't missing out on family dinner, either. Bristol said she would calm Audrey down, and then we could come over later to help them brainstorm about what to do next."

"She should move here," I deadpan, knowing in my heart that Tyson's Creek is exactly where Audrey and Love need to be. Bristol and Leia have been begging her to move here for years, but it's ramped up even more since I told them I was coming home to recuperate after my injury. Bristol even brought out the big guns, claiming that once her baby is born, they're going to need all their aunties around to help them grow up.

"We all know that, but you know we need to convince Audrey that it's a good idea, as well. But I don't doubt that she and Love will be on their way here once school gets out." She flashes me a quick smile before grabbing some clothes off the bed and thrusting them toward me. "Now, hurry and get dressed. You also should blow dry your hair with the round brush. Loose curls will look best with the shirt I chose for you."

"Do I get a say in what I wear?"

"Nope. Just put it on and be happy I'm here to help you."

"Bossy."

"Yes, and you love me for it."

"Yes. I do," I respond before walking back into the bathroom to get dressed.

eleven

Vance

"Here goes nothing," I mumble to myself as I grab the bottle of wine and two bouquets of flowers for Mrs. Grymes and Selina. I picked them up from the store on the way here. I know both are going to declare I didn't need to bring them anything, but there's no way I was showing up here without something to offer as a thank-you for inviting me.

Coming over to the Grymeses' house for family dinner isn't anything new. I've been doing it for years; I even came while Selina was away in New York. But the fact that she'll be here tonight, especially after what almost happened at the dance studio, is exactly why I should have declined their offer to come to dinner.

Selina has been doing anything in her power to ensure we aren't even in the same room together for an extended period. If it were anyone else, I'd back off and give them space. But Selina is different. I've been waiting for over a decade for a chance to win her back, and I'll be damned if I let this chance slip through my fingers. Selina has no plans on staying in town long term, although her actions say otherwise. Either way, I need to remind her of how good we were together and to allow herself to open her heart to me again.

"It's just dinner at the Grymeses'. Nothing different from what you've done for most of your life," I say to myself before turning to the mirror and examining my reflection.

I run my hand through my hair, trying to tame the tousled mane on top of my head. My hair seems to have a mind of its own. Instead of the tousled, windblown look I usually have, it's a complete mess. Pieces are pointing in different directions, no doubt from how many times I've run my fingers through it in the last hour. Turning from left to right, I try desperately to tame my hair, making sure there isn't a single strand out of place. My eyebrows are pulled down in concern as I run my hand along my beard, attempting to smooth down the scraggly pieces of hair sticking in every direction.

"I really should've gotten a haircut," I mutter, just as I feel a firm hand grip my shoulder, causing me to spin around quickly.

"Hey, Vance. It's good to see you," Mr. Grymes says, a knowing smile spread across his face. "You look fine."

Mr. Grymes wasn't only the girl I was in love with's

father, but he was mine, as well. He and Mr. B were always there for me, teaching me what it means to be a good man. He taught me all the things a father would teach his son, and so much more. I thought that after Selina left for New York, things would change, but true to his word, he was always there for me, no matter what I needed. Whether it was a shoulder to lean on or someone to talk to when life got tough, he offered advice whenever he could. I always felt weird talking to him about Selina, but he never passed judgment. He always said that he refused to choose sides because he loved us both dearly. The only thing he wanted was for the two of us to find happiness, even if that meant it wasn't with each other.

"Thanks," I reply, my cheeks heating slightly from embarrassment and suddenly feeling very overdressed. I decided to forgo my usual work boots and jeans for a more polished look. I own exactly one pair of dress shoes—that thankfully still fit when I put them on a few hours ago—and paired them with a pair of light khaki pants and a royal blue dress shirt. The exact opposite of what Allen is wearing. I should've known that tonight wasn't going to be anything different for him. He's the picture of comfort in his dark-wash jeans and white polo shirt tucked into the waistband. To him, this is just a regular family dinner, nothing out of the norm.

"I feel like I'm twelve years old again, coming to the house to tell you how in love with your daughter I am."

"You were much shorter then." He chuckles softly, his green eyes shining with mirth. "There's no need to be nervous, Vance. I've watched you grow into a man worthy of my daughter's love."

"Unfortunately, that's where you're wrong, sir. I'll never be worthy of Selina, but I'll strive every day for the rest of my life to be a better man for her."

"What's up with this 'sir' nonsense, son? Call me Allen, just as you've done since you graduated high school."

"That was before I was trying to convince your daughter to fall in love with me again." I chuckle darkly, adjusting the two bouquets of flowers in my arm slightly.

Allen is the least intimidating man I've ever met. Even when Selina and I started dating, he was laid-back about almost everything besides making his daughter cry. If I ever did that, I knew there would be hell to pay. But today feels different. It's like I have to prove myself to him all over again, so making a good first impression is important.

"You say that as if she ever stopped loving you." He reaches his hand out toward me, and I grip it in my hand before giving him a firm handshake. I eye him skeptically for a few minutes, trying to make sense of his cryptic words.

"You're thinking too much about this, Vance. Let's make our way inside. You know how much Patricia hates when we let dinner get cold." Allen smiles before he releases my hand and strides to the front door.

I follow closely behind him, pausing for a few moments to calm my nerves before stepping through the front door. Although I've been in this house a million times, something feels different today. Maybe it's the anticipation of seeing Selina again for the first time in a week, but there's a charge in the air. A feeling that what happens tonight could change everything between Selina and me for the better or ruin any chance of us reconciling with each other.

"What's for dinner tonight, Mrs. Grymes? I'm starving." I force a smile as I enter the open-concept living room-kitchen combo behind Allen.

"My name is Patricia. Mrs. Grymes was my mother-in-law. Now, come give me a hug and kiss."

Patricia is almost the exact opposite of Selina. At one point, they had the same long brown hair, but she isn't tall like her daughter. We used to tease her about not even being tall enough to get on the kid rides at the carnival when it came through town. She's also dressed for comfort today, wearing a pair of black leggings and an oversized shirt that comes down to her mid-thigh.

"As if I was planning on doing anything else," I reply, placing my gifts on the counter as I make my way around the island. She immediately envelops me in a warm hug, her head barely coming to the center of my chest as she wraps her arms around me. My shoulders sag in relief as I plant a kiss on the top of her head. "Aren't you the most beautiful woman I've ever seen?"

Patricia Grymes has always doted on Selina and all her friends, me included. Although I had my mother with me for most of my childhood, Patricia and Allen were the ones who gave me a family. I love my mother with all my heart, but spending time with the Grymeses was like being a part of a family. Our bond goes beyond me once being Selina's boyfriend. We are family. We may not be related by blood, but the Grymeses and Bennetts are the family I chose. The people who I know will give me the shirts off their backs, and I'd do the same for them.

"Flattery will get you everywhere." She snickers before pulling back, her hand cupping my cheek softly. "But remember, there's no need to be nervous, honey. Selina still loves you; we can all see it. You just need to be patient with her. She's afraid of a lot more than just getting her heart broken."

If anyone would know what Selina was feeling, it would be her mother. Selina and her mother are very close. Selina used to tell her mother everything, and I mean *everything*, but she never used it against us. I can't deny the chemistry that sparked between us at the dance studio a few days ago. There's still something there between us. I can feel it in my soul, but hearing Patricia confirm my suspicions gives me hope. It might be a little easier to win Selina back than I originally believed.

"I hope you're right," I whisper, pulling her in for a tight squeeze before grabbing one of the bouquets off the counter and handing it to her. "For you, milady."

She takes them from me with a smile, pulling them to her nose before inhaling deeply. "I should chastise you for bringing them, but I know my words will fall on deaf ears."

"It would. I also brought a bottle of your favorite wine." I motion my head toward the bottle sitting to the right of Selina's flowers.

"Good thing I made your favorite for dinner. Think of it as a thank-you for an amazing gift."

Patricia Grymes makes the best chicken pot pie this side of the Mississippi River. People have promised to name their firstborn children after her for a chance to sneak a peek at her recipe, and she always refuses. She's made it for me a handful of times, but it's been over a year since the last time I had it.

I immediately drop onto one knee and grasp her hands in mine. "Please leave Allen and marry me, Patricia. Then I can have chicken pot pie every day for the rest of my life."

Selina strolls into the room, coming to a stop a few feet away from us. "So, now you want to spend the rest of your life with my mother, huh?"

I push to my feet and turn toward the familiar,

sultry voice as my eyes scan Selina's body, looking exactly like the girl I fell in love with all those years ago. Her long chocolate-brown hair cascades down her back, framing her face. Her long, gorgeous legs look as if they were painted into the pair of ripped dark-wash jeans she's wearing. She has on red patent leather heels that catch the reflection of the lights in the room as she makes her way closer to me. To finish the ensemble, she's wearing a loose-fitting low-cut shirt the same color as her shoes, showing just enough skin to make my mouth water.

"My eyes are up here, Vance." Her eyes are bright with amusement as a sensual smile spreads across her face.

"Can you blame me?"

"I don't. She looks smoking hot," Leia chimes in as she comes into the room, walking right past me and planting a kiss on Patricia's cheek. She whispers something into her ear, which causes them both to laugh loudly.

"Do I even want to know what you two are over there giggling about?" Selina asks, as I wrap my arms around her waist and bring her close to my chest.

"You look beautiful," I whisper into her ear before burying my nose into the crook of her neck and inhaling deeply.

Selina's entire body sags into my embrace as she wraps her arms around my waist, sliding her hands into my back pockets like she used to do when we were younger. We stand there for a few minutes, enjoying being in each other's arms again before Leia's voice breaks the spell. "My stomach is about to eat itself! Momma G, please tell me that dinner is ready."

"We can eat as soon as you and Selina set the table."

"We're on it, Mom," Selina replies as she unravels herself from my grasp and veers toward her mother.

My eyes remain locked on her as she moves around the kitchen. The two of them work together, grabbing everything they need to set the table for dinner and disappearing into the dining room to the left of the kitchen.

"Don't forget the flowers," Allen says as he claps me hard on the shoulder, causing me to jump slightly.

"Right. The flowers." I grab the bouquet of flowers I picked up for Selina off the island and walks into the dining room.

Selina and Leia are arguing quietly on the other side of the table. Each one points to a different seat, their hands waving wildly in the air as they argue. "Anything I can help with?"

Both their heads swivel in my direction. Selina's cheeks turn a delicious shade of pink as her eyes drop to the table in front of her.

"We need you to pick a seat," Leia huffs, crossing her arms over her chest.

"Where is Selina sitting?" I ask, wanting every chance I can get to be near her.

"See! I told you he was going to say that." Leia rolls her eyes before pulling out the chair to the right and plopping down into the seat.

"I just wasn't sure where I fit into family dinner anymore," Selina murmurs, barely loud enough for me to hear. "I know you guys have been having dinner together while I was in New York and probably have a certain way that you do things. I don't want to intrude."

"How can you intrude on your own family dinner?" Patricia says from behind me as she places the casserole dish containing the chicken pot pie in the center of the table.

"I think someone is nervous," Allen says as he places a basket of rolls on the table and takes a seat at the head of the table to my left.

"Dad!" Selina whines before pulling out the chair beside Leia, taking a seat, and dropping her head into her hands.

"What? I'm only saying how I feel." He chuckles as I make my way around the table and place the flowers on the table in front of Selina.

"There's no need to be nervous, sweetheart. It's just dinner, no strings attached," I say as Selina's head snaps in my direction, our gazes locking. Our eyes remain glued to each other, the air crackling with energy as I lean toward her and plant a kiss on the top of her head.

"Thank you," she mumbles before bringing the flowers up to her nose and inhaling.

Leia mouths, "Good job," over Selina's head and flashes me a thumbs-up, causing me to chuckle softly before I move toward my place between Allen and Patricia on the other side of the table.

I could've taken the seat on the other side of Selina, but something tells me that wouldn't have gone over very well. Selina seems to be just as nervous as I am about this dinner, hopefully for the same reason. The last thing I want to do is corner her or make her feel uncomfortable in her own home. Sometimes a little space is necessary to ensure you get what you want.

"Selina. Please say grace," Patricia says as I take my seat between her and Allen.

"Yes, ma'am," Selina responds as we all bow our heads, and she prays over our meal.

I've never been a religious person. Bowing my head at dinner as Allen blessed the food was something I did, but I've never once had anything I was particularly thankful for until now. I never wanted Selina to get injured while dancing. But she did, and of all the places she could have gone to rehab, she came home to Tyson's Creek. I can't help but wonder if there was someone else pulling the strings, leading the two of us into each other's path again.

Thank you for a second chance with Selina. I'll do

everything in my power to ensure things work out this time.

"Amen," we all say in unison before filling our plates with the delicious meal Patricia prepared for us.

In between mouthfuls, we each take turns catching up on what has been happening with everyone since the last time we had dinner. Leia tells us how her dad is doing after his most recent health scare, and Selina and I fill her parents in on how the renovations at the studio are going. We don't dig into anything heavy until it's time for dessert.

"So, Vance, are you seeing anyone right now?" Patricia asks as she places an apple pie, judging by the smell, in the center of the table. "I heard there's a new girl that works at Just the Drip. Maybe you should ask her out."

"Are you being serious right now, Mom?" Selina groans, clamping her eyes shut tightly before dropping her forehead into her hands.

"You aren't being very subtle there, Momma G." Leia snickers, patting Selina on the back as her eyes focus on mine.

I have two choices. I can completely ignore the question because everyone at this table knows Selina holds my heart, or I can take a chance. I've hinted to her that I'm still in love with her, but not once have I just come out and said it directly to her. Patricia has given me the perfect opportunity to ensure that Selina has no doubts about where I stand when it comes to her.

"I'm sure whoever the girl you're talking about is sweet, but there is only one woman who has held my heart since I was five years old. She's it for me."

"How can you know how you feel about her after all this time? People change. They grow up and sometimes become completely different people than you knew when you were younger. Maybe that five-year-old little girl isn't the same person you gave your heart to all those years ago," Selina mutters, her head still resting in her hands as she continues to avoid looking at me or anyone else in the room.

"No matter who you are right now or the things you've done, I've never stopped loving you, Selina. I had to let you go to survive. The pain of not being near you consumed me, making it almost unbearable to get out of bed every day. I wrote you that letter saying goodbye so I could move forward, but that doesn't mean I stopped loving you. I spent every day since you left begging the stars to bring you back to me."

"Letter? What letter?" Selina's eyebrows pull down in confusion as she looks at her mother. "Mom. What's he talking about?"

"The letter I have had sitting in my nightstand drawer since the day he gave it to me. You forbade us from telling you anything about Vance or anyone here in town after Lydia passed away. I was just respecting your wishes, honey. You can have it whenever you want."

The room fills with tension as Selina stares at her mother; a myriad of emotions flash across her face as she tries to process what her mother just said. I didn't know that she never gave Selina the letter I wrote to her, but deep down, it makes sense. My heart aches at the missed opportunity, but I can understand it. Lydia told me that Selina was afraid to see me before she left for New York after graduation because she knew she'd break. If that was the case, why would she want to get a letter from me, especially one where I pour my heart out to her?

"I want it," Selina demands as she pushes back from the table and stands. "Leia and I will do the dishes."

Patricia's eyes fill with concern as she watches Selina grab her plate off the table and marches into the kitchen. "Okay."

"Dinner was amazing, Momma G. You outdid yourself." Leia flashes her a sly smile before grabbing her plate off the table and following Selina into the kitchen.

"I'm sorry for ruining dinner," I say the moment Leia and Selina are out of sight. "I just wanted to make sure she knew how I felt about her."

Allen reaches over and gives my shoulder a

squeeze. "It's not your fault, son. I have a feeling Patricia completely forgot about the letter."

"He's right, Vance. I'm the one who should be apologizing."

"No need to apologize." I reach over and squeeze her hand. "I'm going to finish clearing the table and see if I can smooth things over with Selina."

"Good luck," Allen says, as I grab the last few plates off the table and make my way into the kitchen.

Selina is elbow-deep in soapy water when I enter the room, Leia standing studiously beside her, waiting for the next dish to dry and put away.

"I always thought it was weird your parents never used the dishwasher," I say, placing the dishes in my hand next to her at the sink before making my way around to the other side.

"A dishwasher is for dishes. Anything else needs to be cleaned by hand. Mom's orders," Selina grumbles as she continues scrubbing furiously at the casserole pan from dinner. "And the cook never cleans up after themselves. Doing the dishes is how we show our thanks for the food."

"I didn't forget," I murmur, my eyes shifting to Leia, looking for a hint as to what the right thing to say is, but she remains silent. The only thing I get from her is a shoulder shrug, letting me know her guess is as good as mine.

The three of us stand there in silence, none of us

knowing exactly what to say. After a few moments, Allen and Patricia come into the kitchen, carrying the rest of the dishes from the table and the uncut pie that was meant for dessert. "Anyone want pie?"

"We need to head to Bristol's once we finish up here. Audrey needs help figuring something out." Selina doesn't even look at her mother as she finishes the last pan before handing it to Leia to dry.

I haven't heard much about Audrey in the past, but I know she's one of Bristol's childhood friends. Bristol moved back to town with Leia after they graduated college. I know from chatting with Leia that they all became fast friends, having video call gab sessions and movie nights, as if they weren't miles away from each other. Selina even joined in while she was away in New York, but I never dared to ask anything more.

"Oh, no. I hope she and Love are okay," Patricia responds, her voice filled with concern.

Leia bends over, shoving the pan into the cabinet next to the stove before hanging the damp towel over the bar on the oven. "Everyone is okay, but some big decisions need to be made, and soon. The moment we finish loading the dishwasher, we are going to leave, but I doubt Bristol would turn her nose up at a piece of your pie."

"You got it." Mrs. G winks at Leia as she places the pie on the counter and pulls the saran wrap out of the drawer. "You make her promise to share with you and Selina."

"You can bet on it," Leia retorts as Patricia finishes wrapping the pie and slides it toward her.

"You two be safe on the roads tonight. The news said there is a storm rolling in," Allen says as he threads his fingers through Patricia's and leads her to the living room, taking a seat and turning on the television.

"No need to worry, Papa G. If things get too bad, we'll bunker down at Bristol's for the night."

My eyes slide back to Selina, taking in her rigid posture. Her entire body seems to vibrate with emotions as if she could explode at any moment. I'm not sure if she is angry about not getting my letter or the fact that I brought it up in the first place, but I have to smooth things over with her.

"I can load the dishwasher so you two can leave for Bristol's. I need to show the cook my thanks for a wonderful dinner, too." I wink at her before rolling up my sleeves and making my way to the other side of the island.

Selina's shoulders sag slightly as she wipes her hands on the towel hanging from the stove and heads toward her parents in the living room. She whispers something into Patricia's ear before giving her a hug, followed by her father, and heads toward the front door.

"Thanks for dinner, Momma and Papa G! It was

amazing, as usual. I'll make sure Selina texts you if she isn't coming home tonight."

"Thank you, Leia," Patricia replies over her shoulder before shifting her attention back to the television.

"Thank you for loading the dishwasher," Selina says quietly before trying to slide past me, but I grip her wrist in the hand, pulling her to a stop.

"I'm sorry for bringing up the past tonight. This wasn't the place for declarations of love, but I meant every word I said."

Selina pulls her hand from my grasp and continues to the door without another word. I watch her go, willing her to come back and talk to me, but I'm met with the sound of the door clicking shut softly as she leaves the house.

"Don't worry, Vance. She hears you, but I have a feeling she's scared to let you in again." Leia sighs as she grabs the pie off the counter.

"She has nothing to be afraid of," I grumble as I pull the dishwasher open and rinse the dishes before placing them neatly inside the dishwasher.

"That's where you're wrong. She has everything to be afraid of," Leia replies as she follows Selina out the door.

twelve
selina

"Thank goodness you two are finally here." Bristol sighs as we walk through her front door and into her spacious living room. "Audrey will be calling any minute now."

Bristol lives on the other side of town from my parents' house in a single-story brick home. Most people would think it was small, but for Bristol, it's the perfect size. The living room is the first room you walk into, with light-colored wood floors and a fireplace by two oversized windows, which brighten the room significantly during the daylight hours, giving her the perfect place to complete her daily yoga routine before starting her day.

"How is she doing, by the way?" I ask before flopping down onto the large beige couch facing the fireplace.

"As well as expected when your entire world comes crashing down around you."

I hold up the two bottles of wine we brought over.

"Good thing we stopped and grabbed these before coming over. Where are the glasses? I'm in desperate need of a drink."

"Family dinner a little more stressful than expected?" Bristol giggles before grabbing both bottles of wine from my hands and striding past me into the kitchen. I barely resist the urge to laugh as I watch her waddle into the kitchen, trying her best to move around while being eight months pregnant.

"That's an understatement. Apparently, Vance came ready to fight for his girl. Mr. and Mrs. G weren't much help either." Leia rolls her eyes at me as she follows Bristol into the kitchen. "They also sent pie."

"Oh! I love pie." Bristol squeals, handing me a glass of wine, followed by Leia holding a plate with my mom's pie on it.

"They're just trying to butter you up so I don't stay mad at them. Ugh, if they weren't my parents, I'd never speak to them again,"

"Was it really that bad?"

"No. I just found out that they've been hiding a little more from me than I had originally thought." I take a big gulp of wine, sending up a silent prayer that she won't ask me any more questions about what happened.

I know I shouldn't be angry with my mother for doing what I asked her to do, but a goodbye letter from Vance was important. I should've been given the chance to read it and make my own decision about what to do. Not to mention, if I had read that letter, I doubt we would have spent the last fourteen years not speaking to each other.

"And whose fault is that?" Leia quips as she grabs one bottle and fills her glass before taking a seat in one of the armchairs to my right.

"Okay, spill because I have a feeling I'm missing some very important details," Bristol says before opening her laptop that is sitting on the coffee table and lowering herself onto the couch on the opposite side of me.

"The short version is that when Selina stopped talking to Vance, he hoped that things would work out, but when he couldn't take it any longer, he wrote her a goodbye letter," Leia begins, her eyes focused on me.

"Damn. That's rough," Bristol replies before shoving a large bite of pie into her mouth.

"Yes. But to make matters worse, he gave said goodbye letter to my mother, who neglected to mention even receiving it until tonight at dinner." I sigh before downing the rest of my glass of wine and pouring another one.

"She didn't give it to you because you expressly told her you didn't want anything to do with Vance Kirkland, and we were all forbidden from even mentioning his name," Leia huffs before following my example and finishing her glass of wine before pouring another one.

"And why was that?"

"Because I saw him getting very cozy with another woman the night Lydia died."

"The fuck?"

"Yeah. And before Leia jumps in and tells me how stupid I was, I better explain." I run my free hand down my face, trying to find an easy way to explain my stupidity to Bristol. "He was hugging someone, yes, but that was it. Nothing more. Just taking comfort from another human being, who happened to be female, after one of his best friends died."

"Then I don't understand why you cut him off."

"Because she was stubborn and refused to ask the man a very simple question, choosing to jump to conclusions instead."

"Oh..." Bristol's eyes widen in understanding as she leans back in her chair, her hand resting on the top of her basketball-sized belly. "Well, I can understand being hurt, but if nothing happened, then why are you still angry at him?"

"I'm not angry," I quip, not wanting to talk about this anymore.

I wasn't lying when I said I wasn't angry at Vance. It took me a while to understand that even if something happened between him and another woman, he had every right to do so. I left Vance without saying goodbye. He had no guarantee that I would come back or when. It was unfair of me to believe he would wait around for me to come home. It wasn't until months later, probably around the same time that Vance wrote that letter, that I found out that what I saw was a figment of my imagination.

I had just gotten passed over for the leading role in the ballet we were doing that semester, and I was pissed. Instead of going back to my room and sulking like I always did, I went out to a bar near campus and started drinking. At some point during the night, I picked up my phone and started dialing numbers, the very first being Leia's. Thankfully, she answered the phone, but I don't remember the conversation we had. It wasn't until the next morning when I got the detailed message with bullet points of our conversation that I realized my mistake.

"She's scared of letting him in again and then leaving. She worried that history might repeat itself."

I open my mouth to respond, but Bristol's computer comes to life, ringing loudly. "Saved by a phone call. But don't think for one minute that this conversation is over." Bristol's eyes narrow in my direction before accepting the call.

Audrey's face fills the screen, but instead of the bright smile I'm used to seeing, her face is covered in tears. Black streaks of mascara run down her cheeks, probably from crying for hours, and her caramel-colored eyes are dull with sadness. Her curly hair is completely out of sight, tucked into a bright red bonnet that matches the shirt she's wearing.

"Oh, honey," Bristol coos, which brings on a fresh wave of tears from Audrey.

"I don't know what I'm going to do," she sobs before covering her face with her hands.

"Just remember, we have places to hide a body," Leia chimes in as she takes a seat on the floor in front of us, pushing the table back slightly so Audrey can see all three of us.

"I know, Leia, but I don't think that's the best idea. It would be hard to get a body from Texas to Tennessee and not get caught."

"Doesn't matter. We can travel to you and make it happen. Just say the word," I reply as Leia nods in confirmation. "No one gets away with hurting you. Not on our watch."

"I told her you guys would say that," Love says before her face appears on the screen, her wavy black hair hanging into the camera, cutting off our view of Audrey. "I could help. I'm a minor. I think I could get away with it."

"See, even Love is on board with our plan," Leia huffs as I throw Love a conspiratorial wink.

Love rolls her eyes before crossing her long jean-covered legs and flopping down beside her mother, tucking her hair behind both her ears. Love may only be fourteen, but she has a good head on her shoulders, and she's the best adoptive niece anyone could have. There is a slight twinge in my heart at thinking about my other adoptive niece around the same age, Lydia and Connor's daughter, Jade. I don't think Jade and I will ever be as close as Love and me, but I want to ensure that she knows how much I love her, regardless of my sudden appearance in her life.

"No jail time for any of you. Do you understand?" Audrey shouts before grabbing on to Love and pulling her down to have a seat beside her.

"She used her mom voice. She must mean business," Love responds, causing all three of us to snicker.

"Let's get serious, guys. We need to figure out a plan for Audrey and Love because they can't continue living with Ian. Agreed?"

"Agreed," we all answer in unison.

"Have you asked the cards yet?" Leia asks before pinching me hard on the leg.

I wince slightly, but Audrey doesn't notice, thankfully. I can't really understand what a deck of cards has to do with making decisions, but it's important to Audrey. Audrey's mother taught her how to read tarot cards when she was Love's age, and now she does it before every major decision in her life. She says that it helps guide the path she takes through life and that each time she does a reading, she feels as if her mother is sitting right there next to her, guiding her toward the right choices. Too bad the cards didn't warn her about Ian being a cheating asshole.

"No, because right now, I don't know what to ask them to tell me. My mind is such a mess. I can't believe this happened to me again," Audrey whispers, a fresh round of tears streaming down her cheeks.

"That settles it. You're coming here. You need your family right now, and since we are all here in Tyson's Creek, you can come to us."

"Yes!" Leia, Love, and I all shout in unison.

"I don't know. Love has school, her friends, and has finally found her place at the dance studio in town. I also have my job at the yoga studio to think about. I can't just pick up and move at a moment's notice."

"Mom, school is getting out in less than a month. Ian should be gone until right after school gets out. That will give enough time for you to give notice at the studio, and we can get everything packed or sold."

"But then what? We need to find a place to live, and I need a job."

"We got that covered, too." Bristol smiles, crossing her arms on top of her belly. "You can work at Nurture Space with me. I've been wanting to cut back on classes with the baby coming, and this gives me the perfect opportunity. I was worried about finding someone I trusted to take over classes, but I trust you with my life, Audrey."

"And you can stay at one of the cottages at my place

until you find a place to live. Things are a little slow right now, so you'll be doing us a favor," Leia chimes in from her place on the floor.

Not to be outdone, I chime in with an offer of my own. "And Love can take classes at the dance studio if she wants."

"Yes! I want!" Love screeches, throwing her fist up in the air before turning to her mother. "See? Everything is falling into place. Please?"

"Yeah, please?" Bristol and Leia beg, their hands clasped together while giving Audrey the best puppy-dog look.

"Maybe this is the sign you've been looking for," I chime in, causing everyone's eyes to snap toward me. "The universe's way of telling you that here is your chance for a fresh start. A new place where you can find everything you've always wanted; all you need to do is take a leap of faith."

Audrey is taken aback by my statement, probably because I'm not into this type of thing, but what do I know? I've also been given a chance to start over. A chance to be with the man that I thought had forgotten me.

Audrey sits up straight. A look of determination crosses her face as she swipes at the few tears left on her cheeks. "Okay. We're moving to Tyson's Creek."

We all cheer loudly and talk at once, trying to come up with the best plan of action for Audrey to get here as soon as possible, but then Love yawns loudly, causing us all to freeze.

"Shit. I didn't even notice what time it was. Love should have been in bed hours ago. It's way past her bedtime."

"Mom," Love whines before stifling another yawn with her hand. "It's Friday. I don't have school tomorrow."

"Yes, but you're also a fourteen-year-old girl, and it's almost eleven at night. You need to get to bed."

"Aunties, tell her I can stay up longer."

"No can do, kiddo." Bristol snickers. "This is one of those times I can't save you from your momma."

"And don't look at either of us. Your momma scares me sometimes." Leia holds both her hands up in surrender, causing us all to laugh loudly.

"You heard them, Love. Tell your aunts goodnight."

"Good night, aunties. Love you."

"Love you, too," we respond as Love pushes to her feet and heads off the screen.

"I better go and make sure she actually goes to sleep. Love you guys, and thanks for being there for me."

"Always," Bristol replies as we all blow her kisses and wave goodbye before the screen goes black.

"You really should learn to take your own advice," Leia says as she pushes to her feet and returns to her chair on the other side of the coffee table. "The universe may just be giving you a sign, as well."

"That's right. A do-over. A chance to not make the same mistakes a second time." Bristol eyes me skeptically, daring me to disagree, but I can't.

"You're probably right, but I don't plan on staying in Tyson's Creek after my injury is healed. The moment I get a call for an audition, I'll be going back to New York."

"And? What you need to do is put your big-girl panties on and see where this leads, or better yet, you can ask his opinion this time instead of deciding on your own," Leia chastises me. "You spent years apart because you were too stubborn to ask a simple question. Don't let this chance pass you by again."

Leia is right. This could be Vance's and my do-over, a chance to ensure history doesn't repeat itself, but maybe trying to pick things up where they ended isn't what's best for either of us.

"I wish I knew what that letter said."

"Good thing I had your mom open it and send me photos so you could read it before going home," Leia chirps, shaking her cell phone in front of my face.

"You didn't!" Bristol exclaims as I reach for Leia's phone, but she pulls it away at the last minute.

"I did, and Selina will thank me for it later."

"I don't know if I want to read it."

"Oh, no. You don't get to change your mind now,"

Bristol retorts, grabbing both my hands and squeezing them tightly. "Here are your choices. You can take Leia's phone into my room to read it in private, or Leia will read the entire thing out loud right here."

"Give me the phone." I hold my hand toward Leia, and she quickly unlocks her phone before placing it in my palm.

"Smart choice. We'll be here when you're finished," Bristol whispers, planting a kiss on the side of my head before I push to my feet and stride to the back of the house.

I don't even make it to her room before I slide to the floor and read the letter.

Seli:

I don't know if I can do this anymore. The pain of missing you, of not hearing your voice, has become almost unbearable. I love you so much that it hurts to not have you near me, but I need to move forward. I need to learn how to live my life without you in it.

I know you are off in New York, following your dreams, making new friends, and creating a new life for yourself, but my heart breaks thinking that it doesn't involve me.

I wish that I could have been by your side as you conquered the world. To be there the first time you dance on the big stage in New York, but this seems to be the end for us.

In my heart, you will always be the little girl with two spiral curl pigtails nestled on each side of her head with red bows tied around the top of each one that I fell in love with when I was a little boy.

This is the end of this chapter in both of our lives, but please never forget, I'll always be here, praying and waiting for you to find your way back to me.

I will always love you, Seli.
Vance

Tears stream down my face as painful sobs wrack my body. After all these years, Vance is still waiting for me to come home. When I saw him that night, I thought that was the end. That he had moved on and was done waiting for me, but that wasn't the case. This letter wasn't his way of telling me he stopped loving me but reminding me he has always been here waiting.

A part of me wants to run to Vance and beg for him to forgive me for all the pain I've put both of us through, but an even larger part of me wants to strengthen the locks around my heart so I can focus on getting better. I came home to rehab my ankle and find the pieces of myself I've been missing. I can't even think about being with him again until I do that, especially if following my dream will only tear us apart a second time. Once I manage to do that, maybe I can figure out a way to apologize for everything that has happened and the pain I put us through, but I have a long way to go before that can happen.

thirteen

Vance

"The usual?" Katie asks from her spot behind the counter. Her dirty-blonde hair is piled on the top of her head, a few tendrils falling to frame her face. Her blue eyes shine with mirth as she keys in my order.

A nod is the only response I give her as I slide my card across the counter. Every day, like clockwork, I come to grab coffee for Selina and her lone employee, Emersyn, in hopes of finally gaining her attention for the first time in years. Everyone in town knows my sad story. If I'm being honest with myself, it's pathetic, really. I'm in my mid-thirties and still trying to convince the one who got away to give me a second chance.

Selina has been back in town for a few months, and I've done everything I can think of to get her to give me the time of day. After our kiss in the studio before we got started on the renovations and my declaration of love for her when I had dinner at her parents' house all in the same week, she's been avoiding me like the plague. I can't say that I blame her. I laid a lot of big emotions at her feet, but that doesn't make it any easier to deal with.

"Maybe today will be the day?" Katie flashes me a bright smile as she hands back my card, along with a receipt.

"Maybe," I grumble as I step to the right and wait for my order.

"On your way to see Selina?" Russell chuckles, as he runs a hand through his brown hair and steps up to the counter.

Russell is a muscular man, my height, with the same shaggy haircut he's had since I've known him. We didn't talk much when we were in high school, partly because he graduated a few years before me, but he owns the hardware store across the street. I usually only see him when we need to order some more supplies, but I've spent quite a lot of time on Main Street since Selina came back to town.

"Yup, my daily bribe of coffee is ready to be delivered."

"I figured since I didn't see you lurking around the front of my store today, you may have taken the day off," Russell replies, his brown eyes locking with mine for a moment before he shifts to Katie and places his order.

I shake my head at how ludicrous my plan to get

Selina to talk to me has become. At first, it made sense that I hadn't seen Selina or any of the girls around much. Audrey was uprooting her whole life and moving to Tyson's Creek with her fourteen-year-old daughter. She doesn't know a single soul here besides Selina, Leia, and Bristol. Of course, they'd go out of their way to make sure she had everything she needed to feel welcome.

But after a few weeks of Audrey and Love being in town, nothing changed. Selina even started missing family dinners on Sunday, much to both mine and her parents' dismay. I've opted out of going over the last few weeks, hoping she'll start spending that time with her parents. Mr. and Mrs. Grymes missed Selina more than anyone when she was in New York, and I refuse to take the time they have with her away from them. I can find other ways to accidentally run into Selina.

That's where the plan of hanging out around Main Street, hoping to bump into her, accidentally came around. Now I find myself spending more time waiting for the perfect opportunity to run into her than I do anything else. At first, I would just lurk around Tyson's Hardware, making up some random tidbit I forgot to order or that we were out of at our offices, so I needed to rush down here for it, but in reality, I only wanted to stare out the window, hoping to catch sight of Selina as she came in or out of the dance studio.

Once Russell was tired of me lurking in front of his

store, I switched to Just the Drip, staring out the big front window while drinking my weight in coffee, waiting for Selina to stop by. After a few days, Katie took pity on me and let me know Selina only came into the shop first thing in the morning for a cup of coffee. She told me in no uncertain terms that if I wanted to see Selina, I would have to take the coffee to her.

For the last few weeks, I've been bringing Emersyn and Selina something from the café. A sweet treat, coffee, hot chocolate, anything I thought could entice Selina to take a minute and talk to me. I know I'm grasping at straws, but I've been trying everything to convince her to give me the time of day since she danced back into town, and she hasn't budged an inch. I'm not asking for much, just a coffee date and a chance to get to know her again, but so far, I've had no luck.

"Good luck," Katie says with a smile as she slides the cup carrier across the counter.

"Thanks. I'm gonna need it." I grab the carrier and walk to the door. Luckily, it's not too far before I get to Barre Studio and pull the door open.

"Hey, Vance," Emersyn greets me as I walk through the door, a bright smile on her face as I step inside.

Emersyn is tucked behind the small welcome table in the right-hand corner of the room. To the left, along the outer wall, there are two sets of metal lockers Selina had us install during the remodel. The top two rows of lockers have nameplates with the older dancers' names on them and a lock, giving them space to keep some things at the studio and not have to bring them every day. The other lockers aren't assigned to anyone, giving the younger dancers places to store their dance bags during class. There are comfortable chairs scattered around the room for parents to sit and wait for their dancers to finish class. On the other wall, running behind the welcome area, there are bright-colored leotards, bags, and photos of ballet dancers scattered along the wall to the right of the desk, stopping just short of the door leading into the dance space.

"No classes this afternoon?" I ask before flashing her a smile and setting the coffees on the counter in front of her.

Emersyn's hand reaches toward the cups of coffee in the carrier. "The middle-grade pointe class is starting soon, but something tells me you knew that already."

"Guilty as charged." I reach for the cup labeled with her name and hand it to her before pulling my own from the carrier and taking a drink.

My niece, Jade, and Audrey's daughter, Love, should both be here any minute to start class. I'm ashamed to admit I've used the excuse of dropping off or picking up the girls for their parents as an excuse to see Selina. I know it's sad that I sometimes use two fourteen-year-old girls to get her to talk to me, but both girls are all for it.

"What do you think my chances are today?" I ask, pulling my cup out of the carrier and taking a drink.

"The odds are in your favor." Emersyn winks at me before taking a seat behind the desk. "She's in an amazing mood. She has another appointment with the doctor this morning."

That statement is yet another reminder that I have a limited amount of time with Selina before she is off to New York again. Selina originally came back to town to rehab after her injury, but when I heard she bought Barre Studio from Ms. Cassandra and saw all the renovations she wanted to do, I'd hoped she had planned on staying in town. However, Selina made a point of letting me know at every turn that it was only temporary. She needed a place to rehab after her injury and couldn't let Ms. Cassandra's studio close, but I have a feeling that it's more than that.

Running a business is hard, something I know better than anyone, and it would be very difficult to do it from a thousand miles away. According to Mrs. Grymes, Selina hasn't been happy for the last few years, claiming that dancing has felt more like a chore than anything else, leaving me to wonder if being a prima ballerina is still her dream.

"Good news?" I question, wondering if Selina finally received the clean bill of health she'd been hoping for.

I'd be lying if I said I was hoping for a less-than-positive outcome for Selina. I want her to dance again, but not at the cost of the second chance we've been given. I need more time. Time to get her to open up to me and to remind her of how amazing things were and how they could be again if she would only open her heart to me.

"I would say so," Emersyn responds cheerfully as the front door opens and my niece, Jade, comes strolling into the studio.

"One of those better be for me," Jade says, wrapping her arms around my waist and giving me a squeeze.

"Of course. Seeing you is the only reason I come here anymore, anyway." I wink at her before pulling a cup from the holder and handing it to her. "Where's your old man?"

"Hanging by the door, trying to get a glimpse of Ms. Audrey." Jade giggles as she takes a sip from her cup.

I chuckle softly at my friend's expense. Not that I'm any better than he is. Audrey Wilde is the first woman since Lydia, who has caught my best friend's interest, much to all our excitement.

Ever since Audrey Wilde arrived in town, Connor has been different. When his wife, Lydia, died during childbirth, he shut himself off from the world, choosing to focus on raising his baby girl instead of finding someone to spend his life with. Until Audrey. Now, she is all he can think about.

I tried for years to convince Connor to dip his toe into the dating pool, knowing that he needed someone to love him unconditionally, just like Lydia did, but he never budged. He also took great pleasure in reminding me that I should do the same thing, and I refused as well. I believed that the two of us would end up as two bachelors, constantly wondering how our lives would've been different if the women we loved weren't taken from us. But when Audrey came into town, she threw Connor for a loop, making him feel things he hadn't since Lydia and wondering what he would do. I tried to give him advice, but if you take my current situation, I was not the best person to ask.

"Still hasn't convinced her to give him the time of day?" I ask, hoping my friend was faring better than I am now.

"Nope. Love and I are about to intervene because they are driving us insane."

Love is Audrey's daughter and Jade's best friend. Jade has always been a little skeptical of new people that come into town, but there was something about Love that caught her attention, and they've been attached at the hip ever since. It seems that Audrey and Love were exactly what Jade and Connor needed. I just hope the two adults pull their heads out of their asses and pay attention to what's right in front of them before it's too late.

"I have a good feeling about those two, Squirt. Just have faith." I pull her to my side, planting a kiss on the top of her head.

"Go away, Vance," Selina grumbles as she comes strolling out of the back room.

This woman is a vision, with wisps of black hair brushing against the top of her ears. Her toned body is a thing of beauty as she practically glides toward me. Her luscious lips are the color of a blush rose, competing with her hazel eyes for my attention.

"I thought you said she was in a good mood," I mumble to Emersyn, causing her and Jade to laugh loudly.

"I am in a good mood. Just not in the mood to deal with you." Selina rolls her eyes as she grabs her coffee and takes a sip.

I quickly come to my senses. "Not even a thank-you, Seli? What would your mama say about your manners?"

I lean against the counter, the perfect picture of ease, though I'm anything but. Being this close to her awakens the demon I've kept trapped inside me for years, reminding me once again that Selina Grymes is the only woman for me, now and forever.

"I'm sure you'll tell her all about it during your

weekly phone calls." She takes another swig of coffee. "She misses you at family dinner, by the way."

"I miss family dinner, too, but it seemed like someone was determined to avoid them as long as I was there, so I told your mom I'd take a rain check for the foreseeable future."

"Don't flatter yourself, Vance. I didn't miss family dinner because of you. I have a lot of stuff going on right now."

"I know, but it's nice to dream," I respond, ensuring I have her full attention. "But I'll excuse your rudeness and not tell your mom on one condition."

"How about I just tell you 'Thank you' now because my answer hasn't changed, Vance. I'm not going out with you." She turns and marches back into the back room. "I need to focus on getting back into shape so I can go back to New York. I don't have time for anything but practice and running my classes."

"All I want is to have coffee and have a chance to get to know you again. Is that too much to ask?"

"Vance, everyone knows you want more from me than to just catch up."

"Seli, please put all of us out of our misery and agree to have coffee with him. I'm sure you two have more than enough things to talk about," Connor chimes in from beside me before I can say anything.

"Maybe. Maybe not, but my answer is still no." She

sighs loudly, checking her watch. "Now, if you'll excuse me, it's almost time for Jade's lesson to begin."

Just as she turns to walk back into the studio, Jade comes strolling out. "What did I miss?" She throws her empty cup into the trash. "Did you crash and burn again, Uncle Vance?"

"Tragically," Connor snickers, as he throws his arm over my shoulder. "Come on, man. Let's go grab a beer while I wait for Jade to finish up with her lesson."

"Are you not hanging around to wait for Audrey again today?" Emersyn chimes in, a devious smile creeping across her face.

"I don't hang around waiting for Audrey," he grumbles, running his hand through his hair.

"Just like I don't come here every day to see Selina." I chuckle as we both give Jade a hug, wave goodbye to Emersyn, and stroll out the door to his truck in silence. Connor has been my best friend for most of my life. He knows everything there is to know about me, including how heartbroken I've been since Selina left.

Just like Connor, I haven't given myself to another woman. I've been completely celibate since Selina left town. I've tried to date for a while, but other women never appealed to me because they weren't Selina. Thankfully, Connor understood and didn't give me too hard of a time about holding on to the hope that Selina would come back someday. I was content with my choice to be alone instead of being reminded every time

I was out with another woman of the one that got away. In my heart, no one could ever hold a candle to Selina. If I can't have her, I'll spend the rest of my life alone.

"It shouldn't be this hard, should it?" I question, slamming my fist on the hood of his truck. "She left me, Connor. Left me and this town in her rearview mirror all those years ago, never to come back. But I still love her."

"Anything in life worth having isn't easy," he says as he unlocks his truck and motions for me to follow.

I open the passenger side door and climb in. "Why does she keep turning me down? All I want is an explanation. She at least owes me that much."

"She doesn't owe you anything, man. You were teenagers. She had a dream and went for it." Connor gets in and starts the truck.

"I never once discouraged her from her dreams," I murmur as I gaze out the passenger window.

Sure, we dreamed about what our life would be like in Tyson's Creek, making plans to buy an amazing house overlooking the creek, cut off from the world. I made sure she had space for a dance studio and a Jacuzzi to loosen her muscles after practicing. These dreams are one reason I planned on going into construction. I wanted to give Selina everything she wanted, building it with my own two hands to show her how much I loved and supported her.

It never mattered to me where these things were,

just that we did them together. I never once forced Selina to choose between being with me and her dreams. My heart aches at the idea that she believed I would discourage her from everything. I spent so many Friday nights sitting on the floor of the dance studio, watching her practice for her entrance ceremony. I videoed her practices so she could watch them back and correct any of the small mistakes. I did everything I could to make sure she knew I was always there for her, that I had her back no matter what, but instead of allowing me to continue to support her, she shut me out.

The scenery passes by as we make our way toward Crawdaddy's near the edge of town. It's the best place in town to grab a cheap beer and focus on something other than how much is going on in your life. Before I know it, the sign comes into view, and Connor quickly finds a parking spot.

"But did you ever *en*courage those dreams?" He turns to me as he shuts off the truck. "All you ever talked about was the two of you getting married and settling down. Not once did you offer to go with her."

"I encouraged her!" I shout, throwing my hands above my head in frustration. "I was the one who recorded her audition. I was there when she found out she got into Juilliard and congratulated her before anyone else. I would have followed her to the ends of the earth if she had only asked."

"But did you tell her that? Did you let her know all your plans to follow her to New York? That you had gotten into NYU and planned to get your degree right along with her?"

I know in my heart that he's right. I never once said anything to Selina about my plans or that I even thought about moving to New York with her. We spent so much time talking about our future. I thought she knew I was in it for the long haul.

"No, you didn't. You put all the pressure on her to decide, not once taking the time to let her know how you felt about it. She probably thought there was no other option for her than to leave. You were her entire world, and she couldn't take the chance that you'd resent her for making you follow her."

"I never would've done that."

"Thirty-four-year-old you wouldn't, but think about that headstrong eighteen-year-old boy you were when we graduated. Do you think he would have been content following her around the world for the rest of his life? Giving up on any of his dreams to be with the woman he loved?"

"I hate to admit it, but you're right. Eighteen-year-old me would've been okay with it for a while, but the more time we were away from each other, the more I would have probably regretted my decision."

"That's right. You would have come home after a

few years, full of resentment that Selina followed her dreams, and you were left with nothing."

"Do you think she thought the same things when she left? That she needed to leave for both our sakes, not wanting to taint what we had with each other?"

"I don't know, man. I wish I knew the answer for you."

"Now what do I do? Selina keeps talking like she has one foot out of the door, determined to run away to New York the first chance she has. How am I going to get her to understand that I don't want to trap her here? I just want to be a part of her life. All I want is to be given a chance to love and support her for the rest of our lives."

"How about you try to be her friend first? The rest will come later." He opens the door and heads inside the bar.

"That's the problem. I don't know how much time I have," I reply into the empty cab.

There is no telling how much longer Selina will be in town before she goes back to New York. I lost her once, and I can't let it happen again. But how do you convince someone that you were meant for each other if they don't believe that themself?

fourteen
selina

"**H**ow's my favorite ballerina doing today?" Bristol chirps as she waddles her way into the studio.

Her red hair is piled high on the top of her head, but a few strands hang loose in the front, framing her face. She's wearing a Nurture Space shirt, the logo stretched slightly around the top of her protruding belly, and a pair of black yoga pants. Her green eyes are shining with mirth as the corner of her mouth pulls up into a smile.

Nurture Space is the name of the yoga studio Bristol opened when she moved here after college. It shocked me when Leia told me her college roommate was moving back to town with her, expecting Bristol to return home after graduation. But Bristol was determined to put down roots and create a home for herself. After following her dad around to different duty stations for most of her life, she refused to do it anymore. Her parents live a few hours away from here, in Alabama, but I think that has more to do with Bristol being here than anything else.

I don't think I could ever be far away from my parents after spending so much time in New York. Sure, the city was amazing. I always had something to do or someone to hang out with, but I felt more alone in a city full of millions of people than I ever did when I lived here. It's one of the many reasons I came back here to Tyson's Creek after my injury. I needed to be around people who knew me, the real me, not the shell of a person I'd become after having spent so many years in the city. Now, if I could only get them to stop meddling in my love life, I'd be golden.

I force a smile, flopping down into one of the waiting room chairs. "I'm peachy keen. So, what brings you here on this fine afternoon?"

I already know Bristol isn't here for a friendly visit. Bristol is one of my best friends, but she's also the romantic in our group. She's more invested in Vance and I getting back together than almost anyone, which means every time we're in the same general vicinity of each other, Bristol always seems to call or appear shortly after. Bristol is here to get details. She wants to know how everything went, not that there is anything new for me to report.

I'm not too ashamed to admit to myself—but not to anyone else—that I've been avoiding seeing Vance. Just being near him brings up old feelings that I fought for years to keep buried deep inside me. I want to go back to not caring, to being the unfeeling robot I had become back in New York, but the longer I'm here, the more my heart opens, allowing all my emotions to come pouring in. Love, fear, hurt, passion, pain, and so many more emotions that sometimes it's too hard to breathe. But when Vance is around, everything else seems to fade into the background. My love for him and the regret I feel for the way I've acted come to the forefront.

"Tell Mama Bristol what's wrong." She grips the top of the chair and braces herself before slowly lowering down into the seat.

I stifle a laugh as I watch her struggle to get comfortable. I can only imagine what it feels like to have an extra fifteen pounds strapped to your midsection.

"Shut up. This will be you someday, and I'm going to enjoy watching you struggle." Bristol leans back in the chair, finally finding a comfortable position to sit in.

"There's nothing really to tell. Vance came into the studio to ask me out again, and I turned him down. He left with Connor to go grab a beer or something. I wasn't really paying attention."

"Then why are you sulking?"

"I'm not sulking," I snap back, rubbing the place on my chest above my heart. "Just had a long day of teaching classes and practicing."

"Selina." My entire body stiffens at the sound of her voice.

We both know I'm completely full of shit. I long for the days that Vance pops up in the studio. The way his eyes pierce my soul makes everything else fade into the background. His brown hair perfectly tousled on the top of his head from him nervously running his hands through it, cut shortish on the sides, leaving just enough hair on the sides to run my fingers through. Vance is always wearing a flannel shirt, rolled to his elbows, allowing his tattoo to peek out from beneath it, over a white T-shirt, with his legs encased in a pair of blue jeans and his work boots covering his feet.

He'd march right toward me, but instead of hesitating in wrapping his large arms around me, the scruff of his beard brushing against my skin, he plants a gentle kiss on my lips. He pulls back slightly and smiles before laying his chin on the top of my head and pulling me tightly into his chest. I'd bury my nose in his chest, allowing his woodsy scent to envelop me as I melt into his arms.

I can see it all playing out in my head like a movie, but then the voice in the back of my mind chimes in, whispering all my fears in my ear. Reminding me that so much time has passed, and I'm no longer the girl he fell in love with. That I'm lost, moving through life like a leaf blowing in the wind. My life is in complete shambles from the choices I made, which ruined the best thing I ever had. For years, I've wanted to tell Vance that I was sorry, that shutting him out was the biggest mistake I've ever made, but something always stopped me. The weeks turned into months and then years. Too much time has passed between us. Vance might just want a chance to get to know me again, but I want more. I want everything, even though I know it's too late.

"Earth to Selina." Bristol's voice brings me back to the present.

"Sorry." I give my head a shake before smiling at her, trying to ease the worry I see on her face. "What are you doing here, anyway? Don't you have a studio to run?" I question, hoping to change the subject as I try to sneak a glance out the window.

"Audrey is currently hiding from Connor."

I open my mouth to comment, but she raises her hand.

"Don't ask. It isn't my place to say anything, but something has happened between the two of them. She needs to work things out on her own."

I can only imagine how Audrey is feeling right now after being betrayed in the worst way by her ex. I always had a bad feeling about Ian Hudson, commenting more than once that Audrey could do better, but I never would've imagined that he had a secret family stashed somewhere.

Audrey and Love came here for a fresh start. The

last thing she probably wants is to start a relationship so soon. But I know Connor is a good man, and he'd be good for both her and Love. However, who am I to say anything? I'm doing everything in my power to run from the man I love because I'm afraid of being rejected.

"They both deserve to be happy,"

"They both do." She smiles before motioning toward the front window. "I saw Vance pulling up to Tyson's Hardware when I came in."

"I don't know what you're talking about," I respond, pushing to my feet and walking to the other side of the room.

Everyone in town knows that Vance has been lurking in the general vicinity of my studio since he finished the renovations. Whenever I see him, he says it's just a coincidence, but I know better. Vance wants my attention for some reason, and a part of me wants to give in to him. To go out to dinner and see if the spark is still there. But a much larger part is scared to take that leap again.

"Okay, so you haven't been secretly waiting for him to stop by so you can get another fix for the day?"

"No, I haven't been."

"Then what have you been glancing out the window for since I came in?"

"I..." I start, but slam my mouth shut quickly, knowing I've been caught.

174

"When are you going to put Vance out of his misery?" Bristol jokes, causing my body to shiver with anticipation at the mere mention of his name. I fidget with my hands, nervously glancing at the door. "No need to be nervous. He will come in and ask you out, and you will turn him down again." She tilts her head to the side, eyeing me inquisitively. "Or is there something else going on?"

"Nothing is going on, Bristol. Just trying to be ready for when my students arrive for class."

The door chimes, causing me to jump slightly. Thankfully, it's just a group of my students. I sigh, grateful to be spared from another date request, because I don't know if I have the strength to tell him no this time.

"Okay, enough about Vance. How did your appointment go yesterday?"

"It went well. Everything is all healed."

"That's fantastic!" Bristol squeals, throwing her arms around my neck.

"Yeah. Sure."

"Why don't you sound happy?" Bristol pulls back, her eyes scanning my face.

"I am happy, but I also don't know if I really want to go back," I whisper, finally giving voice to my biggest fear.

When I got the news from my doctor, I immediately called my old company director. He was beyond excited to hear the news and asked when I'd be returning to New York. When I didn't answer immediately, he told me he couldn't make any promises but was hopeful I'd get a call for an audition soon. I should've been over the moon with the news, but the first thought that entered my mind was wondering if I was ready to return.

I originally came back to town to rehab and discover my love for dancing again. Spending the last few months teaching the girls and dancing just for fun, I've done that. Dancing is no longer a chore for me. I wake up every morning excited to see how the girls have grown since our last class. I've been helping some girls choreograph their own dances for the recital at the end of the year and for entrance exams for Juilliard. My heart is full to the point of bursting, and I wonder if I'd feel the same if I left it all behind to chase after my chance to be center stage.

And then there's Vance. I've been resisting his charms for months, but I don't know how much more I can handle. I can't help but wonder what things would be like between us after so much time has passed. It would be easy to agree to go on a date with him. Would it end at that, or would it become something more? Could I really go back to New York without seeing if there was still something between us? Would I even be able to leave?

This is why I keep pushing him away. I've spent almost every night since coming back to town, lying awake, worrying about what I'd do if the company called me in for an audition. If someone had asked me six months ago, I'd have jumped at the chance without hesitation. But now, there's so much more for me to lose by leaving. The studio, my students, and Vance. My heart shattered when I had to leave the boy I once knew, the boy who was the center of my universe, and I was his. I ruined both of us when I selfishly left. I never once explained to him what I was feeling, my worries and concerns. I decided for both of us. Does he hold that against me? Are all his attempts to go on a date with me his chance to tell me how badly I hurt him and ruined all our plans with my selfishness? The Vance I knew would never do that, but what about the man he is today?

So instead of being brave, I hide, letting my fear of the unknown rule all my actions and fighting the pull I feel toward Vance. I've tried to keep my heart hardened at the idea of there still being something between us, convincing myself that there is nothing between Vance and me, but my heart knows better.

Bristol raises her voice slightly over the buzz of voices around the room. "No one said you can't enjoy your time while you're here." She holds her hands out for me to help her stand. "Besides, you guys haven't been together in sixteen years. After that long apart, the date will probably be horrible, and then you can move on."

"That's what I've been trying to explain. I'm not the same little girl that left here with nothing but a dream all those years ago."

"No one thinks you are." Vance slides into the studio behind another group of girls.

The noise level rises exponentially as he winks at me.

"I can't do this right now, Vance." My voice cracks slightly as I turn my back to him and address my students. "Girls, it's time for class to begin. Begin your stretches and be ready to start in five minutes."

"Yes, Ms. Selina," the girls answer in unison before filing into the studio.

"Just one date, Seli. That's all I ask," Vance says for the millionth time, loud enough for everyone in the waiting room to hear.

Suddenly, all the mothers in the waiting room chime in.

"You guys would make the cutest couple!" Loralie's mom says as she throws a wink in my direction.

"Could you imagine what their babies would look like?" someone else whispers.

Vance preens for them, and I roll my eyes. Right, because having children is obviously the main reason two people should get together.

"Although I would love children, I'm not in a position in my life that I feel ready to have them," I respond, hoping to regain control of the situation.

"You're not getting any younger, my dear. Next thing you know, you'll be sitting in a big old house with nothing but cats to keep you company," Ms. Mable says from her seat by the door.

"She would know," Bristol mumbles, soft enough for only me to hear.

Ms. Mable is the town's resident cat lady. Word around town is she had a fiancé who left her without a word, and now it's just her and her cats to keep her company.

"Good afternoon, Ms. Mable. What brings you into the studio today?"

"I want to sign my niece up for classes. Her mom is coming to live with me while she gets back on her feet."

Emersyn pushes past me and takes a seat beside her. "I can help you with that, Ms. Mable. Selina needs to give Vance an answer before starting class."

"When did you even get here?" I cock my head to the side, wondering how she slipped in without me noticing.

This place is a madhouse when students are coming in for class, but I usually notice everyone who walks through the door. Thankfully, a few of the parents lost interest in whatever was going on between Vance and me and left the room. Vance and Bristol are whispering to each other near the other side of the room. One or two parents are sitting in the chairs, their eyes focused on their phones as they pretend not to be listening to what's going on around them.

"About a minute after Vance asked you out for the millionth time." She smiles brightly at me before motioning to Vance. "Are you going to answer the man?"

"Traitor," I mutter under my breath, crossing my arms over my chest.

"Come on. You should at least give him a chance." Emersyn mumbles, her eyes focused on Vance as he approaches.

"Fine!" I shout. "I'll go out with him! Just... please, for the love of God, leave me alone."

"Me?" Bristol scoffs as she points at herself.

"No. You and Emersyn can stay." I spin in Vance's direction, fighting the urge to stomp my foot like a toddler. "You, get out."

"Seriously?" Vance smirks as the door swings open, and Connor comes in with Jade and Love.

"Are you here to harass Selina again?" Connor bumps Vance's shoulder before turning and speaking to Bristol.

Unable to contain his excitement, he smiles brightly before throwing his arm over Connor's shoulder. "She finally agreed to go out with me."

"I just wanted him to go away," I mutter and cross my arms over my chest.

"All that pestering finally paid off." Bristol snickers.

"Selina said they can bring us home after class," Jade says as she threads her arm through mine.

"I did?"

"Yup, you did. You also said you would hang out with us so my dad and Audrey can have some time alone together." Jade winks in my direction, and I smile.

Jade is the perfect combination of her mother and father. She is average height, with legs for days, and long dark hair just like Lydia, but she has Connor's green eyes that are currently sparkling with excitement. I should be angry that she's involving me in her plan to push her dad and Audrey together, but I can't find it in me. She has made it her mission to force her dad and Audrey together if it's the last thing she does.

She reminds me so much of her mother that it makes my heart ache. She isn't as reserved and introverted as Lydia was, but she loves with her whole heart. She wants to ensure that everyone around her is happy and living their lives to the fullest, including herself. I was worried that she'd keep me at arm's length because I'd been absent for all these years. Connor said he told her stories about her mother and me, but I was worried she would resent me for staying away so long, but that just isn't Jade. She welcomed me with open arms, wanting to know everything I would tell her about her mother.

"Yep, that's what Aunt Selina said. My mom and Connor have a lot of things to discuss." I send up a silent prayer of thanks as Love pipes in from my other side.

"I guess your date now includes two teenage girls." Connor gives Vance a look of sympathy, and Vance slaps him on the back a few times.

Vance walks toward me, planting a kiss on my cheek. "I don't have a problem with that at all. I'll be back soon, Seli."

A shiver runs down my spine as he gives my hand a squeeze before walking out the door.

Overwhelmed with everything that took place over the last few minutes, I ask Jade and Love to run the class through warm-up exercises and then duck into the back room, closing the door tight behind me and leaning back against it.

"What the fuck was I thinking?" I say into the empty room as I slide down to the floor and wrap my arms around my knees.

I've been doing everything to keep him at arm's length and protect my heart. Bristol could be right. Going on a date with Vance could finally convince him that things have changed, that I've changed. But is that what I really want? Do I want Vance to let go, to stop believing that we were meant to be together? No, that's not what I want.

I want him to fall in love with me all over again. To

apologize to him for breaking us apart, for staying gone for so long, even though I knew it was a mistake. I want to tell him I can dance anywhere, that I came back to Tyson's Creek to find myself and rediscover my love for dancing. It wasn't all for him, but I came back to town craving his soothing presence. I want to tell him that even with the distance between us, I always knew he was there, silently supporting me to grow and become a better person. I want to show him with my actions that my heart still belongs to him, but I don't know if I'm strong enough to hear his answer.

I was a coward and ran away from all these questions when I was eighteen years old, and even now, I want to run again. It would be easy to claim that I need to focus on getting into shape so I can go back to New York. But it would be a lie. I'd be lying to myself the same way that I did when I was younger, but if Vance doesn't feel the same, it will break me beyond repair.

"Knock, knock," Bristol says as she tries to push the door open.

I slide forward just enough for her to come in, then push it closed once again and lean back against it.

"I would get down there with you, but we both know I may not get back up," she quips.

We both laugh softly as she walks toward one of the chairs, slowly lowering herself down to take a seat.

"What's on your mind?" she asks, waiting patiently for my answer.

"This is a bad idea," I finally say.

"How do you know unless you try?"

"I didn't come back to town to get back together with my ex, Bristol. I need to focus on getting back in shape and making all my dreams come true." I bang my head on the door a few times.

"Remember that sometimes life gives us a do-over. I would hate for you to pass up this chance and regret it for the rest of your life."

"I won't regret it." I'm not sure if I'm trying to convince her or myself. "Look, I have a class to teach. Are you staying or going back to check on Audrey?"

"I need to go, but think about what I said, Seli."

"Not you, too," I groan. "My name is Selina. Seli was the lost little girl who left Tyson's Creek with nothing but a dream."

Bristol wraps an arm around my shoulder and pulls me in for a side hug. "But who said you couldn't be both?"

She flashes me a small smile before waddling out the door.

I don't know what it is about Tyson's Creek, but no matter how many times I try to escape, somehow, I always come right back to where I started.

* * *

"You ladies ready to go?" Vance says cheerfully as he leans against the doorframe of our dance space.

He's changed out of the clothes he was wearing earlier, and his hair is damp from a recent shower. Instead of his normal attire of dusty work boots and a flannel shirt, he's wearing an almost new button-up shirt with the sleeves rolled to the elbows and dark jeans fitted perfectly to his muscular legs.

"Of course. We just need to change first," Love replies.

She grabs Jade's hand and pulls her toward the changing room at the front of the studio, leaving Vance and me alone.

"Didn't your mama teach you not to stare?" He chuckles.

I drop my head to my chest. Nothing like ogling a man to make things awkward. To maintain some of my dignity, I ramble off ideas for what we can do with the girls, trying to look anywhere but at Vance.

Vance steps into my line of sight, causing me to stop my rambling and look into his eyes. "Change of plans. Connor texted me and asked if I would drop off Jade and Love at the house. Something about things with Audrey not going as planned."

My shoulders sag slightly at the news. I'm sad that things are going badly between Audrey and Connor, but mostly I'm sad to be missing my chance to see where things stand between Vance and me. I know I need to tell him how I feel, or I'll regret it forever. However, I don't want to just lay out all my cards on the table. I hoped that this date with the girls there would've worked as a buffer, allowing me to feel out the situation before putting my feelings into words.

"No problem. I could use the extra time to work on my pirouettes," I respond, trying to hide the disappointment in my voice.

"Oh, no. You aren't getting rid of me that easily. You promised me a date."

"Why are you pushing the issue so much?"

Vance stalks toward me. "I just want to spend time with you, Selina," he says with nothing but anguish in his voice. "I miss you."

My breath catches in my throat as I straighten my back, unwilling to give in. "It's been over fifteen years, Vance. Surely, you don't expect things to just go back to the way they were?"

I back up slightly, eager to get away from him.

"You're the one that ran away, Seli. Forgetting about me and everyone else in this town." He continues to stalk toward me with passion in his eyes.

"I never forgot about you," I whisper as I back closer to the wall. "I tried. God knows I tried. That's why I had to leave, Vance. If I'd met you that night, I would have agreed to anything you wanted, but I wanted my dream more."

I brace myself, waiting for him to answer. I was

always afraid to tell Vance that I wanted more than the house by the creek surrounded by a white picket fence. I wanted that for our future more than anything, but I also wanted to dance. Now that I'm older, I know that there was room in my life for both, but at the time, it was a one-or-the-other decision. I followed my dreams of becoming a famous ballerina and tried to forget the small town I grew up in and the love of my life. Now I have the chance to have both, but it all depends on Vance's response.

Vance's hand cups the side of my face, and I lean into it, relishing the feel of his calloused hands as they caress my skin. "I never wanted to stand in the way of your dreams. I just wanted to be a part of them," he murmurs.

"What if everything goes to shit?" I breathe.

"What if it doesn't?" he retorts, leaning his forehead against mine.

"I don't know if I'm staying," I whisper. "I got a clean bill of health from my doctor yesterday and called my company director. He said I should expect a call for an audition soon."

He needs to know that even if something happens between us, I may still be leaving. Even though my heart yearns to stay here with him, there is a part of me that wants to try dancing again. I've worked most of my adult life to be center stage. If I give up now, it will feel as if I'm flushing all my hard work down the drain.

"Seli," he whispers into my ear, sending a shiver down my spine.

"Don't call me that." I push slightly on his chest, trying to get him to release me.

But he pulls me closer, brushing his lips against mine.

Unable to control the feelings swirling in my body, I lean forward, pressing my lips softly against his. Both of us moan as he pushes me harder into the wall and devours my mouth. He dominates our kiss, nipping and sucking my lip between his before thrusting his tongue into my mouth.

I wrap my arms around his neck and pull him closer to me. Nothing but pure, unadulterated desire courses through my veins. Without warning, he grips my ass, pulling my leotard tightly against my swollen nub as he lifts me off my feet and pins me against the mirror.

"Do you feel that? How much I want you? Need you?" he growls.

I wrap my legs around his waist, and he thrusts his cock against me, sending shock waves of pleasure through my entire body as the seam of his jeans grinds into my drenched center.

"More, more, more," I chant as I use my arms to glide my pussy up and down his shaft.

Suddenly, there is a knock at the door, and we both freeze. Vance's head drops to mine, and his eyes clench shut tightly as he lowers me to the floor. I take a deep breath as I step away from him, my eyes looking anywhere but at him.

"Don't shut me out, Seli."

I scurry to the door and pull it open. "I'm not."

Jade smiles brightly at me, her cheeks pink as Love spins on her heels and heads toward the door. "We're ready."

I feel Vance's arms wrap around my waist. He leans forward, burying his nose in my neck. "We'll be out in a minute."

"We'd better get out of here before we scar them for life when they come looking for us again," Vance mumbles against my skin, planting a kiss by my ear.

"I'm sorry. I don't know what came over me."

Distance. Distance is what I need right now. And a chance to clear my head. If I'm not careful, I could lose myself in him once again, forgetting about everything but the way it feels to be in his arms again.

Maybe this is where you belong.

No. I shake that thought out of my head. I can't get my hopes up. What just happened between the two of us means nothing. It doesn't mean that there's a chance of there still being something between Vance and me. But Bristol's words from earlier filter through my mind.

I've never believed in fate or any of that nonsense, but since my injury, I've been thinking more and more about how things happen for a reason. I was feeling lost and alone in New York, trying desperately to find my passion again, and then I was injured. Was there a bigger meaning or reason for it to have happened, than just me being careless? Maybe I got hurt to ensure that I would find my way home to Vance again. Is that even possible?

"I wouldn't mind something coming over you again, but first, let's get these girls home." Vance runs the tips of his fingers down my arm before grasping my hand, bringing me back to the present. Shocked by the intimacy of the moment, I pull my hand free from his grasp.

"This isn't a good idea," I say once again, trying to ensure that both of us understand what is at stake if we go down this path again. "I'll change, and then we can take the girls home."

I step around him, but Vance reaches out and grasps my hand. "I just want to spend time with you. For once, just let the chips fall where they may. We can worry about everything else later."

The vulnerability in his voice is enough to break my heart all over again. I barely survived leaving him once. I don't know if I could do it again.

I sigh as I take his hand. "Okay."

fifteen

Vance

"Are you two ready to go?" I ask both girls as I stroll into the waiting room. Their heads immediately snap toward the sound of my voice, sly smiles spreading across both of their faces.

"Sorry for interrupting you, Uncle Vance," Jade says before shoving her phone into her pocket.

"You didn't interrupt anything, Squirt." I smile as I stride toward them, taking a seat in the empty chair between them.

"We aren't little kids anymore; we know what happens when a man and a woman find each other attractive," Love huffs, crossing her arms.

"I find Selina a lot more than just attractive," I mumble under my breath.

In my eyes, Selina will always be the most beautiful person in the world. Even though we've both changed a lot over the years, all the things I love about her are still the same. The way her smile lights up an entire room, the way the sound of her laughter is so contagious you can't help but laugh right along with her, the way her eyes hold so much emotion that I get lost staring into them. But she's also just as beautiful on the inside as she is on the outside.

She's been acting like she has one foot out the door ever since she arrived back in town, but someone who's intent on leaving doesn't buy a business. Mrs. Grymes may have told her about the dance studio closing with the hope that Selina would buy it, but she could've said no. But Selina wanted to give the young dancers in this town a haven, a place to call home, just like Ms. Cassandra did for her when she was younger. I know deep down she wants to stay here, but for some silly reason, she doesn't believe she can do both. Sure, it will be hard to run a business and train for a ballet at the same time, but it can happen. She can fulfill her dream of dancing the lead in *Swan Lake* and still have a place here to come back to. I just need to convince her that it's possible.

"We know that, too. You love her."

"You'll find a way to convince her to stay. I know it," Jade and Love answer almost in unison, bringing a smile to my face.

To them, it's that simple. I love her, so I'll know exactly what I must do to make her stay. When, in reality, I have no fucking clue. Yes, I love Selina. I have since the moment I laid eyes on her, but is it really as simple as just asking her to stay? Selina has told me that she was afraid I'd ask her to stay after graduation, but I don't want her to give up on her dreams. I want to be allowed to be a part of them, no matter what that looks like. If she needs to do a long-distance thing until her contract is up, then so be it. If she needs me to stay here and help run the dance studio, I can do that, too. Whatever it is she needs, I'm willing to do it. I know it's going to be hard on both of us, but we can get through it together.

I wrap my arms around both of them and pull them to my side for a hug. "Yes. I do. I love her a lot."

"Didn't you two used to date in high school?" Jade's entire body stiffens as if she's afraid of how I might react to her next statement. "My dad told me how you two would go on double dates with him and my mom."

"Yeah, the four of us spent as much time together as we could. Selina and your mom were best friends, just like your dad and me."

"Do you know why she never came back to see me? Does she blame me for my mom dying?" she whispers, burying her nose in my side.

I plant a kiss on the top of her head. "Selina loves you. We all do. Your birth was one of the best moments of your dad's life."

"And the worst."

"Never," Love chimes in, pushing to her feet and kneeling in front of Jade. "Your dad loves you to pieces."

I can't even imagine what it's been like for Jade growing up. All the sympathetic stares and events that she's had to miss because her mom wasn't here. We've all tried to chip in as much as we can, but there's something about not having your mom that leaves a void inside your heart.

My parents weren't the best role models. My mom worked herself to death, trying to take care of me and put a roof over our heads when I was younger, and I have no clue who my father is. To me, he's nothing more than a sperm donor, someone who blessed my mom with a child. I never really knew who he was, so I never had a chance to miss him.

"Love's right. Your dad will always love your mom, but he didn't lose her completely. He sees her every time he looks at you."

"And there is just enough space in there for my mom and me." Love sniffles before pushing to her feet and turning her back on both of us. "I can't wait for the four of us to be a family."

"Me either." Jade giggles, pushing to her feet and placing both hands on her best friend's shoulders before twisting her around to face us.

Love's hazel eyes swim with emotion as they dart around the room, looking anywhere but at Jade and me. Tears stream down her golden-brown skin as Jade wraps her arms around her waist, enveloping her in a hug.

"We're always going to be family. Right, Uncle Vance?"

My heart swells a few sizes bigger at her calling me her uncle. Love has been so terrified of losing the small family we have all created with each other, something that she's wanted for a long time. Sure, Audrey loves her to bits, but it seems Love wants more for them both. The moment I met Audrey and Love, I knew they'd fit perfectly into our family. The fact that Connor is in love with Audrey is just a bonus, making it a lot easier to explain to people asking about another niece who looks nothing like me. Our family is bonded by something stronger than blood: unconditional love for each other.

"That's right," I answer, as Selina comes strolling into the room. Her head is cast down as she searches her bag for something, completely unaware of what's happened in the last few minutes.

Selina changed into a painted-on pair of jeans and an oversized sweatshirt. The golden skin of her right shoulder calls to me as the tips of her hair brush against it, taunting me, begging me to thread my fingers through it and pull her head back, taking her mouth once again and claiming it as my own.

My mouth waters as I look over and see the peaks of her nipples poking through the fabric of her shirt. Looks like our little rendezvous in the rehearsal room at the studio affected her just as much as me. I can't say I regret kissing her. In fact, the only thing I regret is getting interrupted.

"Sorry I kept you guys waiting for so long, I had to —" She freezes in place, her eyes switching between the three of us before settling on me and narrowing them slightly. "What did you do?"

"He didn't do anything, Aunt Selina." Love sniffles, pushing a strand of her wavy black hair behind her ear and plastering a fake smile on her face. "I was just in my feels for a minute. You know how it is around that time of the month."

"Ah, well, we can make Vance stop at the store for some junk food and chocolate because I can guarantee there's nothing like that at Jade's house."

"Ugh, my dad never has any good junk food in the house," Jade announces before whispering something into Love's ear.

Love nods before grabbing her dance bag off the floor near the chair. "I'll meet you guys in the truck," she murmurs before scurrying out the door, Jade right on her heels.

Selina waits to ensure both girls are out of earshot before turning to me. "Now, what was that really about?"

"Jade was feeling out of place."

"What is that supposed to mean?"

"She was worried you never came back to see her because you blamed her for Lydia's death."

196

Selina gasps as if I struck her, tears welling in her soulful eyes as she shakes her head back and forth. "That wasn't it at all. I wanted to see her, to hold her in my arms. But after seeing you with—" She slaps her hands over her mouth as her eyes widen in surprise.

"Seeing me with who?"

My mind races, trying to make sense of what she just said. Mr. and Mrs. Grymes never once told me about Selina coming back to town, and the last time I saw her was at Lydia's funeral. She refused to make eye contact with me during the entire ceremony and escaped out the back of the church before I could talk to her. I assumed it was because she was upset about losing her best friend, which I understood, but then she went radio silent. Stopped answering my calls and text messages. I tried for months to find out what had happened, but no one could give me an answer. Maybe this is why.

"Never mind. I shouldn't have said anything in the first place. This isn't about me; it's about Jade. I never wanted her to feel abandoned by me."

"I know. And that's exactly what I told her. Lydia was your best friend; you aren't allowed to not be obsessively in love with her daughter."

Selina laughs softly. "I hope you said it more sincerely than that."

"Maybe only a little." I chuckle as she goes to brush past me, but I grab her arm. "Now that we have that out of the way, what did you see that made you cut off your best friends?"

"It's nothing, Vance. We don't want to keep the girls waiting."

"No," I growl, tugging softly on her arm until she drops down into a chair. "You are going to tell me what happened that made you run away from me and everyone else."

"I saw you!" she screams, pulling her arm from my grasp. "I rushed back here from New York the minute my parents told me what happened to Lydia. I didn't even bother going home when my parents picked me up from the airport and went straight to Connor's house."

Selina wraps her arms around her waist, her eyes taking on this faraway look as she recalls what happened that night.

"Connor looked so lost. He didn't say a word when I walked into the room. The only thing he did was stare into space. I tried to stay there and be supportive of him, but I knew there wasn't anything I could say to make his pain go away. It was at that moment I decided I wasn't going back to New York. I was miserable. Dancing no longer brought me joy the way it used to, and I missed you, all of you."

"You were planning on coming home?" I murmur as I reach for her, pulling her against me. Tears spring to my eyes as I bury my nose in her neck, clinging to her body like she could disappear at any moment. "Why didn't you say anything to me, Selina?"

"Because," she croaks, trying to wiggle out of my grasp, but I tighten my hold.

"I don't know what's going on here, but there has never been anyone else in this world for me but you." I lean back, cupping her cheeks in my palms. "I've loved you since before I knew what love was." I kiss the tip of her nose before laying my forehead against hers.

Bitterness courses through my veins that we've lost so much time with each other over a misunderstanding. I barely remember anything about that night besides feeling lost. I wanted to be there for my friend, to help ease the pain he must have been feeling about losing the love of his life, but I was hurting, too. The one person I wanted there was nowhere to be found. I had lost one of my friends, someone I cared about like a sister, but I wanted Selina. I want to feel her body pressed against mine. I want to be able to give myself over to all the emotions swirling inside of me without the fear of being seen as weak or a bad friend. That's what Selina gave me, a place to feel safe to be myself, flaws and all.

"I want to believe you, but..."

"No. There is no *but*, Selina. What did you see that sent you running away from me?"

"After Lydia died, I saw you." Selina clenches her eyes shut, her head swinging back and forth as she struggles in my arms, trying to get away from me. "On Connor's back porch. My parents called me that morning to let me know Lydia was gone, and I rushed home. The only thought in my mind was that I wanted to see you, to feel your arms wrapped tightly around me as you whisper calming words into my ear."

Selina bangs her fist on my chest, tears streaming down her face as she lets all her emotions free. "Instead, I came home to find you with someone else."

"Selina..." My voice breaks slightly as I pull her tighter to my chest, but she pushes away from me. Selina takes a step back, swiping at the tears streaming down her cheeks as her face morphs from pure agony to rage before my eyes.

"Don't touch me," she spits, her entire body shaking with anger. "Why should I believe you? Why did you do all of this in the first place?"

"Because I love you, Selina. You are the air that I breathe. You're the brightest star in the sky on the darkest of nights. It's always been you."

"But why? I don't understand. That night... I saw... you were..."

"What did you see?"

"I saw you in a very cozy clench with someone I had never met before. Just as I walked onto the back porch, she had planted a kiss on your cheek."

"A kiss on the cheek?"

My mind plays everything that happened that day

on a movie reel, trying to find the exact moment that something like this happened, but the only person I saw that night was Emily. Sure, we all went to school together, but I didn't even recognize her when she started talking to me that night.

"But that's not what hurt the most. It was the way you looked at her. Like she was the moon and the stars, the same way you always looked at me before I left."

"Selina." I take another step toward her, but she retreats a second time. "Emily was a girl we went to high school with. I was probably looking at her like that because we had just finished talking about you."

"I didn't know that. I had all these grand plans for when I saw you again. I was going to tell you I wanted to come home that night. I loved dancing, but after a while, I was just going through the motions. My heart wasn't in it anymore because I left it here with you. But when I saw you in the arms of someone else, it broke me. I knew that I had waited too long, that expecting you to wait for me until I fulfilled my dreams was wrong."

"Is that why you stopped talking to me?" I question, letting my arms fall to my sides in defeat. "How could you even think that I'd do something like that?" I question, wanting to understand.

"My best friend in the entire world had just passed away. I'd like to say my mind wasn't in the right place, but that would be a lie. I had always expected you to leave me. Deep down, I knew that the distance between us would have eventually become too much, but instead of doing the right thing and breaking up with you, I was a coward and didn't say a word."

Selina wraps her arms around her waist as she begins to cry uncontrollably. "I was angry and hurt. Just the mere mention of your name would leave me engulfed in indescribable pain, where I couldn't function. So, I asked my parents to stop talking about you. I told Leia that I never wanted to hear your name again. And then I cut everyone else off."

Unable to stay away from her any longer, I stride toward her, wrapping my arms tightly around her slender body. Selina struggles in my arms, her fist hitting my chest a few times before her entire body sags into my embrace. I bury my nose into her hair, allowing all the emotions to pour out of my body into her, hoping that she will finally realize how deeply I care for her.

"Leia and my parents begged me to talk to you. They were determined to prove to me that it was all a misunderstanding, but I wouldn't listen. It took months for me to realize how childish I had been, but by then, it was too late. Too much time had passed. So instead of talking to you, I closed myself off to everything and everyone that would make me remember what we had. What I had lost."

"Selina," I choke out as pain lances through my

entire body at the mention of being with another woman. "I will love you until my dying breath." My eyes lock on hers as I search for answers, any sign that she believes what I'm saying, but the only thing I see is confusion.

"Leia tried to tell me what happened, but I never let her finish. In that moment, all my biggest fears came into view. I always knew you'd find someone better for you than me. Someone to live in that big house by the edge of the creek, sitting on the big porch swing and watching the sun set, your arms wrapped around each other tightly."

"For such a smart person, you really are an idiot sometimes," I whisper against her lips as I thread my fingers through her hair, tugging her head back and exposing her neck to me.

"I have to show you something." I nibble down one side of her neck before making my way back up the other side. "Hopefully, then you will realize how much you've always meant to me. Okay?"

I push to my feet and hold my hand out toward her. She takes my hand without hesitation, threading her fingers through mine. "For the record, Emily gave me a hug because she said it looked like I needed it. My best friend had lost the love of his life, the mother of his child, and there was nothing I could do to help him. I needed that hug that night because I lost someone that day, too. Up until that point, I had spent every ounce of energy I had trying to keep Connor moving, and I barely had a moment to process what had happened. In that moment, the only person I wanted to see was you."

"Okay," she whispers as she strides to the door.

We make our way to my truck, hand in hand, stopping for only a few moments to allow Selina to lock up the studio. I now have a better understanding of what kept Selina away for so long. To think that a small misunderstanding could change the course of our lives is mind-boggling. I can't help but wonder what would have happened if she told me she was coming home that night, choosing to give up her dreams to be here with me. Would things have worked out how we planned? The house, the kids, the perfect life we imagined for ourselves when we were kids? I'd like to think so, but in reality, we could have ended up right here in the same place but without the chance of reconciling with each other. Selina would have eventually resented me for her coming home and giving up on her dream. Minus the pain and heartbreak we both have suffered over the years, I believe we needed that time apart. Time for both of us to grow and become better versions of ourselves.

Instead of spending all these years exploring the world, Selina has closed herself off to everything. New friends, relationships, anything. She didn't want to feel anything for fear of being swallowed whole by her locked-up emotions. I have a feeling this is why she came back to Tyson's Creek. She could have rehabbed her injury anywhere, but she chose to come back home. To the place that grounds her, where she is surrounded by people who understand and love her. I just hope she understands that I'm still one of those people.

"After you, milady," I say to Selina as I swing the passenger side door open, bowing slightly at the waist.

"Thank you, kind sir." She smiles softly before shifting her attention back to the car. "Okay, out of my seat, Love."

"Oh, I thought this wasn't a date. Don't dates sit in the front seat?" Love giggles before sliding out of the car and opening the jump door to climb into the back.

"Yeah, Uncle Vance is insistent that this *is* a date. Is there a particular reason?" Jade questions, then whispers something into her friend's ear.

"Laying it on a little thick, don't you think, Squirt?" I whisper in Jade's direction as I climb into my truck.

"I don't think so. We said we'd help you get the girl, and we plan on doing just that." I should say something, but once Jade makes up her mind, there's no changing it. It might be a lot easier for me if I just wait and see how things play out.

"Vance and I used to date before I went off to school." Selina looks over her shoulder and flashes both girls a smile as I pull out of the parking spot.

"I'd say you did a lot more than just date, Selina." Jade winks at me before shifting her attention back to her teacher. "Uncle Vance says you're the love of his life."

"He told me that same thing," Selina responds softly, her cheeks pinking slightly.

"Does that mean you are going to stay and teach us instead of going back to New York now that your injury is all healed?"

"I wouldn't say it's *all* healed. I've regained my full range of motion. My physical therapist says I should only need a few more sessions, and I'll be back to full strength."

"Great," I mumble, trying to fake enthusiasm but failing miserably.

"We're happy for you, Aunt Selina. But what about us?" Jade questions, her eyes full of worry. "Will you close the dance studio again? Are you planning on leaving us?"

And there is the million-dollar question. I grip the steering wheel tightly as I wait to hear her answer. Selina must have a plan for what she's going to do with the studio. I'm sure Ms. Cassandra might come back and teach a few classes when she's available, but there is no one else. Emersyn could maybe teach one or two classes during the summer, but once classes start back at the university, her time will be limited. Besides, I doubt Selina would ask her to, anyway.

Selina has made no secret of her plans to go back to New York and dance, but we never once talked about what that meant for the studio or for us. On one hand, I'm elated that Selina will be able to dance again because I know that's what she wants. But on the other hand, I know that means she'll most likely leave town again soon. The question is for how long. I'm sure this is why she was so insistent on keeping her distance from me—her fears of what she might say if I asked her to stay. I need to make sure that she understands I don't want to keep her here like a caged bird. I want to take this journey with her, no matter where it leads.

"We never know what the future holds, sweetie," Selina whispers, glancing at me quickly before focusing out the window on the scenery passing by.

The air in the truck grows heavy, each one of us waiting for someone to speak. "Time to change the subject," Love mutters, shifting toward Jade. "How much do you want to bet my mom is at your house?"

"That's not a safe bet." Jade rolls her eyes and then meets my gaze in the rearview mirror. "What do you think, Uncle Vance? Are Audrey and my dad together?"

"I don't know." I pretend to think, knowing the girls want nothing more than to be partners in crime forever. "Maybe. Maybe not. We can't tell the future. But I know your dad is head over heels for Audrey."

"I bet you a hundred bucks she's at my house." Jade winks at Love quickly before turning her attention back to me.

"You're on," I respond as we pull into Connor and Jade's driveway.

"Hold on. You need to text Connor before we go inside." Love leans forward between the seats, a huge smile covering her face. "I got a text from Aunt Bristol. She said to tell you to text Connor before we go into the house."

Both girls giggle as they put their heads together and begin whispering to each other.

"I think you just got hustled." Selina smiles at me as I pull out my phone and shoot him a text.

"It's worth it." I chuckle. "I don't think these girls would survive walking in on their parents getting busy in the living room."

I wait a few minutes for a response, but when one doesn't come, I open my truck door and climb out.

"That was more than enough time for them to get presentable," I announce as everyone else begins climbing out. I stride to the front door, knocking loudly before swinging it open. "Honey, we're home!"

We all file into the house, stopping dead in our tracks when we find Connor and Audrey embracing on the couch. Audrey's eyes widen in surprise as we round the corner, attempting to slide out of Connor's lap, but he doesn't budge.

"They better get used to seeing us together because I don't plan on ever letting you go." He chuckles as the girls squeal in delight as they see their parents wrapped in each other's arms.

"I know we asked for this, but can we keep the PDA to a minimum in the house?" Jade makes a gagging noise before plopping down on the couch beside them.

"We are sitting on the couch," Connor gripes, causing Love to giggle.

"Yes, but it might take a little getting used to." Love leans over the back of the couch, wrapping her arms around both of them, pulling them in for a quick hug.

"You owe us a hundred bucks." Love holds out her hand in my direction.

"Why?" Connor asks as he plants kisses on both girls' cheeks. "Tell me you three didn't bet on whether Audrey and I would get together."

I chuckle. "We sure did. I owe them a hundred bucks, and Selina and I are going on a proper date. I call that a win for me."

"It's not a date," Selina sputters, her cheeks turning a delicious shade of pink.

"I told you I had something to show you," I whisper in her ear before pulling it between my teeth and nibbling softly on it. "If you still want to run away after that, I'll take you home."

Selina nods before stepping out of my embrace and walking toward the front door.

"I'll leave you all to it. It's time to lay it all on the

line for my girl." I flash them all a smile before following her out of the door and closing it behind me I quickly jog over to my truck and climb in.

"Now, let's get this party started," I say as I pull out of the driveway and drive further into the neighborhood.

"Where is this place you're so desperate to show me?" Selina questions with confusion written on her face.

"You'll see. I even have dinner ready for the two of us."

Selina points out the window at the trees rolling by. "Dinner? There aren't any restaurants around here."

"I said I have dinner ready for us, not that I was taking you to a restaurant." I smirk as I turn left onto my street. "We're going to my place."

"You own a house?"

"Yes," is the only answer I give her as I pull into the driveway.

Realization suddenly dawns on her face. "You bought it," she says reverently as she stares at the house.

The old farmhouse we dreamed of growing old in sits a few yards away from the creek. It was built in the late eighteen-hundreds, and the town always wanted to use it as a museum, but with it being so close to the creek and outside the center of town, there weren't many people coming to visit other than a few classes of schoolchildren once a year.

When the original owners died, their kids wanted to sell it but had a hard time finding takers. I promised Selina that once we graduated, I would get a job and buy it for her. I'm sure she never took me seriously, but it was fun to plan for our future.

Once she was gone, I needed something to keep my mind off losing her. And this place was a piece of her, of the life we planned on living together, so I thought it would help me through the pain. When Connor suggested fixing up the place, I jumped at the chance and haven't looked back since.

Sitting on a full acre of land, the entire farmhouse is practically brand-new. I tore it down to the studs, redid the electrical, and added everything we needed to have central heat and air. It was originally only two bedrooms, but I expanded it, creating four bedrooms and three bathrooms, a bonus room, and something special just for us.

"Of course, I did. This is the house we planned to grow old in." I reach over and squeeze her hand. "I tore it down to its bones, but Connor and I got it all fixed up. There's still some work to be done, but it's livable."

I release her hand before opening my door and jogging around to open hers.

"Milady." I bow, making a sweeping motion toward the front of the house.

Large wooden pillars stand tall, framing the front porch that runs the entire length of the house. There are two green rocking chairs sitting on the porch, along with a small sitting area on the far side. I've imagined what it would be like to sit out here with Selina like we used to do when we were younger, spending time under the stars and telling each other about our day. Now, I finally have the chance.

"This is beyond anything I could have imagined." She smiles, threading her fingers through mine and pulling me toward the door. Light illuminates the window, casting a warm glow on Selina's skin as I open the door.

Her mouth drops open in shock as the door swings open, revealing the high ceilings and the circular chandelier that Connor and I refurbished a few months ago. To the right is a comfortable sitting area, full of plush leather couches and a gas log fireplace. The entire room is open concept. Every detail in this house has been done to her exact specification of what she dreamed this room would look like once we lived here.

"How did you remember all of this?" Selina says in wonder as she looks around at the entryway of her dreams.

"I remember almost everything you ever said to me, Seli." I step closer, drawn to her like a moth to a flame. "But I had a little help. You remember the journal you used to keep?"

She thinks for a few moments before nodding.

"You left it at home when you left, and your mom

would look through it to help find me answers to any questions I had about wall color or furniture style. Anything that you may have written down that would help me make this into your dream home."

"Is that why you stayed in contact with my parents?"

"Maybe at first, but soon, they became a haven for me. Your parents are one of the few people in this world who understood how lost I was without you." I wrap my arms around her waist, pulling her tightly into my chest. "After you stopped answering my calls and texts, I was determined to move on, but nothing worked. It felt as if my heart was breaking every time, and I needed a distraction from the pain. I couldn't even be around Lydia and Connor because they reminded me of you. And then when Lydia died..." My voice trails off as the ache in my heart intensifies even more.

There are a million questions right on the tip of my tongue, but I swallow them all down. I didn't bring Selina here to bring up past heartache. Instead, I want to show her how much she means to me. That no matter where she is in this world, this place and I will always be here, waiting for her.

Selina turns around quickly, wrapping her arms tightly around my waist as she lays her cheek on my chest. "I'm sorry, Vance."

"That's all in the past now, Seli." I bury my nose in

her hair, and the smell of lavender and honey overloads my senses. "After I bought this place, I wanted to make it perfect, everything you wanted. I wanted to have it ready just in case you ever came home."

"You believed in us that deeply?"

"I've always believed in us, Selina. Even after all this time, the moment I heard you were back in town, I knew that everything would be okay. Our road back to each other isn't going to be an easy one, but anything worth having in life is never easy."

She takes a step back and gives me a bright smile before threading her fingers through mine. "Show me the rest of the house," she says in excitement, bouncing back and forth on the balls of her feet.

I chuckle softly, pulling her toward the back door. "I'll do one better."

We quickly head through the kitchen, not bothering to stop and turn on a light before I pull open one of the doors. She gasps in surprise when she sees that I renovated the sunroom, turning it into an outdoor living space, complete with comfortable seating and a small dining area. It's the perfect place to entertain friends and family on a cool summer day or to just spend a lazy Sunday afternoon, snuggling with a good book. But what catches her attention is the additions I've made to the deck.

"Finding the same wood to match the deck was

hard, but we managed," I mumble as she inches toward the door. "I added a small overhang, just enough to cover the swing with a little space for others to fit. I wanted to make sure you could enjoy it, no matter what the weather was like."

Selina flies out the door, making a beeline for the porch swing that brought her back to the past. This swing holds so much history for us. Our first kiss, the first time we said I love you, and many other firsts for the both of us happened on this swing. There was no way I wasn't putting it in this house. It's a part of our love story, one that I never want to forget.

A single tear cascades down her cheek as she runs her hand along the wooden back of the swing. "When I came home and didn't see this swing on my parents' front porch, I was heartbroken. I thought they had thrown it away, but here it is."

"I have so many good memories sitting on that swing. I couldn't imagine it being in anyone else's possession but mine." I wrap my arms around her waist, pulling her tightly to me. "Your parents gave it to me as a housewarming gift when I moved in. We always hoped you would come home one day and share this place with me."

Selina steps out of my embrace and sighs. "Vance, I don't know what the future holds. The director could call at any minute with the details about my audition."

"Seli, I love you. I have loved you since the first time I saw you. When will you understand that you're it for me?"

sixteen
selina

We stare at each other for a moment, my mind and my heart battling for what to do next. Being with Vance again is as easy as breathing. After seeing him with someone else when I came home for Lydia's funeral, I convinced myself he had moved on, but I was wrong. Vance has done everything in his power to let me know how he feels. He's said it a million times, but until this moment, I didn't believe him.

I've been making excuses for months, trying desperately to keep him at arm's length, for no reason. I was so afraid that he no longer loved me, but I never stopped to think that anything else was possible. He's told me what he feels a million times, but deep down I've been afraid to hope. Afraid that if I opened my heart to him again, he would break it, breaking me in the process.

Not that I could blame him. I was a coward. Instead of asking him what happened that night, I ran, leaving both of us with broken hearts and unanswered questions. We both attempted to move on in our own ways, but here we are, back at the place where it all started. I have to make another impossible decision: dancing or Vance. I love to dance, but damn it, I still love him, too. I've tried to deny my feelings for years, but being back in town with Vance and all our friends is the first time I've felt alive in years.

I know that if I told Vance to take me home, he would. He'd take me back to my parents' house and never bother me again, but is that really what I want? It's been sixteen years since Vance and I have been together, and I've only been back in town for a few months. Am I ready to give up everything I've worked for a chance of finding happiness with him again?

Before I can decide what my next move is, his lips are on mine. My arms wrap around his neck as he steps in close, pressing his body against mine. The muscular ridges of his chest cause my nipples to become impossibly hard as they rub against him. I abandon all logical thought as my body takes control.

Vance's fingertips dig into my skin, holding me against him like he's afraid I'll push him away. He doesn't know that I can't. Not this time. I'm no longer able to resist the pull we have had toward each other since the day I returned to town.

I love Vance Kirkland more than I'd like to admit, but what I need to decide is if I love him more than my career. I will have to give up everything to stay here with him, and I don't know if being a dance instructor in a small town will be enough.

"Stop thinking so much," Vance whispers as he takes my ear into his mouth, biting down gently. "Just feel, Seli."

Electricity pulses in my veins, morphing into a burning need as one of his hands slips beneath my shirt. His calloused fingers brush against my nipples as he wraps his hand around my breast and squeezes. The heat of his palm against my skin brings a moan from my mouth.

"Seli, I need you." The rough grumble of his voice caresses my skin, making goose bumps pebble on my flesh. "We should wait and talk things through, but if I don't get a taste of you soon, I may just go insane," he growls, leaning forward and closing the gap between our lips.

My eyes drift close as he brushes his lips against mine softly, and I gasp when a tingling sensation courses through my entire body. "Show me." My eyes lock with his as he trembles. The need he has for me is so damn clear in his face.

Vance groans loudly, pulling my body tighter to his chest before he leans in for another pass. I hold my breath, knowing that this moment is going to change everything. I just hope my heart knows what it's getting us both into.

I nibble lightly on his bottom lip as he grips the end

of my hair in one of his hands and pulls down, deepening our kiss. His other hand slides down my back, gripping my ass tightly in his palm, and I moan. Vance pulls back from our kiss, pressing his lips to mine gently three times before speaking. "I think a change of venue is in order."

I look directly into his eyes, which are swirling with emotion, waiting for me to give him the okay. He's giving me an out, a chance to stop things before they go any further, but I remain frozen in place.

"Don't make me regret this," I whisper, afraid of what the morning will bring.

Vance wants everything to go back to the way it was for us—the two of us lost in our own world, where no one else exists—but I don't know if that's possible. We're adults now, with responsibilities and people who depend on us. I know I could untangle myself from his arms and leave, forgetting about how things were, but I know deep in my soul that I can't. Fate has given Vance and me another chance. If I don't take it, I'm going to regret it for the rest of my life. I would wonder if the fire burning in my heart for this man a second time was just a product of what we had before, or if it was so much more.

"I don't have all the answers, Seli. What I know is that I love you more than anything. There are no guarantees in life, but I can promise you I'll live every day of the rest of my life making you happy."

Tears well in my eyes as I rise on my toes, pulling on the back of his neck and crushing our lips together for a second time, letting him know I hear him, and I want everything he can give me, even if it's just for tonight. Without breaking our kiss, Vance wraps his arms around me and lifts me, bringing my feet off the ground and striding inside the house. My back hits the wall as Vance pins me there and slams the back door shut behind us. My head drops back with a thump as my eyes drift shut, lost in the sensation of his lips on my skin.

The same fire as before begins burning through me, and I pull myself tighter to his chest. A painful groan escapes as his hips thrust forward, his jeans rubbing against my swollen lower lips and sending shockwaves of pleasure through my body.

"I'll never get enough," he says reverently as he nibbles his way down my neck. "But if you don't settle down, we won't make it to the bedroom," he growls before capturing my lips with his.

"I wouldn't mind a nice hard fuck bent over the couch; it's been a while," I mewl as Vance leans back and grips the bottom of my shirt. He lifts his leg between mine, holding me in place as he rips it over my head. I can't help myself as I grind my pussy on his leg. I'll be surprised if I don't leave a wet spot on his jeans.

"Don't tempt me." He nips at my collarbone before lifting me in his arms once again and heading straight for the stairs. He takes them two at a time before striding into his bedroom, kicking the door shut as soon as we cross the threshold. He immediately drops me onto the bed and stands up to his full height.

"Like what you see?" I question, as I push up on my elbows.

"You're even more beautiful than I remember." Vance kneels on the bed before sliding his hands into my hair and once again captures my mouth. He nibbles my bottom lip, begging for entrance, and I open my mouth to him. He quickly slides his tongue into my mouth as he pulls my hair to get a better angle.

Overcome with emotions, I fall back onto the bed and wrap my arms around him, pulling at the bottom of his shirt. Noticing my impatience, he breaks our kiss and rips his shirt over his head before dropping it to the floor.

Vance's body looks almost the same as it did before I left, except slightly more muscular and a little more hair on his chest. My eyes wander down his body, committing every scar to memory before my eyes zero in on the small script over his heart. I immediately lift my hand, two fingers tracing over the words, questioning their meaning.

"It says *love you always* in Italian." He covers my hand with his own and presses my hand into his chest.

"And the day we met." Tears fill my eyes and slowly trickle down the side of my face. "Why Italian?"

"You always said you wanted to learn Italian, so I figured why not?" He smiles down at me. "I planned to love you for the rest of my life. Although you were gone, I wanted to brand my soul with the reminder of the love we shared."

"How could you love me so much after I left you?"

"Seli, you were following your dream. I never gave up hope that you'd come back to me. And now that you have, I'm never letting you go again. I love you, Selina."

It feels as if the fear of giving up everything grips my heart, choking me, and making it impossible for me to say those three words in return.

"It's okay, Seli. You don't have to say anything. Show me," he whispers before leaning down to capture my mouth again, sliding his hand down my body and quickly unbuttoning my jeans, brushing his fingers across the edge of my panties. I lift my hips, signaling my desire for him to continue.

Vance chuckles lightly as he slowly pushes his fingers between my folds. "Someone has a greedy pussy."

I moan loudly, matching each of his thrusts with my own. "Please," I beg, not even sure what exactly it is that I want.

Vance pulls his fingers from inside me, brings them to his mouth, and licks them clean before gripping the top of my jeans and pulling them off my legs, along with my panties. He wastes no time in spreading my legs wide and latching onto my clit, sucking it deep into his mouth before taking it between his teeth. I writhe in pleasure as he pistons his tongue in and out quickly, shoving my legs into the air to get a better angle.

He continues to nibble on my clit before replacing his tongue with his fingers. "You're so fucking tight, Seli. Your pussy walls are sucking my fingers inside. I can barely move them."

I can feel myself climbing higher and higher toward my release. "Come for me, baby. I want you to come all over my face." He picks up the pace as he finds my G-spot and strokes his fingers across it twice before I explode.

"Fuck, you taste so good. I could eat this pussy every day for the rest of my life." He continues to lap at my juices as I come down from my orgasm before giving one final long lick from the crack of my ass to my clit. "Has anyone ever fucked your ass before?" he questions as his thumb circles the puckered entrance.

Unable to form words, I moan once again. "You want to feel me inside this ass, don't you, baby?" He pushes the tip of his thumb in, and I stiffen in surprise. "Not tonight, baby. I want inside this pussy first."

Vance steps back and quickly toes off his shoes, unfastens his jeans, and pulls them to the ground. Not even bothering to step out of them, he wraps his arms around my thighs and pulls me to the edge of the bed.

"Play with your pretty pussy. I want you to be nice

and wet before I fuck you." Vance grips his cock, stroking himself from root to tip a few times. Unable to resist his command, I rub slow, languid circles on my clit as he watches me hungrily.

"That's it. Slide those fingers into your pussy and think of my cock filling you up. I will fuck you so good you won't be able to move." I arch my back as I enter my pussy, clenching my muscles tightly as I fuck myself with my fingers. My eyes remain focused on Vance as he grabs a condom from the bedside table and slides it on. I close my eyes, attempting to hold off another orgasm.

"Beautiful," he whispers as the bed dips beside me. I quickly pull my fingers from inside me, raising them to his mouth. Without any hesitation, he sucks my fingers, licking and sucking my pussy juices from them before releasing them with a pop.

"There has never been anyone but you, and there will be no one else." Vance quickly sheathes himself inside me, bringing tears to my eyes. Not from the pain, but from the magnitude of the situation.

A feeling of home overcomes me as he fucks me. I raise my hips and wrap my arms around his waist as his cock hits my G-spot once again.

"So fucking good," Vance hums as he picks up the pace. The only other sound in the room is our heavy breathing and the slapping of his skin against mine.

I can feel myself getting closer to my second

orgasm. "I'm going to come," I warn him, unable to hold off any longer.

"Let go, Seli." He moans as he grips my hips tightly, likely leaving a bruise, but I couldn't care less. "Give it to me." I let go, coming hard enough that stars fill my eyes as Vance throws his head back and roars my name, his release following quickly.

Vance falls to the side, pulling me tightly into his chest. "How about we take a bath, and I give you a full tour of the house?"

"Do you have a claw-foot tub?"

"Of course, I do. I wouldn't have dared forgotten." He smirks before kissing the crook of my neck as he inhales deeply.

"Is it big enough for two people?" I ask him, a smile tugging on my lips.

"I'll make it work," he promises before rolling off the bed. "I love you," he whispers before planting a kiss on my forehead.

I watch as he flashes me a smile before sliding his jeans back on, leaving the top button open before he turns around and walks into the bathroom. I know that I still love Vance. If I'm being honest with myself, I still love him with all my heart. But I need to figure out if I'm staying in Tyson's Creek or going back to New York before I utter those words to him. My decision will determine if being in love with each other is enough because, in reality, love doesn't always conquer all.

seventeen

Vance

"You didn't skimp on anything, did you?" She smiles as she saunters to the clawfoot tub, running her index finger along the edge. "I don't think there's enough room for two, though."

"Are you sure about that?" I raise my eyebrow at her in question as I brush past her and turn the water on. I know full well that if either of us wants to enjoy the tub, there is no way we will both fit inside, but I love to watch her squirm. "Don't you want to sit on my lap?"

Her cheeks pink in embarrassment, giving me just the reaction I wanted. "Why don't I go order us a pizza, and you can relax up here in the tub?"

"What? No gourmet meal planned for us this evening?" she teases as she takes a seat on the edge of the tub, her long legs once again on full display as she crosses her ankles.

Images of those legs thrown over my shoulders while I devour her core, lapping at her juices as I make her scream my name for the second time tonight filter through my mind.

"Eyes up here." She snickers as she leans forward and gives me a kiss on the cheek. "Pizza sounds amazing."

I should be embarrassed about being caught ogling her, but I'm not. I shrug my shoulders before shutting off the water and turning toward the linen closet. I quickly reach inside, grab a towel from the stack, and place it on the floor beside the tub.

"If you need anything, just holler. I'll grab us a bottle of wine and be back before you know it."

"You're going to keep me company after all?" she says as she reaches back and unhooks her bra. Her eyes remain locked with mine as she lowers the scrap of lace down her arms, dropping it on the floor.

My cock instantly hardens against my zipper as I stride toward her, pulling her against my chest and slamming my mouth to hers. We both groan as I run my tongue against the seam of her lips, and she parts them slightly, giving me the perfect angle to taste every part of her mouth.

I slide my hand up her back and wrap her hair around my fist, controlling her movements, and grind my cock into her belly, letting her know that, in this moment, there is nothing on my mind but her. "Climb in before I change my mind." I turn on my heels and stride out of the bathroom.

The sound of her tinkling laughter follows as I stride out the door. Once I get downstairs, I order a large supreme pizza, Selina's favorite, and take a seat on a barstool. Tonight has turned into something out of my wildest fantasies. What I thought would be a simple night of trying to get Selina to open herself up to me again has turned into so much more. I don't want to get my hopes up, but maybe Selina and I are finally headed toward our happily ever after.

Selina and I haven't spoken more than a few words to each other since she came back to town months ago. I never understood her need to keep me at arm's length, but after tonight, everything makes sense. Selina thought I cheated on her. She saw me with her own two eyes in the arms of another woman, someone she had never seen before, taking comfort in a way that only she used to provide for me. I can't blame her for jumping to conclusions, but she still should've talked to me about it or any of our friends, for that matter. I want to believe that if we'd had the chance to talk, everything would've worked out, but to be honest, I'm not so sure. Selina and I loved each other beyond measure. I would have done anything to make her happy, and I believe she'd have done the same, but where would that have left us?

Would we have survived the last sixteen years? Would life have gotten between us, leading us down different paths toward the future? I'd like to believe that wouldn't have been possible, but honestly, I don't know. Letting Selina go was one of the hardest things I've ever done in my life—the other being watching my best friend lose the love of his life—but I don't think I could've been there for them both.

Connor was a shell of himself when Lydia passed, going through the motions, but he was no longer living. His heart and his soul died when she did. Everyone was there for him, letting him take the time to heal and helping him take care of Jade. He slowly found his bearings, learning that life didn't have to end because Lydia was gone. Now, he has Audrey and Love. He's finally learning to live again. So, now it's my turn.

Here is my second chance to find happiness with Selina. The time may not have been right when we were younger, but now that she's within my reach, I plan to hold on tight. We have a lot to talk about. We need to take time to get to know each other again, but the love I feel for her will never waver. It's time for us to stop focusing on the past and start looking toward the future. No matter what happened between the two of us all those years ago, we have a second chance to find love and happiness with each other now.

"Penny for your thoughts?"

My head snaps toward the doorway at the sound of

Selina's voice. "I don't know if you're ready for what I'm thinking at the moment," I say as I rub a hand down my face.

I thought she was gorgeous wearing her own clothes, but seeing her standing in my kitchen, wearing nothing but one of my flannel shirts, has got me hard all over again.

"How about that tour you promised me?" She smiles brightly as she strolls further into the room.

"It's not much. The bones are there, but I could use some more furniture." I reach up, rubbing my hand across the back of my neck, suddenly embarrassed.

Bringing Selina here to see the house was the perfect idea a few hours ago, but after what we just shared, it seems inadequate. I built this house with Selina in mind, wanting to ensure everything was perfect before she saw the space, and now here she is. I shouldn't have brought her here before it was ready. This house was originally something I built to keep her close to me, hoping that one day she would come home and see it. But now that we've reconnected, it's so much more.

"Stop thinking so hard, Vance. I don't expect the place to be a perfect replica of what I wanted when I was a teenager. I just want to see your hard work. To see something that you created with your own two hands."

"I created it for you," I whisper as she bends down,

wrapping her arms around my neck. "This is so much more than just a house to me."

"I know." She sniffles before planting a kiss on the top of my head and releasing me. "But I still want to see it."

"As you wish," I push away from the table, wrapping her hand in mine. "You've already seen the kitchen, so maybe we should start with the living room?" I motion for her to veer to the right before leading her down a hall toward the back of the house. I point out the half bathroom on the right side of the hall before ushering her into the living room. A large leather sectional takes up most of the room, opposite my sixty-inch flat-screen television.

"Now, I doubt this was for me."

"No, the big-ass television is for me." We both laugh as Selina pulls her hand from mine, sauntering around the room.

I scan the room, trying to imagine what it would be like to create a home for the two of us between these walls. We chose this house when we were just kids, saying that we wanted to grow old together while sitting on that old porch swing, watching the sun set behind the rolling hills on the outskirts of town, but I wonder if she still has the same dream. And if she doesn't, I wonder if whatever her dreams are could now also include me.

"I didn't do much to this room, wanting to leave it

as a blank canvas for when..." My voice trails off, not wanting to make her feel pressured or uncomfortable.

"When I came home," she responds as she walks around the couch, her fingers brushing against the leather before she takes a seat. "I'm so sorry, Vance."

"You have nothing to be sorry for. I'd be lying if I said I wasn't hurt that you didn't believe in my feelings for you enough to talk to me about what you saw, but there was a lot going on back then. You'd just lost your best friend and were living a thousand miles away, struggling to keep your head above water," I say before taking a seat beside her on the couch. "I believe everything happens for a reason. So, I know in my heart that we needed the time apart, and now fate has given us a second chance."

"Vance," Selina whispers, as tears collect in her eyes. "I don't know what to say. What to do."

I reach out and grip both of her hands in mine. "I know you only planned on being here for a short period, but I also think there's a part of you that misses Tyson's Creek." Selina tries to pull her hands from my grasp, but I hold them tightly between my hands. "Please don't run from me. Just think about it, okay? I don't want you to give up your dreams. I just want to be a part of them. Wherever they may lead us."

"You're too good to me, Vance," she whispers as our bodies slowly drift closer to each other.

"No, I'm not. But I will strive, every day for the rest

of my life, to deserve you," I say before releasing her hand and pulling her toward me, capturing her lips with mine.

She moans quietly, opening her mouth enough for me to slide my tongue in. I use my other hand to grip her left leg, pulling it so she is straddling my waist. My cock instantly hardens as her warm center slides across my length. "Fuck. If you keep doing that, we won't make it through the rest of the tour."

"I wouldn't mind if round two was a nice hard fuck bent over the couch." She mewls as she grinds her pussy on my leg.

"So tempting." I grip both her ass cheeks tightly in my hands before slapping them lightly, causing her to squeal in surprise as I lift her off my lap and place her on the couch beside me. "I promised you a tour, and a tour you'll get. You haven't seen my favorite room yet." I wink at her before pushing to my feet and holding my hand toward her.

"You're no fun," she grumbles before grabbing my hand and allowing me to pull her to her feet.

I lead her back up the hallway to the stairs. We come to a stop just at the bottom of the stairs, in front of a set of double doors. "I'm plenty of fun."

This is the one room in the house that I built with Selina in mind. I wanted her to have a place to be herself. A place where she can close herself off and forget about the rest of the world—her very own dance studio.

I never could've imagined that she'd come back to town and buy Barre Studio from Ms. Cassandra, giving her the perfect space to dance in. When I built this room, it was a proclamation of the love I feel for her and my commitment to love her for the rest of my life.

I could easily change the room into something else, an office or guest bedroom, but there was a part of me that always believed I'd have a chance to show this to Selina. It is my way of letting her know that even after all this time, she still holds an important place in my life and heart.

"Are you going to open the doors?" Selina's voice brings my mind back to the present.

"Of course." I chuckle humorously as I release her hand and pull the doors open before stepping inside.

"What's this room supposed to be?" she asks as she steps inside.

I take a deep breath, trying to find the right words to explain what this room is meant for. "It's one of the largest rooms in the house, so I figured it'd make a good man cave or guest room, but I built it for another reason."

Selina nods slightly as she looks around the room. The left wall of the room is the front of the house. Two large windows allow the moonlight to filter into the room, giving it an ethereal glow. During the day, the sunlight fills the room with natural light, which creates tiny rainbows on the walls as it reflects off the crystals in the large chandelier hanging in the center of the room.

"This room is for you, Selina," I whisper as I flick the light switch. The entire room is bathed in warm light. "This is your dance studio."

Selina gasps in surprise as she takes in the large wall of mirrors in front of her. Tucked into the right corner of the room is a decent-sized closet with some storage. I covered the pale green walls with different photos of Selina dancing. Most of them are ones I took when we were younger, but there are a few professional ones her parents gave me to make the room perfect for her.

"I had planned on installing one of those fancy sound systems you have at the studio," I say as I wrap my arms around her waist, pulling her tightly into my chest. "The entire room is also soundproofed, giving you the ability to crank the music up and dance your heart out."

Selina spins around in my arms. "I don't know what to say."

"You don't need to say anything," I respond before tucking a stray piece of hair behind her ear. "I'm all in, Selina."

Her eyes widen in surprise, and her mouth opens and closes rapidly as she tries to find a response. I promised myself I wouldn't come on too strong, but after laying my heart on the line, I need to know if she is all in with me, too.

"I don't know how much longer I'll be here, Vance. They could call me for an audition at any moment."

"That doesn't matter to me, Selina. Whether it be here in Tyson's Creek or New York City, I want to be with you. Whatever comes, we will handle it together."

Selina and I stare at each other for a few moments before the doorbell rings loudly, breaking the spell. "Dinnertime!" Selina shouts before sliding out of my embrace and walking toward the front door to grab our food.

There's no chance Selina could have misunderstood my intention. I built a life for us here, a place where we can live our lives together, a place where we can make a home with each other, but I'm willing to give all of that up in a heartbeat if we can be together. Now the only thing left is for Selina to let me in. To choose to take a chance on the love we share and understand that she can have her dreams and love at the same time.

"What do you say to a little fun?" Selina smiles mischievously as I step into the hallway, the smell of cooked peppers and melted cheese causing my stomach to grumble loudly.

"Does it involve eating pizza?"

"Of course. I'm starving, but it also involves shots."

She winks at me before spinning on her heels and making her way into the kitchen.

"Shots are dangerous," I retort as I follow her.

"So are you," she mumbles softly as she drops the pizza onto the table. "One shot for one question. But we're going to need something a little harder than that bottle of wine you promised me earlier."

I'm never one to turn down doing shots, but something seems out of sorts.

If I had to guess how our night would go after I laid my heart out to Selina, this wouldn't have been it, but nothing had gone the way I planned either. I take a few minutes and stare at Selina, my eyes locking on her as I search for answers.

Her eyes are pleading with me to understand. To let her have a reprieve from everything that has happened in the last few hours. Her hands are trembling slightly, turning red at the tips as she clenches them together. Selina is trying desperately to let me back into her life, finally willing to be vulnerable and give me a tiny piece of herself that she's kept locked away for all these years, but she may need a little liquid courage to help.

"Fair enough. Pick your poison." I point over my shoulder to the custom liquor cabinet I had installed. "But we have to eat our pizza in bed."

"A bedroom picnic?" Selina taps her finger against her chin. "You drive a hard bargain."

"It's all about the give-and-take," I respond, hoping she understands the deeper meaning of my statement.

"Deal. But only if you have tequila."

I chuckle as I open the cabinet and pull out a bottle. "Limes or no?"

"Limes. I haven't done shots in years."

I grab two glasses from the cabinet and pour each of us a shot before walking over to the fridge. I poke my head inside and notice two limes sitting on one of the shelves. After sending up a silent prayer of thanks, I grab them both and place them on the counter.

As I search for a cutting board, I ask my first question. "So, why did you stay in New York all this time? You said a few times you weren't happy there, but you stayed."

Selina contemplates her answer for a few moments before responding. "Honestly, I didn't know anything else. I had gone all in when I attended Juilliard. After Lydia passed, I felt even more disconnected from my life here in Tyson's Creek. Dance was the one thing I knew I could do and forget, even if only for a little while. I chose to stay and got it into my head that if I worked hard enough, I could reinvent myself."

I finish cutting the limes and bring them over to the table. We both toss back our shots, and I hand her a lime. She bites down, juice dribbling down her chin. Wanting to know more about her time in New York, I resist the urge to run my tongue across her chin and collect the juices and instead hand her a paper napkin.

"Thanks," she says. "When I first started going to school there, I was the small-town girl everyone loved to give a hard time to, and after a while, I believed them... except when I was dancing. I wanted to make sure I never turned into that girl again."

I finally have an explanation for why Selina never came home after graduation. She could have been a ballerina anywhere, but she chose the farthest place possible from me and everyone she knew. I always thought it was because she was running away from me, but now I know she was running away from herself.

"To be honest, I loved that girl who left town with nothing but hope. But I also love the woman who finally found her way back home."

"Vance..." she begins, but I cut her off.

"It's my turn, but I think a change of scenery is in order."

"That's right, you promised me a bedroom picnic." Selina smiles as she grabs the pizza box off the table, her shot glass, and the plate of limes before heading for the stairs.

"I'll grab some plates and be right behind you."

I want to know everything about Selina's life in New York, but a part of me is afraid that being back here in Tyson's Creek could never compare. Spending quiet nights here on the porch swing, watching the sun disappear behind the horizon won't measure up to the fast pace of the city Selina is used to. She said she wasn't the same girl that she was when she left town, that she's worked to change herself and become someone else. But I can't help but wonder if she was happy.

There had to be a reason that she came home after being injured, and I doubt it had anything to do with Ms. Cassandra needing to sell the studio. That was just her excuse, but I have a feeling the real reason is she's lost. Selina may have wanted to change herself, but I still see glimpses of the girl I fell in love with all those years ago. She's still inside her. She may have buried her deep inside herself, but she's still in there. Now all I need to do is to find a way to coax her into letting her free. Although she set out to reinvent herself, I truly think that what Selina needs is to remember the person she was in order to move forward.

"Hurry up, slow poke. I'm hungry!" Selina shouts from upstairs, causing me to laugh loudly.

"So impatient." I shake my head before grabbing the bottle of tequila off the table and heading up the stairs. I stop in the doorway, my eyes scanning the room as if I'm seeing it for the first time.

I painted the room a neutral beige color, a wrought iron California king-size bed pushed up against the far wall. My bed is neatly made, the gray comforter pulled to the top of the bed with the pillow propped against the headboard. There are two oversized windows on either side of the bed, with two small end tables nestled in front of them. Instead of the mess of clothes thrown around from our first trip to the room, they are neatly folded on top of the dresser pushed against the wall between the bathroom and closet door.

"I picked up a little and made the bed. I hope you don't mind," Selina mumbles before ducking her head.

"Of course not. How could we have a bed picnic if the bed was a mess?" I wink at her before walking further into the room. "Now, let's eat. I don't want to be accused of starving you to death."

Selina laughs as she grabs a plate from my hand before flinging the pizza box open and grabbing a slice. We eat in silence for a few moments before Selina smiles at me, grabbing her shot glass and thrusting it toward me. "Shot time."

I grab the bottle of tequila from the end table beside me and fill both our glasses.

"Okay, lay it on me. Make it a good one." I throw back my second shot before pouring another one and grabbing another slice of pizza from the box.

"Why did you choose construction?"

"What else was I supposed to do with all these muscles?" I wink at her before flexing my arms, making her laugh as she takes her next shot. "Honestly, it seemed like fun. I've always been good with my hands, so why not build houses for a living?"

I can see the wheels in Selina's head spinning as she bites her tongue, wanting to ask an additional question but also wanting desperately to stick to our deal.

"Go ahead and ask, Selina. But I get to ask two questions next time." I pour both of us another shot before throwing mine back.

"Is it enough for you? Never leaving Tyson's Creek and seeing what else the world has to offer besides this sleepy little town?" she asks, her eyes focused on me as she throws back her shot and licks her lips before reaching for the plate of limes.

"Yes and no," I answer honestly. "I regret not going to NYU so I could be closer to you, but I loved being able to build our business from the ground up."

"You got into NYU?"

"I did. I knew when you told me you were applying to Juilliard that I didn't want to be away from you, but I never told you. I foolishly kept it to myself, wanting you to ask me to go with you."

"I never knew that..." Tears collect in her eyes as my hand cups her cheeks. Her eyes drift shut as she nuzzles her cheek into my palm.

"I know. I regretted not telling you every day, but now that enough time has passed, I know it was the best decision for us. Because I didn't go to NYU, I was here for Connor and Jade. I was able to help Connor through his grief after losing Lydia. But it also gave me a chance to grow up and become a better man."

"Unlike me. Is that what you're saying?" Selina's eyes open, locking with mine, the pain of losing her best friend bubbling up to the surface. "I should have been there for Connor, for Jade, for you, but I ran away, closing myself off from the world and attempting to forget everyone who ever cared about me. Hoping by doing so I'd find a way to make the pain go away."

"You dealt with the pain of losing your best friend and me the best way you knew how." I lean forward, planting a kiss on her forehead before resting mine against hers. "I've always and will always be there for you, Selina. No matter what happens between us, you are one of the most important people in my world. Nothing will change that."

"Thank you, Vance." She leans back, brushing her lips softly against mine. "I've been running from the girl I was, determined to reinvent myself, to be someone else, but in reality, I was just afraid. Afraid of what it meant to admit to myself that maybe I made a mistake in going to New York."

"Do you regret it?"

"No. But I regret the way things ended with us."

"They never ended, Selina. Just think of it as a long pause."

Selina wraps her arms around my waist and lays her head against my chest. "Vance, why didn't you find anyone else?" Her words are barely above a whisper.

"The simple answer is, they weren't you. I'd be

lying if I said I didn't try to forget you, but after enough horrible dates, I gave up. I finally realized that I was comparing all those women to you.

"How about you? Has there been anyone else?" I ask, my heart constricting in my chest as I ask.

It's a fair question to ask, especially since she already opened the door, but a part of me doesn't want to know the answer. I'd be a complete idiot if I expected Selina to forget the opposite sex existed, but there is another part of me that wants to be the only man she's shared that part of herself with. No matter what her answer is, it won't change the way I feel about her.

"Before I joined a company, I didn't have time for anything but training, especially another man in my life. But I've been on a few dates, nothing too serious."

I wait for her to say something else, but when she doesn't say anything more, I slide my hand up her leg to the knee before pulling it up and over my hip. "I have to admit that makes me very happy."

She gasps in surprise as I rub my cock against her folds, putting gentle pressure on her clit. "What would you have done if I never came back?"

I roll over, pinning her to the bed with my body. "I don't know. I planned on loving you for the rest of my life. I was thankful for the time we had together, but I also never gave up hope that we might have a chance to be together again one day."

I nibble down her neck before sucking on her breast through the shirt, rolling my tongue around her hardened nipple. I use my other hand to unbutton the shirt as I make my way down her body, stopping at the curly hairs above her clit. I pull her clit into my mouth and suck as I slip two fingers into her drenched pussy, dragging them out slowly before sliding them back inside, playing her like a fiddle.

"Please let me show you how much you mean to me," I growl, my cock begging to be buried inside her a second time. I continue my movements, increasing the pace as I wait for a response, but when nothing comes, I stop.

"Please," I beg a second time, bending my fingers when I find the bundle of nerves that will send her over the edge and brushing gently across them.

I watch as a ripple of pleasure courses through her body. "Yes," she whimpers as I pull my fingers out and slide off the end of the bed.

Selina bites her lip in anticipation as I climb off the bed and slide my pants down to the floor. My cock springs to life as I grip the base and pump my fist up and down a few times to relieve some pressure.

She leans up on her elbows as her eyes travel down my body.

"Hmmm, you are good enough to eat."

I crawl up the bed and give her a searing kiss,

nipping and sucking at the delicate flesh on her neck as I slide her shirt off her shoulders.

"Beautiful," I say reverently as I stare down at the goddess before me. "You have captured me mind, body, and soul."

I trail kisses down her breastbone before wrapping my tongue around her left nipple. Her back arches in the air, trying desperately to push the rest into my mouth.

"Patience, Seli," I murmur.

She groans in frustration as I continue to worship her body, leaving no area untouched by my hands and lips as I make my way between her legs and inhale deeply, her musky scent enveloping my senses.

"Now for my feast." I give her folds one long lick and moan as her flavor hits my tastebuds. I plunge my tongue into her pussy, lapping at her juices as they pour into my mouth. Shoving my arms under her ass, I grip her cheeks and lift her into the air to change the position.

"Oh, God. Yes!" she screams as she wraps her leg around my ears, squeezing my head tightly as she locks them in place.

My need for her grows exponentially as her pussy constricts, pulling my tongue further into her as she comes. I groan as her juices fill my mouth while I lower her back down to the bed, licking her clean before leaning back on my heels and wiping my mouth with the back of my hand.

"I need you," I tell her.

I crawl up her body, rubbing my cock between her lips.

"I promised I would make up for the last time," I whisper into her ear, reaching down and circling her clit with my finger as I grab a condom from the end table and roll it on.

Selina spreads her legs wider to accommodate my body, and I slide into her pussy. A sense of completion overcomes me as I frame her head with my arms, supporting my body weight while I increase my pace.

"Fuck." I clench my teeth, sliding almost all the way out before slamming back in.

"I need more," Selina begs.

I continue to stroke her pussy, and we lose ourselves in the pleasure while the sound of our skin slapping together fills the room.

"Tell me you're close." I moan as my balls tighten, and I climb toward my release. "So tight and perfect." I slide my hand between our bodies and rub small circles on her swollen clit, and her pussy tightens around me. "Come for me, Seli. Come all over my cock."

Without a word, we both erupt. Fireworks go off behind my eyelids as I clench them shut, riding the waves of pleasure coursing through my body.

I don't even bother pulling out. I just roll to the side, bringing her along with me.

"I love you, Seli. Now and forever," I mumble as I pull her tightly to my chest.

I wait for a response, but I hear nothing. When I glance down, I see her eyes are closed. I kiss the top of her head before closing my eyes. As I drift off, I hope that when I wake up in the morning, everything will be as it should be and that I didn't set myself up for heartbreak once again.

eighteen

Vance

I groan as I wake up, throwing my arms over my face to block out the sun streaming through the window.

"Still not a morning person," Selina says as she takes a seat on the bed beside me, a steaming cup of coffee in her hands. She looks beautiful, wearing one of my T-shirts, the neck fitting loosely, showing off her shoulder. "I was going to make you breakfast in bed, but you don't have much food in the fridge. Thankfully, there was creamer for my coffee."

"I don't cook much. The last time I tried, I gave myself food poisoning. I tend to eat out a lot or mooch off Connor for dinner." I reach for the cup and take a healthy sip. "Besides, all I need in the morning is a good cup of coffee and you." I reach past Selina and place the cup on the end table before gripping her arm and pulling her toward me.

Selina laughs before straddling my waist, and my cock instantly hardens in excitement. "Didn't you get enough last night?" She slides her bare pussy along my length, causing us both to moan.

"I'll never get enough of you." She almost growls as I grip her waist, holding her in place. "I want to feel you," I whisper, my eyes locking with hers.

"I haven't been with anyone since..." Her voice trails off, telling me everything I need to know.

"Same for me. The only person I've been with is you," I respond, brushing my lips against hers. "It's your call, sweetheart."

Her eyes lock with mine, searching for something before she nods slightly. Selina raises her hips, reaching between us and sliding my cock into position. Her eyes drift closed as she sinks down my shaft.

Selina's hair cascades down her back, tickling my thighs slightly as she rides my cock in slow, languid motions. "That's it, baby, take what you want. Cover my cock in your cum." She has never looked more beautiful as the sun filters into the room, casting a pale-yellow glow on her skin.

"I'm close," she moans, leaning forward to capture my mouth with hers. In one swift motion, I flip us over without pulling out, quickening the pace. Her walls grip my cock in a vise grip as I piston my hips faster. Ribbons of cum fill her pussy as we come together. I slow down to a languid pace as we both recover from our orgasms.

I pull out slowly, both of us groaning at the loss of

connection, and I slide to the edge of the bed. I grab my cup of coffee and take another healthy sip. "Best wake-up call I've had in years. I could get used to this."

"I need to get home and change before heading to the studio. I have an early class this morning," Selina says as she slides off the bed.

Something shifted in our relationship last night, but I'm not exactly sure what it was. I can practically see the walls around her heart sliding back into place, shutting me out once again, but I refuse to let that happen. Now that Selina has opened her heart to me, I'm going to do everything I can to convince her it was worth it.

"Don't shut me out, Selina. We are in this together, okay?" Selina flashes me a forced smile before heading to the bathroom. "We're going to take a shower, and then I can drop you off at the studio." I give her ass a pinch as I slide by and head into the bathroom.

"Okay." Her face immediately clouds. "I'm sure you have a lot of work to get done."

"I'm sure Connor has everything under control, but I have to check in before coming back to pick you up for dinner tonight." I reach in and turn on the shower.

"Dinner tonight?" she questions as she pulls my shirt over her head and places her hands on her hips. I groan as my cock hardens again. Just looking at her, standing there in all her glory, has me unable to keep my hands off her.

"If you plan on leaving this house, you better get

your ass in that shower." I suck her bottom lip into my mouth as I grind my hard cock into her hip.

"Down, boy." She gives me a playful shove before stepping around me and into the shower.

I quickly follow behind her. "And yes, we are having dinner tonight." Suddenly aware that I'm inserting myself into her life, I amend, "Unless you already have plans."

Selina steps under the showerhead, water cascading down her body before reaching for the bottle of shampoo beside her. "No plans for this afternoon. I'm sure Bristol, Audrey, and Leia will demand my attention for a dish session at some point today. They'll never leave either of us alone until they get some information from us."

"I have a feeling Audrey will be a little preoccupied for the foreseeable future." I snicker as I step closer to her, helping her rinse the shampoo from her hair before reaching down and grabbing the conditioner and running it through her long dark brown hair.

"Connor will at least try to be sneaky about it, but he'll want to know what happened, as well. I promise I'll leave the juicy details for you to tell the girls." Selina's hand swats my chest as I rinse the conditioner out of her hair quickly before shoving her against the tile wall of the shower. "But first I need to have you again."

I lift her leg and wrap it around my waist before

slamming my cock inside her. "Hang on, love. This will be fast and hard."

"Your wish is my command." She moans as I take her again. I swear I will never get enough of this woman.

We made it out of the house with no further interruption from my libido, but only slightly. I dropped her off at her parents' house with just enough time for her to change and head directly to the studio, but not before ravishing her against the side of my truck.

"I really need to get inside, Vance," Selina murmurs, as I nibble down the side of her neck.

I inhale deeply before giving voice to my deepest fears. "I know, but I can't help but feel that if I let you out of my sight, you'll disappear."

Selina has mentioned many times that she plans on heading back to New York when her company director calls. But I can't help but wonder if she will tell me beforehand. Will she give me the chance to come with her, to support her as she follows her dreams, or will she let fear win a second time?

She kisses the tip of my nose before putting some space between us. "I can't miss our dinner date tonight, right? I'll be at the studio all day. You can stop by there or call me whenever you want. If I'm not in a class, I'll answer."

"Okay." I smile, the grip around my heart loosening

slightly. "I'll see you later. Tell the girls I said hi when you see them."

"I will," she replies before heading for the door, but I grip her wrist.

"I love you, Seli," I say with conviction before letting her go.

Selina doesn't say another word as she rushes toward her parents' house and ducks inside. I stand there, staring at the door, waiting for her to reappear for a few minutes before climbing into my truck and backing out of the driveway.

Just as I'm about to turn the corner and head for Connor's, my phone rings. "I was just coming to your house."

"I'm glad I caught you. Meet me at the office. We have some decisions to make," Connor responds, an ominous tone to his voice.

"Is everything okay?" I question, turning in the opposite direction and driving toward the office on the opposite side of town.

"Yes," Connor begins, before sighing loudly. "I got a phone call this morning from a man wanting us to help him renovate an old farmhouse."

"That's amazing! An opportunity like this will put our business on the map for sure."

"You're right."

I turn into the parking lot in front of our office and pull into the spot beside Connor's truck before climbing out. "Okay. Why do I feel like there's a but coming?"

"Because there is."

"Hold that thought. I just parked. I'll be inside in a minute."

I hang up the phone and climb out of my truck. My mind races as I stride toward the door, wondering what his hang-up could be. Remodeling a house is a huge undertaking, but it's not anything we haven't done before. Connor and I have had plenty of practice with my house here in Tyson's Creek. We have a great team of guys working with us and have connections to different distributors around the state. There doesn't seem to be a downside to this, as far as I can see.

"Now, please explain to me how this could be a bad thing."

"The job is for two weeks. He wants us to practically gut the entire interior of the house and rebuild it from the ground up. Kitchen, living room, and renovating a sunroom, as well."

"We may have to hire a few more guys temporarily, but I don't see any big problems with that timeline. We may have issues getting materials they may want, but if the client is realistic about the cost, we shouldn't have any problems." I plop down into my desk chair, crossing my arms over my chest. "Again, what's the problem?"

"The job is in Magnolia."

Well, shit. Now I see the problem. We are a local company, sticking to jobs that are close to home. By doing so, Connor can be home with Jade every night and not disrupt her schedule. However, Magnolia is about a three-hour drive from here, and if there is any hope of us getting the work done in two weeks, we'll have to remain on-site.

"I'm also skeptical about us being able to get all the work done in the time frame he's asked for. I have a few pictures of the place they sent over, and it doesn't look like anything we couldn't handle, but I'm worried."

"You're always in a constant state of worry, man." I chuckle, slapping him hard on the back. "Let me look at these pictures, and we can give the client a call. Once we get a detailed list of everything, we can come up with a game plan and a price for the client. We could be worrying about nothing. If they don't accept our quote, there's no job."

"Sounds good. I just need to call Audrey and let her know I won't be home for a few hours. I told the client we would call them back before dinner."

"Is there any way we could fudge the time a little bit?" I question, rubbing the back of my neck. "I made plans to have dinner with Selina tonight."

"I take it things went well between you and Selina last night?" He's trying to be nonchalant, but I can tell he's on a mission for information.

"Who's asking? You or the ladies?" I smirk at

Connor, not wanting to tell him what happened between us. We didn't do as much talking as we planned, but all the important things were said. "I think she finally understands that I'm all in, no matter what that might entail. We had a great night together. We spent most of the night getting to know each other again."

"I'm glad you finally got her to talk to you. Fingers crossed she's not as stubborn as you are." Connor laughs loudly as he wakes up his computer before searching for the pictures our potential client sent of the house we will be working on. "But I don't think you're going to make those dinner plans."

"Never say never," I reply before pulling my phone out of my pocket and shooting off a text to Selina.

> **VANCE**
>
> Connor has already asked me about what happened last night. Never fear, your virtue is still intact in his mind.

> **SELI**
>
> You're such a goofball. Bristol, Audrey, and Leia were waiting for me when I got to the studio.

> **VANCE**
>
> And?

> **SELI**
>
> And nothing. I had a class to teach. I told them to come back at lunchtime.

VANCE

Why does this surprise me? LOL. Are we still on for dinner tonight?

SELI

Can we play it by ear? Someone kept me up too late last night, so I may just climb into bed after my classes are done.

VANCE

You weren't complaining last night. Just let me know, okay? Connor and I have a proposal to put together for a job, so I'll be at the office for the next few hours. Love you.

SELI

Talk to you later.

"Audrey is champing at the bit to find out what happened last night." I chuckle before shoving my phone back into my pocket.

"I'm not surprised. Now that we've found our way to each other, it seems she's made it her personal mission to ensure her friends are as happy as she is."

"Congratulations, Connor. You deserve to be happy after all these years. I'm sure Lydia is just as happy for you as I am."

"I think she is, too. Now all we need to do is figure out how to convince Selina to give you another shot."

"Did she tell you about her accident?"

"Yes," I murmur. "The doctor gave her a clean bill of health. She should be back to dancing in no time."

"And how do you feel about her dancing professionally again?"

"I'm happy for her. I want to have the chance to watch her dance across the stage with a blinding smile on her face, but..." My voice trails off.

"But what?"

Without looking up from my desk, I voice my greatest fear aloud. "I'm scared that she's just going to pick up and leave again without a word. I know Selina still loves me. I can see it in her eyes, but she's afraid of something. The only problem is, I have no idea what that is."

"Have you asked her?" he questions as he pulls up a gallery of pictures and begins slowly flipping through them.

Each picture shows a different room in the house, each in an even worse state than the last. I'm finally beginning to see why Connor was so worried about taking this job. This is a huge undertaking, but if we pull this off, the word of mouth from this job alone could carry our business to the next level.

"No. She's made it perfectly clear that she doesn't plan on staying in Tyson's Creek long term."

"Really?" Connor questions, turning to me. "But she's putting down roots this time, Vance. She bought the dance studio, she's making new friends, and she's making a place for herself in town again. Even if she wanted to just pick up and leave, she has responsibilities now."

"I know. Maybe she has plans to hire someone to run the studio for her when she leaves or wants to have the business as something to fall back on if she's injured again."

"And you don't plan on asking her what her plans are?" Connor pins me in place with his eyes as I search for an answer to his questions. "I'm going to take your silence as confirmation you plan on making the same mistake you did when we were kids. You need to stop expecting her to be the only one to put her heart on the line. You need to show her how much she means to you, even if that means following her to New York."

"But we have the business. And you and Jade need me."

"Don't you dare use me or my daughter as an excuse for being afraid. You say you are all in and are willing to move miles away from the only home you've ever known for Selina, but actions speak louder than words."

"You're right. It's time for me to man up and have a serious conversation with her. I made the mistake of letting my fear stop me from getting my girl once. I don't plan on making the same mistake again." I pull Connor in for a one-armed hug before digging my knuckles into his hair. "Now, enough talk about the status of Selina's and my relationship. Let's get a plan put together for this client in Magnolia so I can make it to my dinner date."

nineteen

selina

"I t's lunchtime," Leia deadpans as she comes barreling into the studio, Bristol and Audrey hot on her heels. "You are going to tell us all the details about your date with Vance."

"They looked mighty cozy when they left Connor's place last night. I'd be shocked if she made it home before now," Audrey chimes in as she quietly locks the front door behind them.

This is the third time these three have popped into the studio since I arrived this morning. Each one of them wants to know all the sordid details, wanting to dissect every moment we spent together in search of a deeper meaning.

I can't blame them either. I've been replaying every moment of last night in my head on repeat since I walked into my parents' house this morning. My skin flushes as memories of the night we spent together play through my mind on a movie reel. Last night awakened a need for him that is both overwhelming and frightening all at once. I've never connected with another man in the way I connected with him, and I probably never will.

Much like Vance, I attempted to date after I got into the company, but no one ever measured up to my memory of Vance. They weren't tall enough, their hair wasn't soft enough, or their eyes weren't brown enough. I tried to convince myself that I was just picky, not wanting to settle for someone who didn't deserve a chance at my heart, but eventually, I realized that wasn't it. I was still in love with Vance, the boy that stole my heart when I was a little girl. No matter how much I tried to reinvent myself and bury the small-town girl from Tennessee, a large part of me refused to let her go.

"What's there to tell? He took me to his house and showed me around. We did some shots and had pizza."

"That's it?" Audrey questions as she threads her arm through mine, leading me toward a row of seats on the opposite wall. "That sounds like the most boring date in history."

"For real. I expected him to take her on a tour directly to his bed." Leia snickers before plopping down on the seat on my other side.

"Did he manage to change your mind about leaving?" Bristol questions as she waddles towards us, her hand resting on her lower back.

I take a moment, giving serious thought to the idea of spending the rest of my life here in Tyson's Creek. Being able to teach other girls to follow their dreams, no matter what the cost, the same way Ms. Cassandra taught me. That idea alone makes my heart swell, but then I remember everything I will have to give up if I stay.

Dancing the lead in a ballet has always been my goal since I auditioned for Juilliard. Ever since that day, I knew that dancing was what I wanted to do with the rest of my life. Being under the lights and dancing my heart out is an adrenaline rush that I've only felt one other time before: the day I told Vance I loved him for the first time.

Not knowing how to answer that question, I turn to Audrey. "How did things go with you and Connor last night, Audrey? You two seemed pretty cozy when Vance and I left."

"Amazing. Let's just be glad Vance texted before you all came in the door. You would have had a vastly different welcome if you had come in a few minutes earlier."

"I'm happy for you. Now, when's the wedding?" I ask.

I'm not just saying that, either. I'm genuinely happy for her and Connor. I'm glad they finally found someone to spend their lives with. For me, it's been nothing but dance for years. I almost forgot what it felt like to have someone else cherish me so much. That is, until last night.

"Don't change the subject," Bristol says as she awkwardly attempts to lower herself into a chair. "Audrey has already given us the details from her night while you were on your date. Now it's your turn."

Leia and Audrey laugh softly, causing me to sigh loudly. "Nothing happened. We had pizza and chatted."

"Chatting doesn't lead to you not coming home until this morning."

"How did you know I didn't come home?" I question, my eyes swiveling between my three friends.

"Your mom. Someone forgot to tell their mother they weren't coming home, so she called me looking for you." Bristol winces slightly as she runs a hand across her pregnant belly. "Don't worry, I let her know you were on a date with Vance."

"Great. Now I'm going to have to sit through the Spanish Inquisition when I get home, too."

"Anything else you want to tell us?" Leia asks, throwing her arm over my shoulder and pulling me to her side. "All you did was talk all night long?"

"I mean, we haven't truly spoken to each other properly in sixteen years. There's a lot for us to catch up on."

"No one is disputing that. But you honestly want us to believe that a man who has loved you most of his life, who has been practically stalking you for a date and built your dream home, only wanted to chat with you?"

"I could see Vance doing something like that," Audrey chimes in, giving me a small smile before shifting her attention to Bristol and Leia. "I think it's sweet."

"It is sweet, but so is Connor, and we all know what happened when you showed up at his house and told him how you really felt," Bristol deadpans, causing Leia and I to laugh at Audrey's expense.

"Touché," she grumbles before laying her hand on my shoulder. "I tried, but you're on your own with this one."

All three ladies stare at me, waiting for me to give them any more information. I could keep my mouth shut, but they'd never let me hear the end of it. "Something might have happened." I sigh, not wanting to talk about it, but knowing neither of them will relent until I do.

"Come on!" Bristol whines. "Let me live vicariously through you. The three of you are having more sex than I will be for the foreseeable future. These stories will get me through."

"Umm, you mean the two of *them*. My dating life is drier than the Sahara Desert." Leia chuckles humorously.

"He showed me around the house, and it's amazing.

It's everything I imagined it would be, and so much more. Apparently, my mom found an old diary of mine, where I planned out how I wanted to turn the house into a home, and he followed the plan to the letter, leaving anything I hadn't specified neutral."

"Now we're getting to the good stuff," Audrey responds, rubbing her hands together in anticipation. "What else happened?"

"We may have had sex..." My voice trails off, my cheeks heating in embarrassment. "A few times."

"How many times?" Bristol chimes in.

"So many I lost count. No one has ever made me feel so cherished in my entire life. It makes me wonder if he really does still love me after all these years."

"Vance has never been serious about being with another woman. Sure, he went on a few dates and gets plenty of attention, but he never takes them up on their offers." Leia grabs my hand in hers, squeezing it.

"I know. He told me he tried dating for a little while, but they weren't me."

"How romantic." Leia swoons, causing Bristol, Audrey, and I to roll our eyes. "I can't wait for you two to settle down together and maybe have a kid or two."

"Kids have never been in the equation for me." Suddenly, my eyes widen in shock as I realize Vance and I had unprotected sex a few times over the course of the night. The first few times last night were thought out, but this morning was different. Even though we talked about being clean, and how we haven't had any other sexual partners, I didn't even consider the chance of me getting pregnant. I curse internally as I begin mentally calculating where I am in my cycle.

I jump in surprise when Leia fires off questions at a rapid pace. "Are you two back together? Are you going to stay now? Did he ask you to marry him?"

"Marry him? Jesus, Leia, what fairy-tale world do you live in? We went on *one* date. I hardly think that's appropriate," I respond as I push to my feet.

"Seli, I hate to break it to you, but that man has it bad. He bought a house for you," Bristol says as she holds her arms out for me to help her stand.

"He bought a house for *himself*."

"Yes, a thirty-something, self-proclaimed bachelor who hasn't even had so much as a date in the last five years bought himself that big house. *Your* dream house," Bristol says sarcastically as I pull her to her feet.

I head toward the front door, wanting to buy myself some time and think through what the girls are saying. These three have been firing nonstop questions at me since they walked through the door a few minutes ago. Sure, some things they are saying are true, but there must be a logical explanation for everything.

"I understand what it looks like to the three of you, but I never planned on staying here long term," I remind them, unlocking the door. "All I'm waiting for is a call for an audition, and then I'll be on my way back to the city."

"What if that call doesn't come?" Audrey questions, causing me to spin around on my heels.

"I don't know," I whisper, wrapping my arms around my middle. "I've asked myself the same question a million times since I came back to Tyson's Creek, but I still don't have an answer."

"Take it from personal experience. You don't want to miss out on the man of your dreams because of fear."

"I never said I was afraid."

Bristol throws her arm over my shoulder. "You didn't have to. I understand running a dance studio in your hometown wasn't what you dreamed you would be doing at this stage in your life, but things change. Dreams change."

I open my mouth to respond, but then I hear my cell phone ringing. "Hold that thought," I say to my friends, then answer the call. "Hello?"

"Selina Grymes?" an unfamiliar voice asks.

"Yes, this is Selina," I reply as a sense of dread settles in the pit of my stomach.

"This is Stefanie from the New York City Ballet office. We would like you to come in for an audition tomorrow. A principal dancer for this season's ballet was injured, and the director isn't set on giving the understudy the role. He specifically requested you be called for an audition. We've scheduled your audition for nine tomorrow morning."

"Yes, I understand. I'll be there."

The moment I have been waiting for has finally arrived, but I'm not feeling the way I thought I would. My chance to get back on the big stage is within reach now, but the only thing running through my mind is having to say goodbye to Vance once again.

Did he mean it when he said he was prepared to give up his entire life to follow me around the world? Well, not in those specific words, but the sentiment was there. But how can I ask him to do that? How is that fair? Vance shouldn't have to give up his entire life for us to be together.

Stefanie's voice brings my mind back to the present, reminding me that this is what I hoped for. I can't let anything, or anyone, get in the way of following my dreams. I was perfectly happy with my life before I let Vance back into it, and I'll be fine after I leave. Nothing has to change.

Making up my mind, we exchange a few more pleasantries before I hang up the phone. Then I turn back to my friends, who are both waiting with bated breath. "That was the ballet. They need me to come in for an audition tomorrow. I have to get a flight booked."

I pull up all the different flight apps I have on my phone and scramble to find a flight. I know it's going to cost me an arm and a leg to get a last-minute ticket, but

I can't let this opportunity pass me by. Luckily, I locate a flight leaving this afternoon and purchase the ticket immediately.

"Are you sure you want to go?" Bristol questions, echoing the nagging voice in my mind that's urging me to take a minute and think things through.

Maybe there's a way for me to have Vance in my life and continue to dance, fulfilling both of my dreams in the process. Vance said he was willing to do anything to ensure things work between us this time around, but is it even fair for me to ask?

"This is the chance I've been waiting for since my injury. It could be my last shot at fulfilling my dream." My head shakes back and forth as I drop my chin to my chest, not wanting to see the sympathetic looks on their faces I know are there. What more do they want from me? I've been waiting for this chance for most of my life. I can't turn it down for a chance of things working out between Vance and me, can I?

"*Have* to or *want* to?" Bristol challenges before wrapping her arms around me.

"*Have* to." I press the palms of my hands to my eyes, welcoming the pain, needing it to tether me to the here and now. "Plus, it's just an audition. There's no guarantee I'll get the part. I'll probably be back in town, teaching class in no time, but I have to try."

"Who is going to teach the classes while you are

gone? The girls can't go months without class," Bristol mutters softly, tightening her grip.

"I'm sure I can call Ms. Cassandra to help, and Emersyn is more than capable of teaching the classes in my stead."

"You seemed to have thought of everything." Audrey sniffles before wrapping her arms around Bristol and me. "It's like you've been planning this or something."

"I never intended on staying here forever, Audrey. I always knew I was going to head back to New York when the company called me in for another audition." Tears pool in my eyes as Leia joins our group hug.

Each breath feels like pure agony as their grips tighten around me. A gut-wrenching sob escapes me as I bury my nose in Bristol's neck. Snot and tears collect on her skin, but she never releases her hold on me as I try to regain control of my emotions.

"You're going to do amazing," Leia chokes out, her voice thick with emotions.

"We'll hold down the fort here and make sure everything is perfect when you return," Audrey whispers from somewhere beside me. "Just promise to come back to us."

"Come back to all of us. Especially him," Bristol whispers, tears streaming down her face as she rests her forehead against mine. "We'll all be here waiting when you get back."

"I will," I reply with conviction as we untangle our limbs from each other and break apart.

All three of them flash me a weak smile before heading out the door without another word. It would be easy for me to turn down this audition and stay here in Tyson's Creek, but I know I'll always wonder what would have happened if I had gone. I need to see this through, or I'll regret it for the rest of my life. With my mind made up, I stride toward the front desk and grab my cell phone from my bag. I take a deep breath before pulling up his phone number. My finger hovers over the call button before it suddenly vibrates in my hand, signaling an incoming text message from Vance.

VANCE

> I hate to do this, but I need to take a rain check for dinner. This proposal is a lot more complicated than I planned. I love you.

SELINA

> No worries. I need to head home to pack. I got the call for my audition. Wish me luck.

VANCE

> When do you leave?

SELINA

> This afternoon. They need me back in New York tomorrow.

VANCE

Okay. Good luck! I'd say break a leg, but that doesn't sound right. I know you'll do amazing. I love you.

I know it would be easy for me to profess my undying love for Vance and promise to be with him forever, but I can't. Not now. If he loves me as much as he says he does, waiting a few more months for me to finish what I started and then come home won't be a deal-breaker for him. At least I hope it isn't.

twenty

Vance

"**I**s it going to get easier?" I mumble into my empty room as the sun filters in through my bedroom window.

I attempt to sit up but immediately fall back into bed as I wait for the room to stop spinning. When I opened my eyes yesterday morning, I felt as if I could take on the world. I had finally laid my heart on the line and told the girl of my dreams that I wanted to spend my life with her. But that all came crashing down the moment Selina responded to my text.

I tried to pretend nothing happened, that my world wasn't slowly crumbling around me, but I'm sure everyone noticed. I tried to go through the motions. We presented the proposal to our client in Magnolia and won the contract. Instead of heading to Magnolia in a few days, as we planned, I told Connor I could head that way tomorrow, wanting to put as much space between me and Tyson's Creek as possible.

I didn't want to face the sympathetic looks from our friends a second time. I need to find something to take my mind off Selina being gone, something to stop me from spending the entire day checking my phone, waiting to hear from her. I reach over and grab my cell phone from the end table and pull up her number, trying for the millionth time to find the words to explain how I'm feeling, but I come up empty.

I thought I was prepared for her to leave again, but I didn't expect it to happen so soon. I wanted to have more time to get to know her better, allowing our love for one another to bloom again, but it seemed the universe had other options. But things are different this time, even if only slightly. Selina didn't leave without telling me. She let me know she was going for an audition and gave me a chance to tell her how I felt one last time.

I meant it when I wished her luck. I want Selina to have everything she ever wanted. The only thing I was asking for was to be included in her dreams, and once again, I'm left wondering if telling her how much I loved her was enough to convince her I was all in. That no matter if it was in New York or here in Tyson's Creek, we could figure anything out together; she just had to choose to let me in.

My phone buzzes in my hand with an incoming call. I take a deep breath before looking at the screen, hoping it's Selina, but it's Connor. I sigh before swiping across the screen and answering.

"Hello."

"Hey, man," Connor says, his voice rough with sleep.

"Hey," I croak as I roll back in the bed, laying my head on the pillow and throwing my arm over my eyes. "What's up?"

"I'm hurting this morning. I called the client and let them know you wouldn't be there until this afternoon." Connor groans, and I hear the rustling of sheets through the phone. "Are you sure you don't want me to come with you?"

If anyone understands why I drank my weight in alcohol last night, it's our new client, Finn Buckley. Finn seems to have stuck his foot in it with his girl, Marissa, as well, and now he is buying and renovating her dream house, hoping to convince her he's worth her time. Man, does that sound familiar? I wouldn't go as far as to say I bought the farmhouse for Selina alone, but she had a lot to do with it. I'd be lying if I said I wanted her to love that house as much as me, using it to convey how much she means to me. But it seems to have backfired. I just hope Finn has better luck than I did.

I try moving again, but blinding pain shoots through my head, making stars dance before my eyes. "Yes, but remind me to never drink again."

"Until next time life throws either of us a curveball, right? We're too old to be drinking like this anymore," Connor complains.

I hear Audrey's voice in the background, and then I hear muffled voices through the phone for a few moments.

"Who says we're old?" I retort, a few more voices filtering through the line before Connor responds.

"I'm putting you on speakerphone since everyone wants to hijack our conversation."

"So, what's this nonsense about being old?"

"It's a proven fact, according to our fourteen-year-old daughters and the pounding headaches you two have complained about." Audrey giggles softly. "Hi, Vance."

"Hey, Audrey. You may have a point." I groan before rolling to my side. "It sounds like you two have better things to do this morning than chat with me. Get some rest, Connor. I'll call you when I'm on the road and headed to Magnolia." We say our goodbyes before I hang up the phone and finally find the courage to move.

I slowly sit up and swing my legs over the side of the bed, pausing for a few moments. Once the pain subsides, I push myself to the standing position and slowly make my way to the bathroom in search of some pain medication. Anything to stop the pounding in my head. I don't turn on the light as I rummage through the medicine cabinet, grabbing the bottle of ibuprofen and shaking two pills into my hand. I throw the pills into my mouth and wash them down with a small gulp of water, using the cup on the counter.

As I turn to head back to bed, I catch my reflection in the mirror. Gone is the easygoing man without a care in the world. He's been replaced with someone who has nothing left to smile about.

Although losing myself in way too many bottles of beer last night helped for a little while, I'm still no closer to finding a solution to my problem. I could call Selina and ask her directly where we stand, but I'm afraid. Afraid of her putting the last nail in the coffin and ending my years of hope that she would come back to me.

"Stop being so dramatic," I say to my reflection before getting into the shower.

Lying around in bed will only give me more time to focus on everything that is going on and worry about what might happen, which will do nothing for my state of mind.

I shower quickly and dress in a dark pair of jeans and a flannel shirt rolled to the elbow, before grabbing my duffle bag from the bottom of the closet to start packing. I know Connor called Finn and told him I wouldn't be there until tomorrow, but maybe finding something else to focus on is just what I need. Once I have enough clothes for a few days and all the essentials, I zip my bag closed and grab my keys and wallet off the end table. I pause for a moment before grabbing my phone and unlocking it. I scroll down to Selina's number, hesitating for a few moments. Shaking my head, I shove it into my back pocket.

"If she wanted to talk to you, she would have called. Just wait until she comes back, and you can discuss things with her then," I say out loud as I head toward the closet and shove my feet into my work boots before heading down the stairs and out the door.

Once I'm in my truck, I head directly for the coffee shop, in desperate need of some caffeine. I head right for the front counter and place my order, leaving no time for conversations with Katie behind the counter.

She gives me a skeptical look but thankfully says nothing as she rings up my order.

Since the morning rush has passed, I get my coffee in no time and am headed toward the office. I know Connor said I could take my time getting up to Magnolia, but sitting around and worrying about Selina isn't helping anything. I might as well head up to Magnolia and make sure everything is ready when the rest of the crew arrives.

Our company, Ace and Hammer Construction, is located on the outskirts of Tyson's Creek, almost exactly between the center of town and my place. We have more than enough space to store all our equipment and any materials we order specifically for a job. I swing my truck into a spot right in front of our offices before climbing out. The entire place is deserted, which isn't unusual, making it the perfect place to lose myself in work.

After shutting off my truck, I climb out and head right for the front door, pausing for a few moments to unlock it and shut off the alarm system. The inside of the office isn't anything special. There is a small break room off to the right of the door, where the guys can eat their lunches and relax between jobs. Straight in front of me is Connor's and my desk, each one pushed off to a corner, facing the middle of the room. It seems like an odd setup, but I figured it would be easier for us to have conversations if we were facing each other.

After taking a quick sip of my coffee, I stride to my desk and take a seat before pulling out my laptop. Now is as good a time as any to get started on searching for a few vendors closer to Magnolia where we might be able to source material. I stay that way for a few hours, only stopping once or twice to go to the restroom and grab another cup of coffee before my stomach rumbles loudly.

I check my watch and calculate if I have time to make a stop at Crawdaddy's before heading out of town and to Magnolia. It might be cutting it close, but a big, juicy burger with all the fixings sounds amazing right now, so I shut everything down quickly and head out the door. I quickly climb into my truck and head back through the center of town, passing the diner and a few other shops before spotting the neon sign a few miles in front of me. I pull into a spot and head directly inside, grabbing a stool at the end of the bar.

Crawdaddy's is what I'd call a typical sports bar. On the weekends, it plays live music and has an entire wall lined with neon signs. The wraparound bar sits in the center of the room, with small tables scattered around and a dance floor tucked into one corner beside the jukebox. There are also some pool tables near the back, making this the perfect place to come when you want to forget your problems.

"Well, well, if it isn't Vance Kirkland." Beckett, the owner, chuckles before dropping a menu onto the bar in front of me. "To what do I owe this pleasure?"

Beckett also happens to be Emersyn's older brother, although you would never know it by looking at them. They're stepsiblings, but Beckett is just as protective of his little sister as any brother would be. Beckett is six feet tall, with a broody personality and no patience for stupidity, so most people find him intimidating just by looking at him, but anyone who knows him knows he's nothing but a big softy.

I eye him skeptically, waiting for him to ask me something about Selina because there's no way he doesn't know that Selina has left town again. Beckett narrows his eyes at me for a moment before running his hand through his dark hair and resting his elbows on the bar. Most people in town would ask prying questions, wanting to know how I'm handling her leaving again, but Beckett won't say a word, allowing me to share as little or as much as I want.

"Are you going to order something, or are we going to have a staring contest?"

"Just want a burger before I head off to Magnolia for a new job."

Beckett whistles softly, grabbing the unopened menu. "You guys must be doing well if you're getting job requests from all the way in Magnolia."

"I can't complain."

"We've got a new microbrew that I think you might like, if you want to try it," Beckett says as he throws a towel over his shoulder, resting both arms on the bar and leaning forward slightly. "It's from Big Beach Brewing, called Dixie's Heart. I'd love to get your opinion on it."

"Sure. Why the hell not?" I respond, fully aware that having anything else to drink won't help my hangover. "But only one."

Beckett nods in response before striding toward the draft station to grab my beer. He is back in a flash, and I take a healthy drink, letting it sit on my tongue for a few moments before swallowing.

"Not my favorite, but I think it'll be a good seller."

"Fair enough," Beckett says, then heads to check on another customer near the end of the bar.

I look around the bar, hoping to notice a familiar face, but come up short. Not wanting to sit here alone, I pull my phone out of my pocket and dial Connor's number.

"Hey," Connor says over the loud voices in the background.

I pull the phone away from my ear. "Having a party you forgot to invite me to?"

He doesn't miss the sarcasm in my voice. "Asshole. I was just getting ready to call you. We're having a barbecue at the house. Audrey invited Bristol and some girls from class over. Why don't you head over? You can help add some testosterone to the place."

"Nah. Thanks, man. I'm just grabbing a burger over at Beckett's place before heading to meet Finn."

"Well, tell Beckett thanks, but no thanks, because we don't need to be in Magnolia until tomorrow."

"And I told you I don't need a babysitter. I'm perfectly capable of handling Finn Buckley on my own." I chuckle before taking another healthy pull from my glass. "Thanks for the invite, but I'm just going to eat my burger and head to Magnolia. There's no sense in wasting another day if we don't have to."

"All right. If you change your mind, you know where to find me," Connor says.

"Thanks," I reply half-heartedly before hanging up the phone.

I know he means well, but the last thing I want to do right now is hang out with my best friend and his family. I'm so happy that he finally found love again with Audrey, but I don't need their happiness shoved down my throat. I have no idea when or if Selina is going to come back, let alone whether she wants to be with me. The night Selina and I spent together a few weeks ago could easily have been a one-time thing for her, although I made it clear that I wanted something more.

"You look like a guy who has a lot on his mind." The barstool to my left scrapes against the floor as the owner of the voice sits down.

"You could say that," I reply, taking another sip of my beer as Beckett places my burger in front of me.

"Thanks," I say before picking up my burger and taking a healthy bite as Beckett takes my neighbor's order and writes it down.

"So, you and Selina, huh?" Beckett asks, and I nod, not wanting to have this conversation right now. I came here to forget about my problems, not to be reminded of them. "How's she doing? I haven't seen her around since she moved back home."

"She's doing well. She just headed back to the city for a big audition. She's hoping to get back in with the company she was in before her injury." I take another big bite of my burger.

"Good to hear. I remember you always were sweet on her when y'all were younger. Are things working out a little differently this time around?"

"Who knows..." My voice trails off.

Thankfully, a rowdy group of people comes barreling into the bar and grabs his attention.

"Well, when you see her, tell her to stop by and grab a drink on the house," Beckett tells me.

"Will do, but I don't know how much longer she plans on being in town," I mumble around the large bite of food in my mouth, then wash it down with another gulp of beer.

After a few moments, my neighbor breaks the silence. "There are only two reasons someone would sit in the bar during the middle of the day."

"And what are those?"

"Getting off a graveyard shift or a broken heart. Which one is it?" he responds as Beckett places his drink in front of him. He nods his head in thanks before continuing. "You look more like someone with a broken heart."

"What makes you think that?" I bite back, grinding my teeth together to stop from shouting. If I wanted to have a social hour and discuss my feelings, I would have gone to hang out at Connor's house with everyone.

"Body language. The moment he mentioned her name, your whole demeanor changed."

Beckett sets my new beer in front of me.

"You seem a little tense."

"Just got a lot on my mind." I shove the last bite of my burger into my mouth and drop some cash onto the bar. "Thanks for lunch." I give them both a half-assed salute and turn to the door but pause when I hear the stranger's voice.

"If you love her, tell her."

"I told her I loved her, but she left anyway." My voice scratches against my throat from all the emotions clogging it.

"What did she say?"

I shake my head, unable to form the words. My heart feels like it's been ripped out of my chest a second time. "She didn't say anything." I sigh before heading back to the bar and reclaiming my seat. "She and I have a past, a very painful one at that. I've spent the last sixteen years regretting the day I let her walk out of my life. This time, I laid it all on the line, letting her know exactly how I felt, but she still left me."

"Okay, so what are you going to do about it?" he asks, placing a hand on my shoulder and giving it a small squeeze.

"I don't think there's anything else I can do at this point. I told her how much she meant to me and that I was all in. What else is there?"

"Actions speak louder than words." The stranger takes a sip of his beer, his eyes locking on mine as shame fills me.

I told Selina of my plans to go with her to New York when we were younger, how I just wanted her to ask me to go with her, but how is that fair? Selina doesn't know me from Adam any longer. Neither one of us is the same person we were in high school. How can I expect her to blindly trust someone she barely knows anymore?

"Fuck," I groan, my shoulders sagging.

"I see you get it now, don't you?" he questions before motioning to get Beckett's attention. "You need to show her you mean everything you say. That she isn't the only one having to sacrifice something for you to be together."

If I want different results, I have to try an alternate approach. I let my pride get in the way when we were younger, but not this time.

"I have to go." I jump off the barstool and head for the front door without a backward glance. I barely make it out the door before I pull my phone out of my pocket and dial Connor's number again.

"Can you handle the proposal for Finn? I can be in Magnolia in a few days," I blurt out, not even bothering to say hello.

"I already told you I'd go with you to get things

started. Mrs. Buckley only expects one of us to come tomorrow anyway," he tells me. "What's going on?"

I ignore his question. "Great. I need to head out of town for a few days or more. I'm not sure."

"Where are you going?" he asks, but it sounds like he already knows the answer.

"New York." I hang up the phone and pull out of the spot, pointing my truck toward the airport.

I lost Selina once. I don't plan on letting it happen again.

twenty-one
selina

"I'll have the chef's salad with Italian dressing on the side and no onions, please," Brittany tells the server before looking over in my direction.

Brittany Hayden and I have been friends since I joined the dance company right after graduation. After I got the call to come in for an audition, she was the first person I called. Having had to give up my space in company housing after my injury, I needed a place to bunk while I was in town for my audition. Thankfully, she had her own apartment here in the city and a guest room for me to stay in. Not only did she give me a place to stay, but she made a point of filling me in on everything that had happened here in New York since I headed home.

As soon as I arrived, she whisked me off to the practice room to show me the audition piece. Luckily, it was a piece from *Swan Lake* that I have been dancing throughout my rehabilitation, knowing that if I could land the jump that caused my injury, my fear of being hurt again would be nonexistent. By the end of the night, Brittany said I was dancing like I never left, with a grace she had never seen in anyone before. She has been here for me every step of the way, running through the audition piece with me yesterday after-noon and this morning until my audition. After my audition, she immediately whisked me off to lunch at her favorite restaurant in hopes of occupying my mind while I waited for the call to let me know if I got the part.

The server clears her throat loudly, bringing me back to the present. "I'll have the same." I give her an apologetic smile as I hand her my menu.

She flashes us both a smile before striding toward the front of the café. I glance at my reflection in the mirror, noticing the minor changes in my appearance.

"Are you nervous about the audition?" Brittany asks, giving me a reassuring smile.

"Of course. Who wouldn't be? I haven't danced professionally in months. I still can't believe they called me in for an audition. It should have been you dancing up there today instead."

She reaches across the table and grips my hand, giving it a small squeeze. "Nonsense. Don't think anything of it. The director specifically asked for you to audition before she decided. The part could go to any of us."

"Let's just hope I have the spark she's looking for."

Memories of my audition filter through my mind as I pick apart every moment, wondering if what I put forth was enough. If I'm finally going to make it to center stage like I've always dreamed of.

"Of course, you do. They wouldn't have called you if no one believed you would be the perfect person for this role." Brittany gives me a small smile before she picks at the piece of bread on her plate. "How have things been for the last few months, Selina?"

"Rehab was hard, but I made it through," I respond quickly before taking a sip of my water.

"Rehab and getting through the audition are all you've talked about since you arrived, which I understood. But now that the audition is over, spill the beans, girl."

I give her a small smile. "There's nothing to tell. I bought the dance studio in town from my old dance instructor and have been teaching ever since."

"It must be amazing watching all those young girls grow as dancers."

"You have no idea."

I regale her with stories of all the girls that come through my studio. I tell her about teaching them how to pirouette and the excitement I felt the first time one of them completed a sauté without falling. Brittany listens to all my stories, not once interrupting me or making light of all the accomplishments my students have made since I started teaching. As our server arrives with our food, I finally pause.

"I didn't mean to monopolize the conversation, Brit. How are things going for you? How is it dancing as Odette in *Swan Lake*?" I ask, eager to hear of my friend's success.

She was originally slated to dance opposite me as Odile before my injury, but once we knew how serious my condition was, it was an easy decision. She would dance in my place, and her understudy would perform as Odile.

"It was amazing! I have always wanted to be in *Swan Lake*, although I don't think I did that part justice after spending months watching you dance," she mumbles as she stabs her fork into her lettuce.

"Nonsense. You danced beautifully. Better than I could have with a bum ankle." She gasps in shock, causing me to laugh. "You didn't think I'd leave before watching you perform at least once, did you? I was at almost every performance before I left for home."

We eat in silence for a few minutes. "And what about men?" Brittany asks with a smile.

I pause mid-bite, not wanting to have this conversation with anyone, let alone Brittany. "Who has time for men?"

"That means there's someone." She motions for me to start speaking.

I sigh. I don't have the faintest idea how to explain

what is going on with Vance and me. "There's nothing to tell. My ex and I reconnected for the first time in years." I take a sip of my water and send up a silent prayer that she'll drop the subject, but no such luck.

"And?" she presses. Suddenly, it's like a light bulb goes off in her head. "Wait a minute! Your ex from high school?" she screeches loudly, drawing stares from some other patrons.

"Yes. Now keep your voice down, or I won't tell you anything."

She pretends to zip her lips and throw away the key, then leans forward, places her elbows on the table, and rests her chin in her hands, letting me know I have her full and undivided attention.

"Before I came back to town, I hadn't spoken to him since I left town after graduation. When I went home for my best friend's funeral, I had planned on telling him I wanted to come home, to try and rekindle what we had, but I saw him in the arms of another girl."

"That son of a—" she growls, her hands balling into fists on the edge of the table.

"No, let me finish. It wasn't what I thought, but after that night, I couldn't see a way for us to be together," I start.

"And?" She taps her fingers on her cheeks, showing her annoyance.

"And we reconnected while I was home. I tried for months to get it through his head that I was coming back here the first chance I got, but he wouldn't take no for an answer." I smile brightly as I tell her about his antics to get me to go on a date with him again. "Finally, I gave in, hoping that after all these years, the spark would be gone."

"But it wasn't?" She leans back in her chair and crosses her arms.

"No, it wasn't." I sigh, burying my head in my hands.

The truth is, giving up this part and settling down in my hometown doesn't sound so terrifying anymore. Just sitting here talking about my students has brought me more joy than I could have imagined. As I think about what the future would hold for me there, my heart feels light, as if the weight of the world has been lifted off my shoulders. I came back to New York and hopefully nailed my audition, proving to myself that I could do it. I was hoping for some sense of accomplishment for nailing the audition and fulfilling my dream, but instead, I feel as if something is missing.

"What do you want?" Brittany asks as she slides her chair closer to mine and lays a comforting hand on my shoulder.

"I know I've worked so hard to get where I am today, but something is missing." I sigh as I look to the ceiling, wishing that I didn't have to choose.

"Something or someone?"

"Definitely someone." I smile softly, my cheeks

pinking in embarrassment. "I would love nothing more than for him to walk through that door, but I couldn't ask him to pick up his entire life and move to New York just so I can dance for a few more years."

"How do you know that isn't what he would want?"

I turn my head to the side and look Brittany in the eyes. "I never asked."

She throws her hands up in exasperation. "Girl, this is the shit eighties movies were written about."

I giggle nervously as I take another mouthful and avoid looking into her eyes, although I know she's right. Yes, I've always wanted to be a dancer, but the one thing being home for the last six months has shown me is that there is something else missing in my life. Or, in my case, maybe some*one*.

"The smile on your face says everything." She pauses, making sure she has my attention. "I've only ever seen you that happy when you're dancing."

"Maybe, but this is my dream." I use the same regurgitated answer I've been giving everyone since I came home.

Brittany gives me a soft smile. "You have been a dancer at the New York City Ballet for years and danced on hundreds of stages. If you ask me, that's pretty badass."

Images of what my life with Vance would be like filter through my mind. Nights spent sitting on the deck, swinging in our swing, and telling each other about our days. I can see it all laid out in front of me, and I yearn for it with all my being. I've wanted to be a prima ballerina for most of my life, but it wasn't until this moment that I realized I have something else that I cherish more than anything. More than being in the spotlight.

"Dreams can change," I respond, tears pooling in my eyes.

"They can," she agrees. "Just because this isn't what you envisioned your life being at this point, doesn't mean it isn't meant to be."

Vance has been waiting for me to invite him into my life completely since the day I left. It's time I finally gave him that answer.

"What if I'm too late?" I ask the one question that has been filtering through my mind during this entire conversation.

Once again, I left Vance, not bothering to include him in my decision. What if that's the final straw, the thing that sends him over the edge, and he turns his back on me for good?

"Then he's an idiot," Brittany retorts without hesitation.

"Thank you," I whisper to my friend before pulling her in for a hug.

If it wasn't for her making me open up about every-thing that was going on since I left, I never would have admitted to myself how this injury had changed things for the better.

"Anytime. Just promise to name your firstborn after me, and we can call it even."

"You got it," I reply, just as my phone rings.

I search in my bag and pull it out, noticing the familiar number from the ballet on the screen. I take a deep breath before answering and listen intently to the person on the other end.

"Hi. This is Stefanie from the New York City Ballet. We're delighted to inform you that you have been selected to perform the role of Juliet in this season's production of *Romeo and Juliet*."

I look over at my friend and grip her hand. "Thank you for this opportunity, but my place is with my students," I respond confidently.

"We understand. If there is anything the company can do for you in the future, please let us know."

"Thank you. I have one small favor to ask." I pause and flash Brittany a bright smile. "I know it's not my place, but I would recommend Brittany Hayden for the part. There are very few people I know who can light up a stage the way she does."

Brittany gasps in surprise as tears pool in her eyes.

"I'll pass your recommendation along, but the final decision rests with the director," Stefanie informs me.

"I understand. Thank you." I hang up the phone

and turn to my friend. "I hope they aren't dumb enough to give the part to someone else."

"That doesn't matter right now." She raises her hand to get the server's attention.

Once they arrive at the table, we ask for the check. Once we have settled the bill, we quickly hail a cab and head to her apartment in Hell's Kitchen.

"Now it's time to get you to the airport. You have a man to catch."

We both laugh as we stand from the table and head to the front of the restaurant. Although this trip didn't turn out the way I thought, I have no regrets. I've lived my dream, but now it's time to find my destiny.

* * *

The entire flight home, I try to imagine how my conversation with Vance will go, but none of the outcomes are what I want.

"Penny for your thoughts?" a voice asks from beside me.

I turn to my right and notice an older woman sitting next time me who looks a lot like Betty White. Her silver hair is perfectly styled, one side pinned behind her ear by a beautiful comb, a soft smile on her face. "You look like you have a lot on your mind and could use someone to talk to."

I contemplate brushing her off but decide against it.

Having someone to talk through all these emotions in my mind with might be helpful and alleviate some of my nerves about seeing Vance.

"I'm headed back home to see someone I hurt pretty badly," I reply as she lays her tiny hand on top of mine. "I just hope he isn't tired of waiting for me to make up my mind."

"If he loves you, he'll wait until the end of time for you to be together."

"I hope so, but I've kept him waiting for a very long time. I kept putting my dreams before everything else, not once asking him what he thought or felt. Expecting that he'd wait for me to come home."

"Did he?"

"Did he what?"

"Wait for you, dear." She flashes me a knowing smile before squeezing my hand. "I'm pretty sure I can already guess the answer to that question."

Vance has every right to tell me to get lost, that he's tired of waiting for me to decide if I want to be with him. I honestly can't blame him if he did tell me that, but instead of telling me to get lost, he waited for me to come home, just like everyone else I shut out of my life before I headed to New York.

"Yes, he waited for me." I smile down at her. "I finally realized that I was making choices for him. I never had a conversation with him about whether he'd be willing to come with me to New York or if he would wait for me. And, as it turns out, I didn't have to ask because he waited anyway. He waited for me to decide if I loved him enough to come back to him. I just wish it hadn't taken me so long to realize it."

"Attention, passengers. We are approaching the Chattanooga Metropolitan Airport. Please fasten your safety belts and put your seats and tray tables in the fully upright and locked position. We'll be landing shortly," the flight attendant announces over the loud-speaker, and my heart drops into my stomach in antici-pation of the encounter that awaits me when I get back to Tyson's Creek.

"Nervous about seeing him again?" the older woman beside me asks, noticing my change in demeanor.

"No. Well, not exactly." I give her a forced smile. "I'm more afraid of what's waiting for me when I land."

"Don't you mean *who*, sweetie? That man would be a fool not to see how much you love him."

"I do. Very much so," I reply as the landing wheels meet the ground, jolting us slightly, and the engines work to slow us down.

She gives my hand one last squeeze. "If it's meant to be, it will be."

"I hope you're right."

A few minutes later, the plane comes to a stop at our arrival gate, and I unbuckle my seat belt and stand.

"Do you need any help?" I ask her.

"No, thank you, sweetie. I have to wait for my wheelchair."

I nod as I slide past her, grab my travel bag from the overhead compartment, and exit the plane. As I step out into the main terminal area, I spot a familiar pair of eyes staring back at me.

"What are you doing here?" I ask, pulling my bag to a stop in front of Vance.

He rubs the back of his neck and shows me a boarding pass. "Coming to get you. I let you get away once. I wasn't going to do that again."

Tears trickle down my face as I say the first thing that comes to mind. "Can we have a do-over?"

He stares at me skeptically as he takes a step closer, framing my face with his hands. "A do-over?"

"Yes. I know I messed up all those years ago, leaving without a word, but I realized something when I was in New York."

"What's that?"

"I went to New York looking to fulfill a dream, but once I got there, I knew something was missing." I wrap my arms around his neck. "You."

I hold my breath, waiting for him to reject me like I imagined he would. But instead, he pulls me tightly into his chest, pressing a gentle kiss on the top of my head.

"It feels like I've been waiting my entire life for you to say that."

"The wait is over, Vance. I love you." I rise up slightly on my toes and kiss him softly. We stand there in our own little bubble of happiness until I hear a familiar voice behind me.

"I see you found your heart," the older woman from the plane says with a smile as she reaches back and grasps the hand of another gentleman.

"What are you doing here?" Vance asks, looking at the gentleman pushing her chair.

"I came to get my girl, just like you." He tips his hat in my direction before looking back at Vance. "I'm glad you decided to take my advice."

Vance grasps the man's hand and gives it a firm shake. "Me, too."

Then the elderly man grasps the handles of the wheelchair and heads toward the baggage claim.

"What was that about?" I ask Vance as he leads me toward the airport exit.

"We met at Crawdaddy's today when I was on my way out of town."

"Out of town? Where were you going? How long did you plan on being gone? What about..." Vance chuckles softly as he places his hand over my mouth.

"I was heading to Magnolia for a job we just bid on. Not for long, just to do some preliminary work before Connor and the crew arrived later in the week. But that man gave me the little push I needed to come get what

I wanted. To prove to you that I was willing to do anything for us to be together."

"It seems like we both needed a little push in the right direction."

Vance and I will go through our ups and downs as we try to find our footing with each other once again, but there is one thing I know for certain: Sometimes a do-over is all you need.

twenty-two
seth

I hit *end call* on the satellite phone I've been using.

"Maybe next time," I mumble to no one as I push off my bunk and head toward the mess hall.

There's been an ache in my heart ever since I deployed. I spend most of my time missing the only person I've ever given my heart to. Sure, we only spent one night together, but that night meant everything to me. I knew the moment the sun came streaming through the window that morning that my heart would only ever belong to her.

The connection I feel toward her has only grown stronger since I woke up that morning. The moment I laid eyes on Bristol Reid, I knew she was someone special. The more time we spent together, and the more I got to know her, I could see our future playing out before my eyes. Bristol is the type of woman I can see myself settling down and starting a family with. When we are together, all my worries and troubles turn into nothing but background noise.

It took me months to get Bristol to admit the attraction we felt toward each other. To give me a chance to show her she meant the world to me, even if there was no guarantee that I'd return. I knew deep in my soul that if I didn't find out how delicious she tasted as I licked the salty sweat from her skin, or how it felt to have her pressed tightly to me as she moaned my name, I'd regret it for the rest of my life. However, now that I know all those things, the idea of never having them again tears me in two.

Bristol wanted one night together, no strings attached, but to me, it was so much more. I knew I was shipping out in a few weeks, but it didn't matter to me. I wanted—no, needed—to know everything I could about Bristol, or I'd have regretted it for the rest of my life.

"Finally decided to join the land of the living?"

The only response I give Brady is a grunt as I grab a tray and begin piling on food.

"So talkative today." He rolls his eyes as I head toward a table in the back. "Seriously, man. Who pissed in your Wheaties?"

"Just trying to figure out what the hell I want to do when my contract is up," I mumble as I shove another bite of food into my mouth.

I've spent the last two decades in the Marines,

trying to find my place in the world. I've traveled across the world fighting for my country, which gave me a sense of belonging for the first time since my parents passed away. But I always felt like something was missing. There was a part of me that was still searching for that one thing that would bring me back to life.

"You could always come home with me," he responds matter-of-factly, as if he hasn't just handed me my heart's desire on a silver platter. "My dad told me they're looking for guys at the station. Since we're in the military, all we have to do is pass the civil service exam and then attend the academy. Nothing too hard."

Having no family of my own, I had nowhere to go during leave periods or holidays, so ever since I met him, Brady has always invited me to join his family. But I had no way of knowing that this last trip would change the direction of my life forever.

"Maybe." I try to remain calm as images of reuniting with Bristol again filter through my mind. She told me we couldn't be anything more because she couldn't live with not knowing if she was the most important person to me. That if given the choice, I'd choose her over everything else. Maybe this is my chance. "But don't you have to wait for a date to open?"

"Yeah, but I doubt you'd have to wait too long."

"Where am I going to stay?" I question, knowing I have enough money saved to buy a small house somewhere, but I don't want to make any rash decisions.

"As if my parents will let you stay anywhere but with us. Besides, you can crash with me in the apartment above their garage. It's nothing fancy, but it's more space than we've had in a long while."

The Thomases welcomed me with open arms the first time Brady brought me home during a stand-down, a time of rest and recovery the command gives us after deployment, and they ensure I always feel like part of the family every chance they get. Hell, his mom even sends me care packages over here in the sandbox, claiming she wants to brighten my day just a little more.

"But seriously, where else are you going to go? I'm the only family you have." A mischievous smile crosses his face. "Besides, this will give you a chance to prove to your girl you're not going anywhere."

I made the mistake of telling Brady about what Bristol said after our first meeting. Instead of laughing in my face, he seemed to understand where she was coming from. We spent a few nights racking our brains, trying to find the perfect plan to convince Bristol that she was the most important person in my life, but we always came up empty. Maybe this is my chance.

"Bristol is not my girl," I mutter as I stand up, grab my tray, and turn toward the exit. "She made it perfectly clear she wanted nothing else to do with me after that night."

Brady grasps my shoulder, pulling me to a stop. "But you never told her everything, did you?"

I shake my head, wrenching my arm from his grasp. "She has no idea we're coming home for good in about six months."

"I'm sure someone has told her that we are coming home. Tyson's Creek is a small town; I'm sure someone has said something," he continues.

"That doesn't change anything," I mumble to myself as I empty my tray into the trash and stomp off toward my tent. I'm tempted once again to dial her number but decide against it, stuffing the phone under my pillow and closing my eyes. Maybe I can grab a quick nap before I have watch in a few hours.

"Damn it, Seth. Stop being so stubborn!" Brady shouts as he smacks my boots and pushes my feet off the side of my bed, then plops down in their place. "I've never known you to give up so easily."

"I make decisions that could cost someone their life almost daily. I have to be sure about them," I growl before sitting up and resting my elbows on my knees.

"Would it kill you to take a chance?"

Brady waits for me to answer, but I remain silent.

"I know how much she means to you. Ever since that party at Tranquility Retreat, you've been different. You've been looking forward to your life after the military."

"What the hell is that supposed to mean?"

"You've never thought about getting out. You've never once said anything about what you wanted to do after retirement until that night. Now you're trying to make plans for the future. Plans that could easily include Bristol if you let them."

"When did you become so fucking demanding, man?" I smirk in his direction.

"Demanding or not, the only thing I'm asking is that you think about it," Brady responds as he strolls toward his bunk on the other side of the tent. "You don't want to spend the rest of your life wondering if things could've been different."

It's hard to admit that he's right, but I know deep down that he is. Being a Marine is all I have ever known, but since meeting Bristol, I want something more out of life.

I throw both hands behind my head before leaning back on my bunk and crossing my feet at the ankles. I close my eyes and attempt to imagine what it would be like to run into Bristol again now that time is on our side.

If I managed to find some way to get Bristol back into my life, I could never let her go again, even if I tried. Brady is right; if I moved to Tyson's Creek, it would only be a matter of time before we run into each other. Not everyone is given a second chance to make an impression on the woman of their dreams, so I need to seize this opportunity and make the most of it.

I tried to say goodbye to her once, but now our paths are about to cross again. I'm sure she'll be shocked to see me at first, but if I play my cards right, maybe we'll be a couple before the year is out.

"Wishful thinking," I mumble into the empty bunkhouse as I give up on getting a quick nap before watch and decide to head toward the gym.

Maybe Tyson's Creek is where all my dreams will come true... or maybe I'm just setting myself up for another heartbreak.

epilogue
selina

When Vance and I returned to Tyson's Creek about a month ago, it seemed as if nothing had changed, but I was different. The idea of settling down once again in my small town didn't feel as suffocating.

Vance insisted we spend some time together, just the two of us, before announcing our relationship to the world, and I agreed wholeheartedly. After being apart for those few days, I was starved for his love and attention. We spent an entire week holed up in his large farmhouse, only leaving for food, reconnecting with our bodies and our souls.

To say I'm still apprehensive about how fast things are going with him would be an understatement. Vance and I have gone from barely saying two words to each other to being in a full-blown relationship in a matter of a few months. I'm sure there are people out there who would say things were moving fast, but this is the perfect speed for the two of us. After spending so many years away from each other, why wait any longer to start our lives together?

Couple that with my recent surprise, and panic isn't a strong enough word to describe how I'm feeling. Yep, I'm pregnant. I guess I shouldn't really be surprised, given the number of times Vance and I have spent enjoying each other's bodies since that first night we spent together. We haven't talked about having children just yet, but Vance has made no secret of how badly he wants to have a ring on my finger and my belly round with his child.

It seems surreal that I'm finally able to have everything that I've ever wanted—Vance, a chance to have a career that I love in dance, and now, raising a family in the dream home the love of my life built for me. I used to believe that there was no way I could be happy in my small hometown on the Tennessee-Alabama border, but here I am. I guess someone really can have their cake and eat it, too, as the saying goes.

The sad part is that I've only had about twenty-four hours to get used to the idea of being a mother. Noticing the warning signs, Bristol encouraged me to take a test yesterday morning. Two pink lines showed up in no time, and I had no idea how to feel until the panic set in. Bristol did her best to keep me calm, calling in reinforcements from Audrey and Leia, but it seems my niece or nephew decided that was the perfect time to make an appearance.

Bristol's water broke right there in my parents' kitchen. After that, it was nothing but frantic phone calls to all the rest of our friends, and we rushed to the hospital. Rebekah was born a few hours ago, weighing in at seven pounds, twelve ounces.

"She's beautiful," I say as I look down at the precious little girl in my arms.

"I agree with you, but I'm a little biased."

I lift my head and notice the content smile on Bristol's face. If I didn't know for a fact that she'd spent the last twelve hours in labor, I would have had no idea. Bristol looks the exact opposite of tired, with her red hair tied in a messy bun on top of her head.

"When are you going to tell him?" she asks as I place little Rebekah back in her arms and take a seat in the chair beside her bed.

"Soon," is the only answer I can come up with. The events of yesterday are still a blur in my mind. "I know he'll be ecstatic about having a baby, but are we ready?"

"Ready? There is no ready, Seli. Look at me." Bristol gives me a reassuring smile. "I never wanted to be a single mother, but life had other plans. Now, I just want to make sure I'm the best mother I can be to my little girl."

"Have you thought about telling Seth?" I probe gently at the sensitive subject.

Bristol was beyond secretive about the name of her baby's father until a few weeks ago. Overcome with the panic of being a single mother, Bristol finally confided in Leia and me. It seems she wanted to keep it a secret in case he came back into town, not wanting him to find out from someone else he was going to be a father, but when she never received any contact from him, she decided to never speak of it again. No matter who helped Bristol bring Rebekah into this world, we would all be there for her, ensuring that she was the most spoiled little girl in all of Tyson's Creek, that is, until our little one arrives in about eight months, give or take a few weeks.

"Even if I wanted to, I couldn't. I made the mistake of telling him it was a one-time thing. Who would have thought that the one time I tried to do something reckless, it would turn out like this?" Bristol stares out the window, lost in thought.

I give her time to collect her thoughts before breaking the silence. "Do you want to find him?"

"I don't know."

"Why don't you contact Brady? You said they were in the same unit, right? Leia was talking about him coming home soon when I came in."

Talk about a small town. Brady is the only son of the town's midwife. He also happens to be friends with Seth, Rebekah's father. Through a series of events, Bristol and Seth hooked up and created this miracle, but he has no idea.

"Maybe," Bristol says before quickly changing the

subject. "You need to tell Vance sooner rather than later. The longer you wait, the harder it will be."

"Tell me what?"

We both spin toward the door, and my mouth drops open in surprise as Vance steps into the room.

Vance

Selina immediately turns toward the window as I step into the room.

"These are for the new mama," I say as I place a large bouquet on the table beside her bed. "And this is for the little miss."

I hand Bristol the small gift bag and run my hand over the top of the baby's head. Images of Selina sitting in the same position, holding a baby with her dark hair and my eyes filter through my mind. I shove my hand into my front pocket and grip the ring box I've been carrying around for days. She has said repeatedly how she thinks we should slow down and get to know each other again, and I respect that, but after almost losing her a second time, I want to tie her to me in every way possible.

"How adorable," Bristol squeals as she pulls a tiny onesie out of the bag, spinning it around for Selina to see.

Selina snickers quietly before covering her mouth and turning back towards the window.

"Why don't you two head out to the hallway? I think this little one is ready to eat," Bristol says, throwing a wink in my direction before gesturing wildly with her free hand.

"Did I miss something?" I question as my attention shifts between the two women.

Selina turns to her friend before grasping my hand.

"I need to talk to you," she whispers, pulling me toward the door.

I send Bristol a look of panic, unsure of what's going on, but she just shoos me out the door.

Selina leads me to a small waiting room at the end of the hallway before dropping my hand and heading for the window. I wait for her to explain, but I can't take the silence anymore. My heart pounds in my chest as I imagine all the worst-case scenarios.

"Are you leaving?" I croak, the emotion clear in my voice. She shakes her head, not even bothering to turn around and look at me. Air whooshes from my lungs as I sigh in relief. "Then whatever it is, we'll face it together."

Her shoulders tremble as her head connects with the window, causing a soft thump to echo through the hall.

"What's wrong, Seli?" I rush to her side and wrap

my arms around her waist, pulling her tightly into my chest. "You can tell me anything."

Selina pulls in a big breath. "I'm pregnant."

My entire body freezes in shock. "Pregnant?"

My head spins as I process the information she's given me. My heart swells with love, overcome with happiness and the sense of peace I have been longing for all these years. Finally, Selina has given me the last piece of myself that I have been searching for.

"We're having a baby," I say out loud as a grin spreads across my face.

Her body stiffens in my arms as she rambles. "I know we didn't plan on having babies right away. Hell, I just came back to town for good. This wasn't what I'd planned, but I really want to keep this baby, and I would love for you to be a part of his or her life. I understand if you need some time to think about things."

I quickly spin her around and give her a quick kiss. "Marry me," I say with conviction.

Her eyes widen in surprise as she attempts to pull away from me. "Wait. I just told you we're having a baby, and that's your response?"

She pushes against my chest, and this time, I let her go.

"Yes," I insist. I watch her pace from one end of the hall to the other, mumbling to herself and flailing her arms wildly in the air.

She pauses and turns in my direction. "You under-stand marriage is for life, right?"

"Yes."

She continues pacing. "And you want to keep our baby?"

"Yes." I stride forward, stepping directly into her path.

She smacks into my chest, and I wrap my arms around her to ensure she doesn't fall. "Can you give me anything besides one-word answers? I'm being serious!" she screeches as she pounds on my chest with tears trailing down her face.

"Yes, I do." I smirk at her before pulling her back into my arms. "See? That was three words." I kiss the top of her head, then rest my forehead against hers. "Marry me."

"I'll have to think about it." She buries her nose in my chest and inhales deeply.

After a few moments, her entire body relaxes.

"I'll wear you down," I tell her, as I pull the box from my pocket and flip it open.

"It took you six months last time," she responds, lifting her head and looking into my eyes.

"But it worked. And if we're married before our new little one is born, then I call my mission a success." I cup her face and wipe the remaining tears from her cheeks with my thumbs.

"Is that what I am to you? A mission?" she huffs as

she tries to step out of my embrace, but I refuse to let her go.

"No, Seli. You're everything," I say reverently before taking her lips in a soft kiss.

"I can live with that," she mumbles against my lips, as I grip her left hand and slide the ring on it. She pulls back, takes a quick glance at the ring, and then throws her arms around my neck, pulling me in for a deeper kiss.

If someone had asked me months ago if this was the outcome I saw for Selina and me, I'd have answered yes without hesitation. I always knew Selina was the other half of my soul. It just took her longer to figure it out and make her way home. But I'm just glad that she finally realized she never had to find a place to belong, and she didn't have to be someone else, because there was always someone who loved her just the way she was: me.

the end

I hope you enjoyed *Love You Still*! Wondering what happened to Vance and Selina after the end? Scan the QR code for instant access to a bonus epilogue for your new favorite couple. Just use the QR code below.

Already subscribed? Just check your last newsletter for the link to my bonus material! If you can't find it, you can simply resubscribe and the scene will be yours in minutes!

aj alexander
messy emotions. big heart energy.

USA Today Bestselling Author AJ Alexander has been writing romance since 2018. She loves writing small town romances with found families and all the nosey nellies that help her characters find their happily ever afters! She lives in Arizona, otherwise known as the surface of the sun, with her husband, two daughters, two cats, and a lovable golden retriever.

When she isn't writing you can find AJ reading, binging the latest true crime documentary on Netflix, or binging the latest Korean Drama or Anime that's released. AJ is a cynical hopeless romantic that believes in love at first sight, that bigger is always better, and everything should be put off for a nap.

Come find her in the wild! There's nothing she loves more than connecting with my readers.